MAXINE
BANKS
IS
GETTING
MARRIED

BY **LORI AURELIA WILLIAMS**

Roaring Brook Press
New York

Text copyright © 2010 by Lori Aurelia Williams
Published by Roaring Brook Press
Roaring Brook Press is a division of Holtzbrinck Publishing Holdings
Limited Partnership
175 Fifth Avenue, New York, New York 10010
www.roaringbrookpress.com

Distributed in Canada by H. B. Fenn and Company Ltd.

Library of Congress Cataloging-in-Publication Data

Williams, Lori Aurelia.
  Maxine Banks is getting married / Lori Aurelia Williams.—1st ed.
    p. cm.
  Summary: When seventeen-year-old Maxine's best friend gets married, Maxine
suddenly decides that she and her boyfriend Brian should too, but things do not turn
out the way she expected, and both she and Brian realize that they are not as grown
up as they thought.
  ISBN 978-1-59643-513-1
  [1. Marriage—Fiction. 2. Honesty—Fiction. 3. Family problems—Fiction.
4. Maturation (Psychology)—Fiction. 5. African Americans—Fiction.] I. Title.
  PZ7.W66685Max 2010
  [Fic]—dc22
                                                          2010008184

Roaring Brook Press books are available for special promotions and premiums.
For details contact: Director of Special Markets, Holtzbrinck Publishers.

First Edition October 2010
Printed in August 2010 in the United States of America
by RR Donnelley & Sons Company, Harrisonburg, Virginia

1 3 5 7 9 8 6 4 2

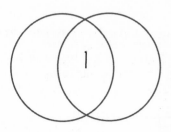

My best girlfriend Tia just got married. She married her longtime boyfriend Doo-witty. Tia's mama didn't want to let Tia get married because she was barely seventeen, like me. But when her mama found out that Doo-witty got an art scholarship to a school in New York, she knew that Tia's heart would be completely broken if she couldn't go with him. So Tia and Doo-witty got hitched. They had their ceremony down at the Tabernacle of the Blessed Redeemer, where Sister Ashada recently became the lead minister. Tia's mother and Grandma Augustine did all of the decorations, including Tia's beautiful white satin gown and lace veil. The pews of the church were decorated with home-made red velvet bows and fresh red roses from their garden. Me and Tia's little sister, Shayla, were bridesmaids, and Shayla's friend Kambia read an original prayer. Everybody in the neighborhood came. The sanctuary was so full that the ushers had to seat people in the balcony. The entire event was wonderful—the ceremony, and the reception with the four tier Italian Cream wedding cake. There was much love and happiness going around on that day. My friend Tia got treated like a queen, and ever since her wedding I've been thinking that I want to be treated like a queen too. All last night and this morning I psyched myself up for what I'm getting prepared to do today. As soon as I finish getting dressed and prettied up, I'm going to go and see my boyfriend, Brian. Then, before he even gets a chance to shower and shave, I'm going to ask him to be mine. I haven't worked out all the details of the wedding and marriage, but I know it will be okay because he loves me as much as Doo-witty loves Tia. I believe when two people love all crazy like that, the only thing to do is take some vows and promise to spend the rest of your life together. After I spray on Brian's favorite perfume, I'm going to put on his even more favorite purple halter dress, the one that I wore to the seventies soul dance, and then I'll match the dress with my purple three-inch slingbacks. The shoes will hopefully make me look taller and leaner, and the dress will show off my curvy waist and full bosom. I know I'll look hot once I'm all fixed up, and Brian will think I'm hot too. He won't be able to take his eyes off me when I tell him what I have planned for our future.

I slipped into my dress and curled my hair. I guess I was hot inside and out, because I was sweating, and by the time I got to Brian's my curls were limp and damp. I didn't look all that alluring anymore. I prayed that my appearance wouldn't bother my future husband.

I took out the key that I use to water the plants when Brian and his dad go on business trips, and opened the door. I knew that Brian's dad was away again, but I still tiptoed through the house. I went straight to Brian's room and pounced on him. He slowly turned over and opened his eyes.

"Wake up, sleepy head. I want to talk to you about something," I said.

"Maxine, what's up? Give me some sugar?" he said and yawned.

I leaned over, and we shared a quick kiss.

"Is that all I get?" he asked.

"Until you brush your scuzzy teeth."

"So it's like that. All right," he said, getting up. He threw his spread back and sat on the side of the bed in his black knit boxers and muscle shirt. He looked too hot like that. "Guess what? I got some good news about you and me."

"Good news? What kind of good news? Baby, what are you talking about?" he asked and yawned again.

"I'm talking about you and me, being like Tia and Doowitty. I've been thinking about it for a while. I've been thinking about how we can live by ourselves. You know, handle our business and do our own thing."

"Do our own? What? Baby, what you talking about, getting married or something?" he said, wiping the sleep out of his eyes.

"Yeah, that's what I'm talking about. What do you think?" I asked, excitedly.

He got a big grin on his face. "I don't know. You and me married, huh? We be getting our wedding on, and everybody be showing up, giving us presents and stuff."

"Yeah, it will be so cool," I said, bouncing up and down on the bed.

He stroked his chin. "Yeah, it could be, I guess, if we can pull it off."

"You know we can. I'm making money working at Bobby's on the weekend, and your boss at the card shop is about to make you an assistant manager. That will mean a bunch more cash in your paycheck."

"Not a bunch, but more, for sure. Still, I don't know. Where we gonna live? My daddy might be okay with it, if he ain't got no choice, but do you really want to be dealing with him all of the time? You know my mama ain't going for it, and I'm guessing a big part of this is trying to get away from your own mother."

"Yeah, you're right about that," I had to confess. Besides being a little jealous of my girlfriend and her new husband, I really wanted to get away from our families. Brian's dad loves him, but he likes to have everything his way, and when someone disagrees with him there is usually hell to pay. As for my mother, she is the biggest reason why I want to get married and leave home. Her boyfriends have always come first. When there's a new man in the house, Mama's attention is completely focused on him, his wants, his needs. My great-aunt Freda says that Mama was like that from a teenager. "When she started dating that was the end of my spending any kind of time with your mama. She and I were real close, like me and you are now, but a new boyfriend always meant that I couldn't get her to visit me for weeks or sometimes even months. It's just the way it is with some women. They men mean everything to them. There ain't no room for anybody else."

It certainly is true with Mama. I can't count on her for anything, if somebody with a beard or a mustache is around.

"I don't know how we gonna do it, Brian. First, I just want you to say that you really want to see it done."

He put his arms around my waist and pulled me to him. "I guess I hadn't thought too much about it. Anyway, I love you. I want whatever you want. You are my girl. If you say you want to be married, I'm cool with that," he said, and gave me a huge kiss. I returned it, even though he still needed to brush his teeth.

"Are you sure?" I asked, when we pulled away.

"You know it. It's gonna be you and me girl. I'm gonna be standing up there in a tux, looking all GQ for my favorite girl."

I hugged him tightly, thinking about how he really would look. Brian isn't what you would call handsome. He has a nice body, but overall he is an average-looking African-American guy, and you wouldn't pick him out in a crowd of young guys his age. What I love about him is the way he treats me like a queen. My girlfriends all get jealous when they see the things that he does for me. When I need something, he never lets me down, no matter what he has to go through to get it. Last year I was playing volleyball at school when some girl went to hit the ball and ran right into me. I fell and broke some teeth, and my mouth was a mess. When Mama took me to the dentist, he told her that it was going to cost a fortune to replace or fix the teeth. Mama asked the other girl's mother to help out, but her family was even poorer than ours. As soon as Brian found out that the girl's family wasn't going to pay, he said he would help us with the bill. He took on extra hours at his job. He was exhausted most days when I saw him, but with all of us pulling together we were able to pay the entire bill off before the oral surgeon even started working on me. I felt blessed and loved to know that I had a boyfriend who would sacrifice so much to help me. That's what I love about Brian, he has never left me hanging. I want to get married in a beautiful white wedding dress like Tia, but as far as I'm concerned he can show up to our wedding in jeans and a basketball shirt. I just want him there, saying his vows and sharing the moment with me.

"So we really gonna do this? You're sure?" I asked.

"Yeah, we gonna do it, but you know your mama ain't gonna like it. She freaks out when we alone in your room. She not gonna be happy with us wanting to be alone together forever."

"Mama will be cool, baby. Don't worry about it. It's gonna work out. I just have to figure out a way to put it to her."

"Well, you put it whatever way you need to. Do whatever it takes, and we can work the rest out later." He yawned again. "Since you done woke me up, I might as well get dressed and get to work a little early," he said, getting up.

"Okay," I said. I leaned down and we shared another kiss. I didn't wrinkle my nose at his breath. I figured I was going to have to get used to it, if I was going to wake up each morning beside him. Brian gathered some clothes and went off to the bathroom. When I heard the shower turn on, I sat down on the bed and took a deep breath. What was I going to do about Mama? All I could think is how my mama has photos of me in every room of the house. Some are those boring posed ones that you take at school and your local discount superstore, but most of them are snaps she's taken of me on special or fun occasions. There are at least twenty photos of my birthday parties in various frames sitting in the living room and thirty-five Christmas photos in the hallway and her bedroom, but you won't see Brian in any of the photos, even though he was present when most of them were taken. "Mama, why don't you take some pictures with Brian in them?" I asked, each time she took a snapshot.

"Maxine, I ain't wasting my film on that boy. You the only one who thinks he put all them stars up in the sky. You photograph him."

"Mama, be nice."

"Maxine, I am nice. I just don't need no pictures of anybody but you. Can you understand that?"

Of course I could understand. Brian wasn't her kid, she didn't need a photo of him. Still, I knew her reasons for cutting him out of family memories was because she never really wanted me with him. Mama has always thought that Brian wasn't the guy for me because of his family. She doesn't really get along too well with his dad, and she hates his mother. It's mostly because his parents both have money and professional jobs, but Brian's mother also got into it with Mama once at one of my birthday parties. When she came to pick Brian up, they got into an argument about Mama's boyfriend. He was more friendly to Brian's mother than he should have been, and Brian's mother didn't like the attention. She told him off, and when Mama got involved Brian's mother told Mama that she should go back to school and get some professional job training, so she wouldn't need some player to pay the rent. Mama exploded all over the place that afternoon, and after that it was a long time before she let Brian come over. When he did come back, she started treating him like she really didn't want him there. Things have gotten a little better lately—a little. I hope and pray it's enough to let her say yes to my getting married.

Back at my house I busied myself with washing a load of clothes while Mama slept. I washed and hung out some sheets and watched them blowing softly in the breeze. Mama loves pastels, but the sheets are dirty dishwater gray because Andre likes them. I can't stand the brother. He's always worried about what Mama does with her money. If I ask her for some money, he always has to ask me what I'm going to do with it, and if he doesn't like my answer he tells her not to give me the cash. Then there's his babies' mama, LaTrice. He got two little boys by her, and she's always coming to our house acting a fool with him about child support. The last time she came I was the only one home. She started going on and on about how Mama and me was taking money that was supposed to be for her kids. I got into a bad argument with her, and I had to physically push her out of my front door because she started swinging. Later, when Andre asked her what happened, she lied and said I started the whole thing, so Andre punched me over it, and Mama didn't stand up for me at all.

"How you gonna let him treat me like that?" I asked, crying.

"Maxine, he didn't hit you that hard, plus you know Andre got a short temper. Next time his ex comes around don't get all up in her face. Just be cool about it," she said. I was pissed off for days. Then Mama got mad at me for being pissed off. She told me that Andre was the only dad I had and that I should be trying to get along with him. I've never really known my real dad, but he sure as heck isn't Andre. My aunt Freda says that he was some nice guy that Mama was hooking up with, but all he did was work and didn't like to go out to the clubs much, so Mama started going out with somebody else and dropped him. Aunt Freda says that Mama told her once that she'll always regret breaking up with my dad. He would have been a good father and a good role model, if she had let him stay around. Now all she has to look forward to are poor substitutes.

I watched the sheets until I heard Mama get up and start her morning routine. When I went inside, she was sitting on the sofa with a half-eaten cereal bar and the latest issue of *Jet* magazine.

"Maxine, where you been?" she asked.

"Washing and hanging out clothes."

"No, I mean before that, you know I sleep light. I heard you going out of the front door."

"Oh, I went to see Brian."

"What for? What were you doing over there so early?" she asked suspiciously.

"Just talking."

"About what? Maxine, what you got to talk to Brian about this early?"

"Just stuff."

"Just stuff. What kinda *stuff* requires you slipping around to his house before the sun is barely up in the sky?"

"I don't know. I only went to tell him that I love him."

She rolled her eyes. "Is that all? Look, Maxine, every time I see you, you all over that boy. He knows how you feel. You ain't got to go slipping out of this house to meet up with him."

"I wasn't slipping, Mama. I thought you were still asleep."

"I'll just bet you did," she said, giving me a glare.

"Come on, Mama, don't be all funky this morning. I got something to ask you."

"What is it?" she asked, adjusting her bandanna over her pink foam rollers."

"It's about me and Brian."

"What about ya'll? What is it now? And just so you know, this is my day off. I ain't got time for no foolishness."

"Aw, Mama, I ain't talking about no foolishness."

"Well, what is it? Spit it out," she said, screwing up her lovely brown face.

"Mama, come on."

"Don't 'come on' me. You got something to say, Maxine, say it."

"It's about me and Brian. We been thinking about it, and we want to be married."

She dropped her magazine and looked like I had just driven a bus through the living room. "Maxine, have you lost your mind? You ain't nowhere near ready to be nobody's bride. Do you hear me?"

"I hear you, but why not? I'm not a kid anymore, Mama. Me and Brian been together for ages."

"Been in school together for ages, been hanging around this house sucking face and being silly together, that's what ya'll been for ages. Ya'll ain't been doing nothing that makes me think you ready to be a wife. You may not be a kid no more, but you are far from being an adult."

"Not that far, Mama. In case you hadn't noticed, I've been getting really grown up."

"No, what you been getting is too grown. You think you some kind of woman, to tell me what to do in my own house," Mama said, getting up off the sofa.

"I'm not trying to tell you what to do, Mama. I'm trying to tell you that me and Brian are in love and we want to be together, like Tia and her boyfriend."

"Like Tia—Lord have mercy. I should have known what this was all about. I knew that little fast-tail friend of yours was gonna send you off in the wrong direction!" Mama yelled.

I rolled my eyes. "Mama, don't go there. You ain't got to call Tia out."

"Why not!" she hollered. "Ain't she what this is all about?"

"No, Mama, I just told you, it's about me and Brian. We want to be together."

"You are together, Maxine, but what you ain't gonna be is together and *married*. You can't do that without my permission, and you ain't gonna get it. You're way too young."

"No, I'm not, Mama!" I said angrily.

She pointed her finger. "You can get as mad as you want, but I ain't changing my mind. And that's it, Maxine," Mama said, starting to walk away.

I grabbed her arm, and she turned around like she was gonna knock me into the field across the street. "Maxine, who you think you jerking?" she asked.

"You have to, Mama. I'm going to have a baby," I blurted out.

"A baby? A what?" She looked like that bus had ran through the house and plowed right into her.

"A baby, a freaking baby! Are you completely out of what's left of your mind?"

"No, I took two of them tests last week, Mama. They both

came up positive," I said, shocked at my words. I didn't know where they were coming from, but I didn't care.

"Positive!" Mama said. "Well I'll be, Maxine, how could you be so careless and dumb? How you gonna come up in my house with a big belly and no husband? Why weren't you careful? I didn't raise you like that. I raised you to have more sense than the average girl in this hood!" she said, stamping her foot.

"I am the average girl in this hood, and I'm trying to get a husband!"

"You supposed to have one first!"

"So was you, but you didn't. You didn't have a husband before *or after* you had me, but I'll have Brian because he's gonna always be around!" I fired back.

She looked stunned. "Every man is always around, Maxine. They around when your belly gets huge; they around when the baby comes out, so they can look like the proud papa; they around for the baptism, cause they scared God gonna get them if they don't turn up at the church; and they around when the baby start to crawl, so they can tell everybody how fast they growing; and they sho' around for the first birthday party, so they can send them cute pictures to all they friends and relatives. They around for all of that Maxine, but don't expect them when you got to buy baby clothes and diapers, and sho' don't look for them when you got to write a check to the day care. They ain't gonna be around for any of those things. So, if you fool enough to be carrying a baby, you better be smart enough to start making some kind of plans to give it away. 'Cause, honey, love don't mean squat when ain't no money in your hands."

"I'm not giving away my child, Mama. Letting somebody else take care of your child might be your thing, but it ain't mine," I said, knowing full well how much the words would hurt.

"Don't go there, Maxine. You told me you wasn't gonna bring that up no more. I'm sorry that I let you go for a little while. I was a lot younger and a lot dumber when that happened. I made the wrong decision and I'm sorry about that, but you 'bout to do something that's gonna get you in a mess for sure."

"I'm already in a mess, Mama. Ain't that what this conversation is about?"

"The conversation is about you wandering around with a baby and no man!"

"I got a man, and I ain't even worried. Brian ain't like one of your men. He will help me do anything I need him to do."

"Brian, Brian? I'm so sick of Brian. Maxine, are you really basing your future on that boy? Honey, let me comb my hair and take you down to the crazy house right now. Lord knows you need to be locked up!" she said, throwing her hands up in the air.

"Very funny, Mama, but I know I can count on him."

She shook her head. "Shoot, you better count on finding that baby some good parents, that's what you better do."

"Brian and I will be good parents, and I wouldn't ever let somebody else take care of a child that I should be taking care of myself. Like I said, that's not *my* thing."

"Okay, you know what, fine. I'm done with this conversation," she said. "I'ma go get me another cereal bar and a cup of coffee. Do what you wanna do. If you trust Brian, you go on and marry him. Give your child a father. Just don't come crying and complaining to me when you got no money and nothing but baby poop in two hands."

"I won't, Mama. Me, Brian, and the baby will be just fine," I said.

"Whatever, little girl. I'll let you be married, because I'd rather see you with a husband, than struggling without one. I don't know how you gonna pull this whole marriage thing off, but I ain't gonna stand in the way of it."

"It's gonna be fine, Mama," I said.

"Maybe, but I want you to know that I'm really disappointed in you, and ain't no wedding going change that. You know I got three sisters, just like me, ain't none of them ever made it down the aisle. I told you a long time ago that I didn't want that for you. I wanted you to be married, but not like this. This kind of marriage can't ever work."

"You don't know that, Mama," I said.

"I know it. My daddy married my mama because she was pregnant. They stayed together for years, but they were never happy. My mama said that her whole marriage she was always afraid that her husband would find someone that he really loved and run off and leave her with all of us kids. That's why she worked so hard trying to make him happy all the time. In the end, all that trying just made her bitter. I hope it doesn't make you bitter too."

"I'm not Grandma, Mama, and I'm also not you."

"No, I guess we ain't never been too much alike. I remember when you were a little girl, I couldn't even pick out an outfit for you. If I tried to buy you a pink dress you would say that you wanted a blue one, even though blue looked just awful on your skin. We would end up getting into a big fight in the store. In some ways, we always been at odds, Maxine, but I hoped we were on the same page with this." With that she walked off to the kitchen.

"I'm sorry, Mama," I mumbled underneath my breath, and I meant it. I didn't want to lie to her. I simply wanted her to give me my freedom. I opened the front door of the house and went outside. The sun was fully up, spreading its bright rays across a cloudy blue sky. I should have felt toasty, but my mood was keeping me lukewarm because I had lied to get what I wanted. To be honest, I couldn't believe how easily Mama gave in once I told her that she was going to be a grandmother.

I remember the morning I discovered my period, Mama came into my room and told me that from now on I had to be careful. She talked about not letting boys take advantage of me, and I never have, and that includes Brian. He helped see to that. He made certain that no matter what we didn't rush things. The first time was when we were barely fourteen. We had gone to our friend Jabari's house to play his new Nintendo and eat some popcorn and slices of German chocolate cake his mother had made. It was just supposed to be a simple fun afternoon, and it was, until some older kids showed up.

The kids were friends of Jabari's sister, Nisa. Nisa wasn't home, but Jabari was trying to be cool and asked the kids to come in and hang anyway. Things were fine until we figured out that the older kids weren't interested in just playing videos. They had other games in mind, the kind of games that most parents hope you don't play until you're married. Before we knew it, couples were messing around everywhere, except for me and Brian. We continued playing Quake, and soon moved on to a version of a 007 game that Jabari had gotten for his birthday. I think deep down we both wanted to leave, but we didn't want to look like babies in front of the older group. So we stayed, and it wasn't long before the group realized that we weren't doing the things they were doing.

"Hey, little dude, you scared of that girl or something?" a short boy in a yellow Kobe Bryant T-shirt asked Brian.

The curvy girl he was fooling around with broke into laughter, and the whole room soon joined in, including Jabari, even though he didn't even have a girlfriend yet.

"I ain't scared of nothing," Brian said.

"Well, you act like you are. Why you playing games with that girl, when there are better things that you could be doing? You understand what I mean, dog?" the boy asked.

"I got ya, man, but we don't have to be doing what ya'll doing to have fun," Brian said.

This time all of the kids laughed.

"Aw, man, this boy is inn-o-cent. He had never had his stick dipped," the boy said.

Brian's face turned red, and mine would have too, but I wasn't gonna let some guy I didn't even know make me feel bad about myself, or my man.

"Yeah, he has. We just like to keep our business to ourselves," I lied.

"Is that right? Well there's a bedroom over there. Go on little man, handle your business *in private*," the boy said, pointing to the open door of Nisa's bedroom.

"Yeah, man, go do what you have to do. Don't be a such a female, dude. What are you some kind of sweet boy or something?" asked another boy with a huge silver-and-rhinestone watch on.

Everyone laughed again.

"Man, just leave me alone," Brian said.

"Well, go do your thing then, man or, shoot, let me do it 'cause I can handle my shorty *and* yours. I got it like that," the boy with the watch said.

"I'm not a shorty and don't make me throw up!" I snapped.

The boy laughed.

"Let's go, Brian," I said, grabbing my purse to leave.

"Aw, man, you gonna let your lady tell you what to do? No wonder you ain't hitting that. Go on out the door, sweet boy," the boy with the Kobe shirt said.

"Drop dead! We're not going!" I snapped.

Before I even knew what I was doing I was pulling Brian behind me into Nisa's bedroom. As soon as we got in there, I slammed the door and sat down on her messy unmade bed fuming.

"Maxine, what the heck are you doing?" Brian asked, confused.

"I'm stopping them from talking about you!" I said.

"And how are you doing that, Maxine?"

"You know how."

"No, I don't."

"Well, shoot, they dogging you out. It ain't fair. It ain't nothing special about what they doing. We can do it too," I said.

He looked more confused. "We can what? Maxine, have you lost it?"

"No, of course not, baby. I just want them to stop teasing you, that's all," I said.

"By giving in to their nonsense? Maxine, baby, we didn't come here for this. All we came to do was chill and play some games," he said, shaking his head.

❦ 17 ❦

"I know that."

"Well then, don't trip."

"I'm not trippin', they trippin'. Don't you want to? I mean, I thought you wanted to anyway," I said, a little hurt by his response.

"Girl, you know I do. I love you, but you just going to be upset if we do this today. You're not ready for this, and I'm not going to do something that both of us is gonna feel real bad about later," he said.

"I won't feel bad, I love you. I thought you loved me too."

He sighed. "Look at me, Maxine. What do I have on today?" he asked.

I shrugged my shoulders. "The same thing I got on, a red T-shirt and blue jeans."

"We look like twins, don't we? And you know how much I hate it when couples do corny stuff like that," he said.

"I know, but I don't," I said with a big grin.

"Yeah, and that's why I dressed this way, for you. I did it because I knew it would make you happy. Don't I always do that?"

"Yeah."

"Well, that's because I know what makes you feel good, girl, and trust me, this ain't it. You don't want to do this here, with them fools outside of the door."

"No, I don't. But they gonna keep talking trash about you if you don't look like you manning up," I said.

He grinned. "Girl, my daddy taught me what *manning up* means. Trust me, it don't mean taking advantage of your girlfriend just because some dudes you don't even know are all up in your grill. Girl, this is wack. It ain't for us."

"Are you sure? Because I won't mind, I know everything will be okay if it's with you."

"I'm sure. I mean I really want to, but we don't even do things this way. Do we?"

"Naw," I said.

He pulled me to my feet. We walked out of the room without saying a word, and started playing video games again. Of course the older boys knew that we hadn't done anything, so they really started laying into Brian. Brian didn't say anything back, and the boys soon backed off.

Later in our relationship, when we hooked up for real, it was under much different circumstances, and we were very, very careful. I didn't want there to be any accidents. I didn't want Mama to be upset with me, like she is now.

Brian needed to be told about the new plan. I went back inside the house. I walked to my room, picked up the phone off of my nightstand, and dialed it. It rang three times and Brian picked it up.

"What's up, Maxine?" he asked.

"We're gonna have a baby," I said, calmly into the receiver.

"What?" he asked.

"I told my Mama that you and me are gonna have a child."

"What? You're not for real are you?" he asked in a panicky way.

"Naw, I'm not for real, but Mama don't know that, and what she don't know won't keep us from being married."

"I guess it won't," he said. "I don't know about this though, Maxine. You can't pretend something like this for too long."

"We don't need to do it for long, Brian. We just need to do it long enough to plan a wedding and go down the aisle. This will work. Trust me," I said.

"Maxine, I ain't never trusted anybody in my life, but you. If you say we gonna have a baby, we gonna have a baby," he said.

"I love you," I said.

"Me too," he said, and hung up.

I put the phone down and picked up my History notebook from my nightstand. I found a clean sheet and began writing down everyone I wanted to invite to the wedding. From the kitchen I could hear Mama taking out her unhappiness on the pots and pans that I left drying in the sink the night before. The banging didn't bother me. All I could hear were the wedding bells ringing in my ears, and nothing else.

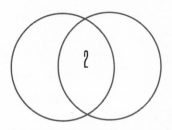

2

When Mama's boyfriend, Andre, first moved in with us he brought his seventy-pound pit bull mix, Bad Girl, with him, and she was bad for real. She would bark and lunge at strangers from behind the fence, and if a stray cat or possum wandered into our yard she would grab it and rip it to pieces. Our side yard soon became a graveyard, and we would spend our days burying some poor animal that wasn't fortunate enough to see Bad Girl coming and get out of her way. Mama hated these burials, and after each one she would threaten to get rid of the dog. One day, while we were burying yet another neighborhood kitten, I asked her why she didn't just up and do it.

"Mama, why don't you just call the animal control people and have her taken away?" I asked.

"Because I can't. That darn dog makes me sick, but I can't get rid of it, and you know it."

"Why not?" I asked.

"You know how much Andre cares about that stupid mutt. He'll throw a fit on me."

"So, what's new about that?"

"Don't start nothing, Maxine. Besides, the dog ain't responsible for what she's doing. She's just a dumb animal. I can't just take her and leave her in the hands of God knows who."

"Are you kidding, Mama? You didn't have any problem leaving me in the care of the state all those years ago!" I snapped.

"Maxine, don't even go there. You know I didn't take you to foster care, the state did that. Don't keep hanging that on me. You know I wasn't the one who fired that bullet," she snapped.

"No, you just loaded the gun and gave it to them," I said.

"Maxine, I had a right to have a life. It wasn't my fault that you didn't get along with Mr. Potter."

"You mean Mr. Pothead, don't you, Mama? Do you remember how he used to spend his afternoons all lit up and how he used to make that cash he was giving you?" I said, digging into the hard black dirt with my shovel.

"Maxine, that's not true. Mr. Potter was a man of God, and you know it. He went to church all the time, and Sunday school. He never missed a lesson."

"He did miss one, Mama. He missed, 'Do unto others as you would have them do unto you.' I remember that from when I used to go to church sometimes with Tia and her Grandma Augustine. I remember Sister Ashada said that you are supposed to treat people the way you want to be treated. I don't think that Mr. Potter wanted somebody beating on *him*."

She threw her shovel down. "Maxine, I'm sorry about what Mr. Potter did to you. I know that his discipline sometimes went a little far. I think he just believed in that other thing they say in church. I don't know exactly what it is, but it's something about your kids will get spoiled if you don't hit them sometimes, and there's something about a rod in there. Mr. Potter just had some old-fashioned ways, that's all. He wanted to do things the way they used to do them back in the day."

"Mama, I don't think it was okay—even back in the day—to hit your kids until they got big bruises and welts on them and couldn't sit down for a week," I said, angrily digging up a big clump of earth. I flung it behind me, onto the kitten whose lifeless body was lying on the ground, carefully wrapped in a couple of twin-sized pillow slips from my bed.

"My God, such a shame," Mama said, turning around to look at the cat.

"Yeah," I said.

"Maxine, I don't want to argue with you about things that went on in the past. I can't change them, and neither can you. Let's just bury this poor animal in peace."

"Whatever, Mama. We shouldn't be having to bury it at all," I said.

"My God, what a shame," Mama repeated.

We buried the cat, and I patted the dirt into place over it with my bare feet.

The next day when I went to school I told Brian about the kitten, and about all the animals that Bad Girl had killed. He said that he was going to call the animal control people, because a dog that would attack other animals might someday attack me. "You don't know. One day you might be the one somebody is shoveling dirt over," Brian said.

I couldn't argue with him. I had to admit I really didn't feel safe with Bad Girl around, so I didn't stop him from making the call. About a week after he phoned, the animal control cops came by our house one afternoon while Mama and Andre were at work. I showed them where the bodies of the animals that Bad Girl had killed were buried, and they took her with them. I didn't expect them to, but one of the cops said that he recognized Bad Girl as a dog that they had labeled as dangerous earlier in the year. They said Andre's babies' mama had called them after Bad Girl attacked her puppy. The puppy had to have major surgery, and Andre was told that he had to keep Bad Girl penned up at all times and away from other animals.

"We're going to go ahead and load her up. Please have her owner call us when he gets home," the lady cop said.

"Yes ma'am," I told her, glad to see the dog go. When Mama came home from her hotel cleaning job she saw the dog was gone and asked me about it. I told her that Brian had complained about Bad Girl and the animal cops had taken her away.

"Good, I wish I had been brave enough to do that myself. If they call here, you tell them don't even think about bringing that mutt back to my house," she said, taking her uniform off.

But it was another story when Andre got to the house. When he got back, Mama acted like she didn't even know what was going on.

"I don't have a clue where she is. My God, I sure hope nothing ain't happened to that dog," Mama said.

Of course I told Andre the truth, that the dog had been taken away. He cursed us all out and went racing down to the pound, swearing that he was going to bring his beloved dog back. I don't think that any of us were surprised when he returned home alone and told us that Bad Girl was going to be put down. That night he and I got into a fight. Brian was there and jumped in the middle of it.

"Man, I called on that dog. You better back off of my girlfriend," Brian said.

"Boy, you better get out of my face!" Andre yelled back.

"I'll get out your face when you get out of Maxine's," Brian said.

"Boy, who do you think you are? Don't think because your daddy got a little cash it means that I won't beat you down!" Andre yelled.

"I'm not afraid of you. Do what you have to do!" Brian yelled back.

The argument soon turned physical, and although Andre is much stronger than Brian, the two them actually went toe-to-toe for a while. They tussled until Andre figured out that he could go to jail for attacking a kid. He let Brian go and stormed off, muttering and swearing. Mama started crying.

Oh, how Mama cried. She really put on a show. She did everything she could to keep Andre from thinking that she had had anything to do with what happened to his dog. Her waterworks went on for days, until her tear ducts completely dried out. It made me sick, but I wasn't surprised. She's good at making certain that she never comes off looking bad or guilty in any situation, and I doubt if that will ever change.

The incident with Bad Girl happened weeks ago, but this morning at breakfast I was once again reminded of how good Mama is at protecting *herself*. Andre was jumping me about the baby he thinks I'm going to have and Mama didn't say or do one thing to help me.

"How you gonna let this girl come up in here with another mouth to feed?" Andre yelled at Mama over the table.

"It's not my dang fault that she got knocked up. I told her to keep her dress down and drawers up. She knew better than to be messing around with that Brian boy without no kind of protection," Mama said, opening the wrapper on her oat cereal bar.

"Apparently she didn't. Apparently she ain't got no kind of a brain in her head, getting knocked up for that rich boy that ain't even gonna be around when her belly is all swollen up," Andre said.

"That's not true!" I said. I took my glass cereal bowl over to the table and threw it down.

"Don't be tearing up nothing you didn't buy," Andre said, mixing sugar into his steaming hot coffee. I wanted to pick the cup up and pour it into his thick Afro.

"So, you didn't buy it either. Great-aunt Freda gave us this bowl for a present. It ain't got nothing to do with you, and neither do I," I said.

"That's a lie. It's got everything to do with me. You talking about bringing another mouth to feed into my house!" Andre yelled.

I just rolled my eyes. Andre didn't scare me. He was just

another bully that Mama was stupid enough to bring home one day.

"It's not your house. It's me and Mama's," I said.

"No, it's mine, cause I'm the one paying the damn rent. Your mama don't make enough money to put mayonnaise on a sandwich."

"Yes, she does," I said.

"Yeah, right, so that's why you think you need to come home knocked up, so your mama can spend the little money she makes buying pampers and milk for some little fool that you don't even need!" Andre hollered.

"You don't know what I need!" I hollered back.

"Yeah, I do. You need your behind beat for being so stupid. You need to quit acting like some kind of dumb tramp!" Andre said through gritted teeth.

I gritted mine even harder. "I'm not a tramp and I'm not asking you or Mama for anything. Brian is gonna take care of me. He loves me!" I said.

"Loves you. Shoot, he might love what you giving him girl, but I guarantee you he ain't gonna love having to take care of no crying ass baby in high school. You wait and see. As soon as you pop that baby out he's gonna book it out of the hospital and never look back." Andre laughed.

"That's not true. Brian would never do anything like that. We're getting married," I said.

Andre's dark eyes widened in shock. "Married, what is she talking about?" he asked Mama.

Mama just shrugged her shoulders and took a bite out of her bar.

"Married! Girl, that little player ain't gonna marry you.

Why would he marry you? You ain't nobody. That boy's family got money. He ain't gonna hook himself up for good with you," Andre said. He threw his head back and roared. He was far from being a bad-looking brother, but with his face all screwed up in an ugly laugh, he looked like some hideous creature from hell.

"Stop laughing. Brian loves me, and we are getting married. Tell him, Mama. Tell him that Brian ain't the kind of boy that would do what he talking about!" I shouted at Mama.

Mama shrugged again, like she didn't even have a clue what I was saying.

"Mama, say something. Tell him what kind of boy Brian really is."

"Yeah, tell me," Andre said sarcastically.

Mama sat there for a long time just looking at Andre, as if she was trying to think of something that Andre wanted to hear.

"Well, tell me. Cause I know this tramp is lying or trippin' or both," Andre said.

"No, I'm not. Brian is gonna marry me, and Mama said it was okay. Go on, Mama, tell him," I pleaded.

Mama shook her head. "Look, I'm trying to eat in peace, that's all," she said.

"I'm trying to eat in peace too. So, tell him, and he'll shut up," I said.

"Ain't nothing to tell," she said. "I don't know what kind of boy Brian is. I don't know what he gonna do."

"That's not true. I told you that he said he would marry me, and you know that, Mama," I said.

"All I know is I got somewhere else I have to be," Mama said.

She got up and left me sitting there with Andre. He threw his head back and roared with laugher again. I threw my spoon down on the table and stormed out.

"You better be going to find someplace to get rid of that crap you done brought into your life," Andre hollered after me.

"The only crap in my life is you," I hollered back.

I went to my room and started dressing, angrier than I had been in a long time, but not at Andre. His words were like being attacked by a single red ant. The pain would be there for bit but it would quickly go away. It was Mama that I was really angry with. She hadn't said anything when Andre called me a tramp. How could she let him do that? I had never even brought another guy over to my house, while every guy she had ever talked to had made it past our front door. My pregnancy was fake, but Mama had been pregnant without a husband at least one other time.

About two years ago, after this dude she was crazy about moved in with us, and then back with his wife in less than two months, Mama started getting up every morning looking like she had been wrestling with the Devil all night, and not being able to keep her breakfast bars and orange juice from being spewed out all over the kitchen floor. When I asked her what was wrong, she just said that she was stressed out from work and it was making her tired and sick to her stomach, but I knew different. There was enough pregnant girls in my school for me to know the symptoms. It wasn't unusual to hear some tired-looking, rumored-to-be-pregnant girl puking her lungs out when you went to the bathroom during first or second period.

Finally, after about a month, my uncle Ernie came over and picked Mama up. They were gone for a few hours and when they came home Mama's eyes were all watery, and she looked like she had been jumped by a hundred gang bangers. I asked her what was wrong again, but she just went straight to her room and stayed there for three days, lying in bed, watching reruns of her favorite Western shows, *Bonanza* and *Gunsmoke*. When she finally came out, she still didn't say anything, but there were no more dark circles under her beautiful brown eyes, and her lovely smooth skin was glowing again.

"Are you feeling better?" I asked.

"Maxine, why do you keep asking me stupid questions?" she asked, slicing fresh strawberries into her oatmeal.

"It's not stupid. I just wanted to know if you're okay. Mama, you looked real bad when you came home the other night and you been in your room for days."

"I know where I been, Maxine. I don't need you to tell me my business. I told you, I'm okay. You just eat your breakfast and quit dipping in my Kool-Aid."

"I'm not dipping, I'm asking, but whatever," I said, putting Parkay on my toast.

"Yeah, whatever," she said.

We left it like that. She ate her oatmeal, and it didn't come back up. I never told her that I suspected she was pregnant, and that I was hurt that she wouldn't even talk to me about what was going on. It was my little brother or sister that she had more than likely left behind at some clinic that day, all because she had made a mistake by being with a guy that she had no business being with in the first place.

Me, I wasn't even like that. I would have never made her mistake.

I slipped into a comfortable summer outfit and I left the house. The sun wasn't blazing yet. It was actually kind of mild and pleasant out, and I tried to calm down a bit when I got into the fresh air. I was going to see my man, and I didn't want to see him with my feelings all jacked up. No matter how Mama and Andre felt about me and Brian we were still going to be married, and maybe one day I really would have his baby. The thought of that filled me with joy. I really would love to have a little Brian or Briana running around some day.

I took the number eighty bus and got off in front of the Redesign Center. It sounded like a place that might have something to do with art or making ugly rooms pretty, but it was really a place for younger boys who were failing academically, and older boys who wanted to get their futures on track. For the older boys, the focus was on job readiness or preparation for military careers, but for the younger ones, the focus was on helping them sort their grades and negative behaviors out, so that they could excel in school. Most of the older boys joined on their own, but there were some that also came to the center as mentors for the younger group.

A few months ago Brian was asked to be a teen mentor at the center. The teachers thought that his good school grades, and the fact that his father was a successful businessman, made him the perfect role model for the kids twelve and under.

At first Brain wasn't too cool with working at the center, because he knew that it was something that his father would definitely want him to do, and also because he didn't see any reason to try and help kids that he said probably just sat in class all day doing nothing.

"Why should I go out of my way to help some fools that won't help themselves until report card time?" Brian asked, but he soon found out that it wasn't true. Most of the students in the center were hard workers who just needed some help grasping what they were already being taught in the classroom. When Brian found that out, he changed his mind about the center and was eager to work there. Besides spending time with me, it is the one thing that he actually enjoys doing.

When I got to the center, I headed for the lounge, where I knew Brian would be waiting for a new sixth grader that he was tutoring in writing. As soon as I opened the door, I saw him sitting in a black vinyl chair looking at a *Vibe* magazine. I walked over and kissed him on cheek, before I took another chair across from him. "Girl, what's wrong?" he asked, looking up from his magazine. I guess some of the anger I had earlier was still showing in my face.

"Nothing, I'm fine. Andre was just being mean again, and Mama wasn't saying anything to him about it."

"What's new about that?" he asked. "I don't know why you don't set that dude straight and let him know he don't run nothing in that house but his mouth."

"I try to sometimes, but it's hard when Mama won't say anything to him. You know that."

"Then say something to her. Let her know you don't like

the way she treats you. She's your mama. She's not supposed to let some dude treat you like dirt in your own house. Dang, Maxine, stand up for yourself."

"It's not that simple, Brian. You know it's not. How you gonna stand up to somebody that never even admits when they are doing wrong?"

"You stand up to everyone else, and for everyone else. I've seen you get into all kinds of people's faces over me, and your girl Tia. Remember last year when that band girl was making fun of Tia because Doo-witty was kinda slow, and you told her that she better back off before you made her swallow her horn."

"Yeah, I know, but it's not the same. She wasn't my mama. Besides, you know how things are because of your father. It's not easy getting into it with someone you love."

"Yeah, I know, but my father ain't never tried to hurt me, or let nobody else hurt me, and that makes a difference."

"I know."

"Do you, Maxine? Baby, I love you more than anything, but you got to learn how to get on someone when they are doing something to hurt your feelings. It's like your great-aunt Freda says, 'You can't just be a caretaker for other people, you got to take care of yourself too.' Do you understand that?"

"Of course I do."

"Well, good baby, because I want to marry a strong sister. I don't want to marry someone who doesn't have a clue how to handle their own stuff."

"I see your point baby, and I get you. I'll get better after we jump the broom," I said, and gave him a big smile. He got up from his seat and returned my smile with a passionate kiss.

"You guys need to cut that out in here," Brian's boss, Mr. Warner, suddenly said from the other side of the room. We looked up and saw him standing by the water cooler next to the door. He filled a clear plastic cup up to the brim and came over to us.

"Did I hear something about jumping the broom?" he asked, and quickly drank his water down, without spilling even one drop on his fly dark green suit. Brian's boss is a super-neat brother. His suits always look like he has just picked them up from the cleaners, and he keeps his hair short and tight in a military hair cut. He's an ex–air force commander, and he runs a boot camp twice a month for the boys who are having the hardest time cleaning their lives up. In the camp, he puts the kids through a tough workout, but Brian says he's even tougher when he helps tutor the kids in the math classroom.

"Mr. Warner doesn't like mistakes. If a kid misses a problem, he makes them keep working it over and over until they get it right, even if it means that they have to keep working the problem until midnight. He says that mistakes are weaknesses, and the center doesn't turn out weak kids," Brian once told me.

I don't know about all that, but I do know that most of the boys who attend the center look up to Mr. Warner, including Brian, who says that he has a lot of respect for someone who could serve his country and then come home and serve his community as well.

"So, did I hear something about a marriage?" he asked Brian.

"Yes sir, you heard right. Me and my girl getting married pretty soon," Brian said.

"Married?" Mr. Warner asked.

"Yes, sir. We are going to get hitched," Brian said, and smiled.

"Really, at your age? What's the rush? If you don't mind my asking," Mr. Warner asked.

"No rush, we just love each other," Brian said.

Mr. Warner stroked his beard. "Well, love is one thing, but marriage, that's something else. I know. I've been married for about twelve years. It's nothing to go into lightly. You really need to be certain that you are making the right choice. Are you?"

"We're certain," I said.

"Why not wait? Why not go out and learn something first, get some valuable experiences in your life. Why the big hurry?" Mr. Warner asked.

"We just want to, that's all," Brian said.

"Yeah. We just want to," I said. I was beginning to feel like we were criminals being questioned by a cop or something. Why was Brian's boss asking us so many questions?

"I'm sure you do—just want to do it—but still, most people your age don't understand what it takes to make that level of commitment so young. There is a huge financial, emotional, and spiritual commitment that comes when two people are joined for life. Do you know that Brian?" Mr. Warner said.

"I—I don't—don't know," Brian said, stumbling over his words.

"Well, do you?" Mr. Warner asked.

"I—I think so," Brian said.

"We do, besides I'm going to have a baby," I blurted out.

"A what?" Mr. Warner asked.

"Oh yeah, uh, a baby," Brian said.

"You're going to have a baby, *with her*?" his boss asked.

"Yes, sir, we have a baby on the way," Brian said.

Mr. Warner's face looked like it was going to explode. "Brian, you know that you were chosen to be here because your school selected you from a long list of students. They chose you because they believed that the boys here could learn a lot from you."

"I know, and they can," Brian said.

"Can they? What is it that you can teach them, how to become a parent before you even get out of school? How to ruin a young girl's life?" Mr. Warner barked.

"No. No, sir. That's not what I think I can teach. It's just that me and Maxine . . . ," Brian said.

"My life isn't ruined," I said, interrupting Brian. I didn't appreciate what Mr. Warner was saying at all. He didn't know anything about me.

"Yes, it is, and so is Brian's, and that's not what I'm trying to teach the young boys who come here. I want them to learn how to avoid some of the pitfalls of this neighborhood, like drugs and gangs, and premature pregnancies. The shame and crime of all these things are just bringing our little brothers down. It's why I came back here, decided to work in the hood again," he said, wagging his finger at Brian.

"Having a baby isn't a shame or crime!" I snapped.

Mr. Warner walked over to my chair and got right in my face. "Do you really believe that?" he asked. "You can't be that foolish."

"She's not foolish, and you don't have the right to talk to her like that. We haven't committed a crime, and the only shame is how you're talking to my girl," Brian said, getting his boss straight.

Mr. Warner backed away from my chair, the whole time looking like he wanted to go all commando on Brian.

"That's right. We ain't doing nothing wrong. You don't have no right to be all nasty to me," I said. I wasn't even pregnant, but if I was it didn't mean that he could talk a lot of trash to me and my man.

"I'm not trying to make you mad or disappoint you, but we haven't done anything awful. We just love each other, sir," Brian said.

"Well, I don't need that kind of love at the center. Look Brian, I've won more battles than I've lost around here with these boys. I've managed to get some of the worst students back on track, and I'd like them to stay on it. I'm trying to win a war here, and I need soldiers that I can trust. I can't hold my ground with a traitor in the mix," his boss said.

"What does that mean?" Brian asked with a stunned look on his face.

"It means, I'm sorry, Brian, but I can't use you around here. I need someone with both brains and common sense. I need someone who can be a true leader for these impressionable young minds. I can't have them thinking that it is okay to screw up," Mr. Warner said.

"That's not fair, sir. I'm good with the kids and I'm one of the best tutors you have," Brian said.

"You used to be, not anymore. I'll let the students know that you will no longer be helping them out," Mr. Warner said.

"Are you for real? Come on man. Just like that?" Brian asked.

"Yes, and I'm really sorry that it didn't work out. I'll call your school tomorrow and ask them to recommend someone else," Mr. Warner said and left the room.

I looked at Brian. My great-aunt Freda would say that he looked like the Egyptians must have looked when they saw the Red Sea closing in on them.

"What just happened, Maxine?" he asked.

"I don't know."

"Did he just tell me that I can't come back because we're getting married?"

"I think so, and because I said that I was gonna have your child."

"That's not fair. I really like volunteering here. And we haven't done anything wrong," Brian said.

"He thinks we have, because of the baby."

"What baby? We're not having a baby, not really. This sucks!" he said, jumping up out of his chair.

"I know. It's my fault. I shouldn't have said anything."

"Well, you're right about that. Maxine, why did you have to tell him about the baby? You ruined everything. Why did you even have to say anything?"

"I didn't mean to. It just slipped out."

"Dang, it's not fair for him to diss me like that. I'm good at what I do Maxine. Those boys really like me. I help them with their schoolwork and all sorts of things. How is he just gonna tell me that I can't do it anymore? I hate this. I didn't do anything wrong," he said, and kicked the chair over.

I bent down and picked it up. "I guess he don't want the other boys to think that it's okay to have a baby before you're married," I said.

"But I'm not. I'm not having a baby!"

"I know, I'm sorry baby. It's my fault. Do you want me to go tell him the truth, Brian? I can tell him that we're not really having a kid, and that I made it all up," I said, trying to calm him down. I walked over to him and put my arm around his shoulder. He brushed it off.

"Would you please? Dang, just go tell the truth," he said.

"I will, if that's what you want," I said.

Brian sighed. He took a moment and collected himself. "No, that wouldn't be right. I'm just confused. It's not your fault. I just need to get my head together. He shouldn't be kicking me to the curb just because I'm not living my life the way he wants me to, plus I didn't like the way he asked me if I was going to have a baby *with you*. I didn't like the tone in his voice, as if he couldn't believe that I would want you to be the mother of my child. I don't even know what he meant by that. He's a snob, and he can go shove his center where the Good Lord split him."

"Are you sure? Baby, you love hanging out here, and I know how much you respect Mr. Warner."

"I love hanging out with you more, and I don't want to hang around someone that doesn't respect me back, or my girl."

"You shouldn't have to," I said.

"I know. Still, I wish it hadn't gone down like this. I wish we didn't have to lie and give stuff up to get what we want. It's a bad way to start our life off. I don't like doing stuff like this," Brian said.

"I don't care if I have to lie and give everything up, Brian, as long as the one thing I'm able to keep is you."

"Yeah, I feel you girl. Plus, if my boss makes me assistant manager at the card shop, I won't have all that much time to hang out here anyway. Shoot, let's go get some barbecue or something. I'm kind of hungry."

"Okay," I said.

We left the center arm in arm. When we got halfway down the street, Brian turned and acted like he wanted to go back. He didn't though, because he knew that what was in front of him was going to be much better than what he left behind.

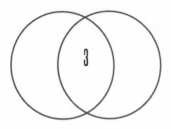

3

Though Mama initially agreed to let me and Brian go down the aisle, she's been putting everything off for the past two months, even though I've been doing everything to convince her to speed things up. I've made myself throw up a few times, and have even faked some dizzy spells. Yesterday I pretended to be light-headed while I was hanging the towels out on the clothesline. When Mama saw me, she came running over and took the laundry basket. "Maxine, give me that dang basket. I don't need you dropping my clothes everywhere. Shoot, why don't you go work on getting your school grades up, or go have fun with your girlfriends. Why don't you go see what them twins, Bonita and Madona, are up to? Maybe ya'll can catch a movie or hang out at that new CD store."

"Mama, my school work is fine, and I don't want to hang out at a store," I lied. The truth is I love shopping with Bonita and Madona. They are identical twins, sort of. If you can excuse the fact that they had a brother born at the exact same time as them so they are really triplets. Their mother sent him to live with relatives after he got involved with a gang. I often wonder what the girls would be like if their brother was still around. Would his being around have stopped them from being the Doublemint Twins? They dress alike, talk alike, and always do the same things, and they are almost as close to me as Tia.

They are plus-sized girls like me, so they know what it's like to never find anything to wear in the junior section. They dress each day in big shirts and baggy pants, because they say it's more comfortable, while I always find something cute in the women's section to fit my curves. The girls are also kind of shy. They don't go out much, and prefer to spend their time reading teen magazines and surfing the Internet. I've never been interested in what so-called teen idols do, and I don't really care what goes on in cyberspace, but when I need someone to talk to, I can always go to the twins. We talk about everything from boyfriends to mother problems. The only thing we don't talk about is school, because the girls go to an alternative center. It's strange really. Madona is an okay student, but her sister Bonita spends all day daydreaming. Last year Bonita flunked five out of six classes, and when Madona found out her sister was failing, she somehow managed to flunk the exact same classes too. The principal at their school thought it was messed up as hell, so he kicked them both out and sent them to the alternative center, so they could have their work supervised and get some counseling. Madona is doing better, but Bonita is still gazing out of the window. It doesn't bother me none that the girls are a little odd about some things. They understand me, and I understand them. The great thing about understanding friends is they know when to let you concentrate on your own life, and your man. They know what really matters to you, but mothers usually don't.

"Mama, I want to be with Brian, that's all. Why can't you see that? Why can't you just deal, and let me and Brian do what we need to do?"

"I am dealing, but what's the rush? You gonna be with Brian for the rest of your life, ain't no need to be hurrying things," Mama said, while I was putting the dinner dishes away.

"There is a need, Mama, and pretty soon you gonna have to admit that," I said.

Since Mama wouldn't deal, I was gonna make her deal. I decided to go to the clinic to get proof, and I asked Brian's cousin Kayla to help me. She's my age, and she's already having her second child. Her first baby was born in Galveston, where her baby's daddy lives. She was heading down to join him, but before she left, me and Brian asked her if she wanted to pick up some cash for moving expenses.

"Are you sure you want me to do this?" Kayla asked me, when we gave her some money from our part-time jobs.

"Yeah, I'm sure. They don't ask for any ID, so all you got to do is go down to the clinic and tell them that you're me. Don't nobody even know me down there, because I go somewhere else."

"Are you sure you need me to do this? You don't think your mama believes you already?" she asked.

"Yeah but, my mama can be stubborn sometimes, and she don't really like Brian."

"Yeah, mamas can trip like that. Look, whatever girl, you know I can use the cash. I'll get your back, but when your mama finds out, she gonna want to beat it."

"It won't be the first time. Anyway, I know she'll be mad, but it will be cool as soon as she figures out that I'm really happy," I said.

She turned to Brian. "I hope she's right. Are you sure you want me to do this?" she asked.

"Yeah, do whatever Maxine wants. She my girl," Brian told her.

"Okay, it's cool cousin. I got you covered. I'll go down to the clinic today," Kayla said.

I can't tell you how excited I was when I heard that. And when she later brought back medical papers saying that Maxine Banks was nine weeks pregnant, I happily handed them over to Mama.

"See, Mama, I can't wait forever. We got to make plans now. You the one who said that you didn't want me having a baby without being married," I said.

I thought, when confronted with the evidence, Mama was going to yell and go crying to Andre. Instead she looked kind of shocked and broken when she saw the paper.

"Maxine, how could you do this?" she asked. She walked over to the living room phone and picked it up. A few seconds later I heard the loud hello of Great-uncle Jerry coming from the receiver.

"You know I don't usually ask for nothing, but I need some cash. Maxine needs to get married," Mama whispered to the only person in our family who actually had any benjamins.

I was glad I couldn't hear what Great-uncle Jerry was

saying. I figured he was as disappointed as Mama was and I couldn't be bothered about it. I wanted to be married, and I didn't care how I had to make it happen. Besides, it would be better for both me and Mama. Eventually Andre and I was going to seriously have it out. I wasn't gonna let him push me around forever. We were in each other's faces all the time. It was a bad situation for everyone, and Mama would end up having to kick one of us out anyway.

"What did Great-uncle Jerry say?" I asked Mama when she hung up.

"What do you think, Maxine? What on earth do you think?" Mama asked. She sighed. "My head hurts from all this drama. You done really caused me stress. Maxine, go ask Tia's grandmother how much she would charge to make you a dress, and after that you better help me find some place for you to get married in it."

"Yes ma'am," I said, running out of the house.

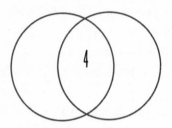

4

We've put off talking to Brian's dad for as long as we could about the baby, but this morning we decided that it was time to throw ourselves on the mercy of the court.

"This isn't gonna be easy. I'm certain that my mother has already told my father what's what. Are you sure you don't want me to do this by myself?" Brian asked me before we knocked on his father's study door.

"I'm sure that I love you, and loving you means that I can't be anywhere else," I said.

"That's all I need to know," Brian said. He knocked, and it only took a second for his father to answer. The angry look in his eyes made me feel happy that I wasn't letting Brian face him alone.

"Your mother told me your news. Son, how could you mess up like this?" his father roared, before we barely stepped in the door.

"I haven't messed up anything," Brian said.

"Of course you have, and you know it. You know the situation your mother and I ended up with, and we were better prepared than you. Your mother had money, and I was about to graduate college with a very bright future. Still, a child born to two unready parents always creates a disaster."

"Disaster! Is that really what I was, Daddy?" Brian asked, hurt.

"No, son, that's not what I meant. I'm simply trying to tell you that this shouldn't have happened."

"Well, it did happen, Daddy. Maxine is pregnant, and I have to step up," Brian said.

"Step up to what? Step up to living without nothing, having bills you can't pay? And what about your schooling? You're not about to quit school," he said, pointing his finger in Brian's face. Brian flinched a little. He's always been intimated by his dad. His daddy is an ex-football player, who spends a lot of time working on his physique. He's also a shrewd businessman who works at a marketing firm, where he handles only the biggest accounts. When he got through with college, he kept it real by building a house in the hood. It's the only thing about him that I admire.

When his father first realized that Brian and I were serious about each other, he didn't like it because I'm only a so-so student. He wanted Brian to be with some girl that always makes the honor roll and he's let me know it on several occasions.

"I know my boy loves you, but I'm concerned about your poor study habits and lack of ambition. Brian is going to go far, and he needs a young lady that's going to help him do it," he's told me over and over.

"What Brian needs is someone who loves him and treats

him good—and that's me," I always say. I was hoping to prove that to him someday. Maybe I still will, after he stops being so pissed about the marriage.

"Daddy, I'm stepping up to my responsibility. Isn't that what you always told me to do?" Brian asked.

"Son, I also always told you to be careful. Don't you remember when I took you down to the drugstore and bought condoms? How could you let me down like this, and yourself? What about the future we planned? You were supposed to finish school and go to college. After that, we planned on you working with me, until you went back to school and obtained a higher-level degree. There were high hopes for your future. That's why I don't understand how you could let this happen!" his dad hollered. This time Brian really flinched. He got a look on his face like he might actually tell the truth.

"It just did. It just happened. We were being careful, but mistakes do occur," I said.

"Maxine, you were the girl who was supposed to love and care for my boy. Now look at the trouble you've gotten him into," his father spat.

"Daddy, Maxine didn't get me into anything. I did what I wanted to do. So just lay off with the attitude," Brian said, standing up.

"Who do you think you are, little boy? Do you even know that the baby is yours!" his daddy yelled again. Brian cringed a little, but he didn't back down.

"I'm not a boy anymore, Daddy. And I know the baby is mine. Maxine ain't even like that. The bottom line is, I'm about to be a real man and a father. You just gonna have to get used to that," Brian said with authority in his voice.

"That's right," I said.

Brian's father looked as if he wanted to slap me into the next universe. Then his face softened.

"Okay. Okay, son. I don't like any of this, but I've always taught you to take care of your responsibility. As long as you agree to stay in school, I'll try to accept this. I'll help you out the best way I can, so that you can eventually still do the things that we talked about. But just know that you have really made a mistake and there's no way to turn away from it."

"I don't want to turn away from it, Daddy. I love Maxine, I want to do right by her."

"Brian, trust me, this isn't the right thing to do. However, I'll back you on it. I love you, and I don't want to see you destroy your life. This is a hard hit, and I'll help you bear it."

"Thanks, Dad. I can do this. I won't let you down," Brian said.

"You've already done that, but I promise that I'll do everything I can to make certain that your life doesn't continue to go downhill."

"It won't as long as I have Maxine," Brian said.

"I hope you're right," Brian's father said.

Me too. I hope that me and Brian are making the right decision. I was glad that Brian stood up for me, and even gladder that I came up with the baby idea. Everything was falling into place. It was going to be exactly the way we planned it.

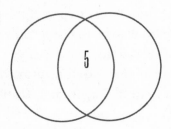

5

t's a week before the wedding and most of the details have all been worked out. I have a fierce white gown with little flowers made of pearls decorating the skirt, and I've ordered a dreamy white wedding cake that looks like it's been draped in lace with violets on the top. Summertime Florist is going to decorate the church with more beautiful violets, purple pansies, and my favorite lavender ribbons. I chose white for Brian's tuxedo and his groomsmen, and he's already picked them up. Tia just spent all her money moving to New York, and can't afford to come home for the wedding, so I asked my girlfriends Madona and Bonita to fill in as maids of honor. They are *so* ready to go.

"Girl, you know we gonna be there for you. When is it? We can't wait," they both said, when I told them about the wedding. So, all I had to do after that was get Tia's grandma to make them dresses. She made two beautiful satin gowns for them, along with two more for my Great-uncle Jerry's granddaughter,

Kiki, and Brian's thirteen-year-old cousin, Demonee. Demonee is the only thing I'm not happy about. Brian's daddy insisted that Demonee be in the wedding, and I threw a fit. That girl sucks the life out of me. Whenever I've been around her she's been ugly acting and disrespectful, which is exactly the way she acted when I asked her.

"Why I got to be in your stupid wedding? You ain't got no relatives of your own?" she asked.

"Yeah, I got some, but you're gonna be my relative soon. I just thought it would be a good way to get to know you," I said.

"Whatever, it's all stupid to me. I could be hanging out with my friends or something on that day."

"Yeah, I guess you could," I said, sarcastically.

"Yeah I could, except I'll be in your dumb wedding, 'cause I know my uncle is gonna make me anyway," is how she ended our conversation.

I fussed at Brian about it for days, but when I saw how cute and sweet Demonee looked in her junior bridesmaid's dress, I decided to drop the matter and hope for the best. Anyway, like I said, most of the details of the wedding have already been worked out, except where we are going to live. Yesterday Brian's dad called him and told him that he had a great solution to our problem. After I finished my boring English homework, Brian and I were going to go check it out. Trust me, I couldn't wait to see what surprise might be hidden in the bottom of our cereal box.

I guess English teachers don't understand how exciting it is to be on the verge of getting married, because it took most of the morning and afternoon to finish my paper. During the time it took me to finish, Brian called twice, because on Sundays he has to go to work kind of early. When I finally told him that I was ready to go, he came over looking a little bit irritated. "Maxine, are you sure you want to do this? I mean, do you really want to get married?" he asked, standing on my front porch in his black work slacks and neatly pressed shirt. The question caught me completely off guard.

"Brian, what are you talking about?" I asked.

"Maxine, I been calling you all morning and you been putting me off. That seems like a strange thing for someone to do who wants to have a wedding."

"I wasn't putting you off. I was doing homework."

"All this time?" he asked.

"Yeah, all this time."

He sighed and suddenly looked confused, as if he didn't know what he was doing. "Maxine, are you really certain about all this? I mean, baby, this is gonna be for real. Do you know that?"

"Of course I know it's gonna be for real, Brian."

"And you're sure that this is what you want? You're sure you want to take this big leap? I mean, because Maxine this is really major. It's gonna change all kinds of stuff. It's scary. Are you scared?"

"No, I'm not."

"For real? I mean, are you really, really certain about this?" he asked.

I grew irritated. "Yeah, I am, and you told me that you wanted it too!" I snapped. "Brian, we done put a lot of work into all this. I done lied to my mama, she done asked all my relatives to help her out. Tia's grandma done made me a beautiful dress, I got a wedding cake, and the church is gonna be all decorated with flowers. I been planning this for weeks. So, how you gonna come ask me if I still want to have a wedding?"

"I just need to be sure," he said.

"Baby, I am sure. There ain't no problem with me. I want a change. You the one who needs to be sure that you still want this. Do you, baby, because that's what I need to know?" I asked.

He hesitated for a minute, and that minute was like a thousand. I actually had time to wonder why I was dumb enough to ask him the question. If he was thinking about calling the wedding off, I had just made it easier for him to do it. Giving a guy a way out was a dumb thing for a girl who really wanted to be a wife to do. I hoped and prayed that I wouldn't pay for it.

"Naw, I love you, Maxine. I just want to make sure that we doing the right thing."

"We are," I said, and gave him a big kiss. He kissed me back, and I could feel the uncertainty coming from his lips. It made me a little nervous, but I knew it was only pre-wedding jitters—it had to be.

"Don't worry. It's gonna be so cool. We gonna have our own house and everything.

"For real?"

"For real, real."

"So what's up? What is the new place really like? Did you see it already?"

"Come on, girl. I'll let you see what it looks like," he said, pulling me by the arm, down the steps.

As we walked hand in hand to our new place, Brian told

me a little more about it. It had two small bedrooms, a little kitchen-and-dinning room combo, and our own living room. There was a nice-sized front yard, and his daddy was having a washer and dryer put into the shed out back. It really did sound like heaven. I couldn't believe what his father was doing for us. I can't tell you how much joy it filled me with to know I wasn't gonna have to live with Mama anymore, or Andre, or Shabba, or Little C, or Dwayne, or Tyrese, or Malcolm, or any of the other dudes that Mama had hooked up with over the years—dudes who seemed like they would be cool, until their mail started coming to our mailbox. Out of all of them, I think that Shabba was one of the worst. He hardly ever worked and spent his days stretched out on the sofa watching sports. When Mama would get on him about finding a J.O.B., he would get angry. Sometimes he would hit Mama, and that was bad, but it was what he did when he didn't hit her that made me hate him. When he kept his hands to himself, he would go into her room and start destroying things. He put his foot through her brand-new TV, cut up her mattress, smashed her lamps, threw her stereo system across the room, broke all of her picture frames, and even punched holes in the wall. Each time he did it, he would say that he was sorry, but it didn't matter. Mama was the truly sorry person, too sorry to throw him out. She stayed with him for nearly two years, until she finally got tired of paying the rental company monthly payments for furniture that she could no longer use.

After Shabba came Calvin, who everybody called Little C. Little C actually had a great personality and took good care of us, but he did it by ripping off the electronics store that he worked for. When the cops came to get him, they seized an

MP3 player that he had given me for Christmas and the big-screen TV set that he had stolen to replace the one that Shabba broke.

Dwayne actually came before Shabba and Little C. He wasn't lazy and he didn't steal, but he just made me wish that I was somewhere else whenever he was around. The minute I would walk in the door he would start on me about my weight. He would call me Little Miss Piggy, and tell Mama that she shouldn't be giving me afternoon snacks, and she would listen. I didn't mind going hungry for the afternoon, but I did mind when he would reach over at dinner time and snatch my chicken leg out of my hand, or take my plate and rake half of my food into his. One time he even told Mama not to feed me for an entire day, because he said that I had eaten too much food the day before. He said he was teaching me how to eat like a lady, but I didn't feel like a lady. I felt like a dog that he could feed or not feed whenever he felt like it. I was happy when Dwayne found another sister and went on his way, but over the years Mama has found a ton of Dwayne's, Shabba's, and Little C's, and I've found a ton of reasons to want to stay away from them.

I had passed the house a million times on my way to see my friends Bonita and Madona, and simply hadn't noticed it. On the outside, it was unimpressive. The white paint was dirty and peeling and somebody had broken down the gate. The grass was so overgrown I kept expecting to see a herd of elk grazing in it. When we stepped up on the porch, we noticed that wasps had made nests over the door.

"Be careful. I'm gonna have to get some of that wasp spray," Brian said.

I barely heard him. I was way too elated. We had our own house. "Can you believe it, our own place? Ooh, I can't wait to see what's inside," I said, stepping closer to the door.

Brian stood there. "Last chance, Maxine. We can call the whole thing off and tell our parents that we lost the baby," he said.

I shook my head. "I don't want to call anything off, unless you do, Brian," I said, a little annoyed that he was bringing it up again.

"Naw, I don't," he said after a few seconds. "Well, here we go then," he said, taking a key out of his pocket and opening the door.

"Ooh, I can't wait to see what it looks like."

And I was impressed. The moment we stepped in the living room I realized that it was a lot better than the yard and the front porch. It was da bomb, at least to me. It was dusty and had cobwebs in the corners, but the living room had nice hardwood flooring, and the previous owners had at least painted the living room walls my second favorite color, aquamarine. The master bedroom was small and actually needed painting, but it had a huge window with a box underneath for flowers. The bathroom had his-and-her sinks and elegant gold-tone features. You could fit only a twin bed in the second room, which would be really cute, once we did a little handiwork. The kitchen was what I liked the most. Brian's daddy had clearly purchased new appliances for it. There was a shiny new stove and a convection oven, a two-door refrigerator, and even a dishwasher that could handle oversize loads.

"The washer and dryer are out back. My dad had to get an electrician to hook them up," Brian said.

"I can't believe it. It's all ours?" I said, giving Brian a hug. I really couldn't get over it. "Let's go look at the washer and dryer, right now," I said.

We started to head out, when a knock sounded on the kitchen wall. We turned and saw some girl standing in our house. I hadn't seen her before. She looked about a year older than me, and was makeup pretty. She was wearing some of those butt-hugging rump-shaker shorts, and a strapless spandex top, with her big boobs spilling out all over the place. Her hair was hanging clear down to her waist. Most of it looked natural, but she clearly had some extensions weaved in. "Can I help you?" Brian asked.

"Yeah, I seen ya'll come in, so I thought I would come over here. My name is Shelbee. Most people call me Shell. I seen ya'll around school. Maybe ya'll seen me too?"

"Not really," I said.

Brian started nodding his head up and down. "Oh, yeah, I seen you last week. You had on that little green dress. My boy was trying to holler at you, but you wasn't even paying him no mind," he said.

"Naw, I wasn't into him. He wasn't my type," the girl said with a big grin.

"Yeah, well, a lot of girls say that he ain't their type. They just like to laugh at him," Brian said.

"Who? Like to laugh at who?" I asked.

"That fool Roy. You know how he his. He always after some hot shorty," Brian said.

The girl blushed. She was fair, and her skin went all pink.

I cut my eyes at Brian. "How do you like the school?" I asked the girl.

"It's cool. It's bigger than my last school. I like that. There's lots of new friends to make."

"Yeah, we got a bunch of cool kids," I said.

"For real. I already met some guys, but not too many girls. Maybe you and me can hang sometime."

"Sure," I said. Then I remembered that she was some strange chick that I didn't even know. Why was she in my house, again? "What did you need?" I asked.

"Oh, me and my family is trying to move into a house down the street. We ordered a whole bunch of furniture, but we still have to put a lot of it together. I was on my way to the store, when I saw ya'll coming up here. Your boyfriend looks kind of strong. I thought I would come over here and ask him to help," she said.

"My fiancé," I corrected. I don't know why, but I felt it was important to say that. She seemed like a nice girl, but she had some nerve, coming up in my place asking my man to help her.

"Oh, your *fiancé*. I didn't know ya'll was like that. Ya'll just my age. I can't believe you are getting married," she said.

"Me either, but we are," I told her.

"What kind of furniture ya'll got to put together?" Brian asked.

"Oh, beds, tables, bookcases, that kind of stuff, and my sister got money. We can pay for the help," the girl said.

"Really?" Brian asked.

"Yeah, my sister told me to let you know that she can help you out with some cash. We just down the street, if you want to come over."

"Look, we really would like to help you, but we're trying to look at our new place together," I said in a not-so-nice tone.

Brian cut his eyes at me. "Naw, wait a minute, Maxine. They offering to pay, and we gonna need some cash. Even with our jobs it ain't gonna be easy to keep the bills paid at this place."

"I know that, but me and you was trying to look at our new life together," I whined.

"Maxine, we ain't gonna have no life together, if we can't make this work," Brian said.

"What about your job?" I asked.

"I'm already late. I'll call Julio and get him to cover for me. I'll just go in tomorrow. Where do you live?" he asked the girl.

"Not too far down the street," she said, pointing toward the road.

"I'll go," Brian said. He pulled me to him and kissed me. "Maxine, I'll see you at your house later. I'm gonna go get us some cash," Brian said, taking off.

"I hope I see you in school," the girl said, following Brian out of our place.

"Yeah, me too," I told her.

I walked them out of the house and watched Brian going with her down the street. I had really mixed feelings. I was grateful that my man was gonna get some extra work, but I didn't like her butting in to our special moment. I didn't like it at all. I sighed and waited for a few moments before going back inside the house. As soon as I walked in, my mood changed. I still had a washer and dryer to see. It was my own washer and dryer—in my own house—and nothing could spoil how happy I was about that, nothing at all.

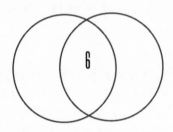

6

Something old, something new, something borrowed, and something blue. Those are the things you're supposed to have for your wedding, to start your marriage off right. During my final rehearsal and dinner, I was blessed with two of them and cursed with the other. The evening started out the way I figure most wedding rehearsals and dinners do. It was exciting and rocky at the same time, because Brian forgot the CD we were supposed to march to.

"Maxine, baby. I gotta run back to the house. I forgot that old Luther Vandross song you wanted to go down the aisle to."

"Dang, Brian, I asked you to get it off of my dresser before we left," I said.

"Maxine, my brain is all over the place these days. I don't know if I'm coming or going, or just running around in circles. I'm sorry, baby. I'll go get it right now."

"Well, hurry up, and don't take too long," I said, noticing

that the wedding party was already breaking out into total chaos. With no music to rehearse to people were just doing their own thing, some of the kids were banging on the piano, while others were playing hide-and-go-seek in the pews. The adults were talking on cell phones or gossiping loudly about family members who couldn't make it to the dinner. There was even an argument breaking out over what girl would go down the aisle with what guy. The entire thing was giving me a serious headache. It was way too much drama and stress. I decided to leave my friends Bonita and Madona in charge and let them run the others through their part of the program without the music, while I folded some wedding programs in the ladies' parlor.

I had a pretty good stack of them in front of me when my great-aunt Freda came in. I smiled all over when I saw her. Aunt Freda is always there for me when I need a shoulder to cry on. When I'm troubled, she gives me advice or just sits and has a glass of iced tea or Coke with me. I feel comfortable with her and I never feel that way with Mama. I think it's because she's easy to talk to, and she loves to joke around with me. She also treats me as if I'm all grown up, while my own mama treats me as if I should still be walking around eating lollipops. There's something else too, something that makes me love her more than anyone else. She treats Brian like he belongs to her too. There's nothing that he can't talk to her about, and I love it. My mama can't say two words to Brian without being nasty, but Great-aunt Freda always treats him like a part of the family. She loves Brian just about as much as I do, and he loves her too. Like me, Brian doesn't have much of a relationship with his grandmothers, so he often goes to Great-aunt Freda when he wants to talk some of his problems out. He says that she listens to him without judging him and nobody in his entire family does that.

"I got you something *old*, Ms. Thing," Great-aunt Freda said, handing me her best pearl bracelet. "My grandma gave this to my mother on her wedding day, and my mama gave it to me. It's pretty long. I figured you could make it into one of those anklets, like I always see you wearing," she said, putting the jewelry around my leg. When I lifted my ankle up, I felt like a really cool princess. The pearls made my leg look off the hook. I couldn't thank Great-aunt Freda enough for bringing it. I loved how special it made me feel, and I would definitely wear it with pride. The bracelet was one of the few things Great-aunt Freda kept from her wedding day. When she was only sixteen, her father, a poor sugar-refinery worker, married her off to his boss. It was a loveless marriage, created by a desperate father, but Great-aunt Freda stayed in it until her husband died of a heart attack several years later.

"Ooh, I'm so glad you're marrying somebody that you love," she said, handing me the velvet box that the bracelet was in. "I hated my husband. Because I was a good twenty years younger than him, he treated me as if I had no thoughts of my own. I wasn't allowed to do anything. Plus, he wasn't all that attractive. He had more hair on his arms than on his head. And, let's not talk about conversation. God! He was boring when he talked. The folks at the sugar refinery used to joke that he could put you to sleep quicker than Tylenol PM."

"Why did you agree to marry him?" I asked.

"I did what I had to do for my family. My daddy had eight mouths to feed, and he didn't make squat. All he had was a daughter who was just about marrying age."

"Like me," I said.

"Naw, not exactly. You love Brian. You'll do much better than me. You always have, that's why I love you the best out of all of my nephews and nieces. You make mistakes here and there, but I ain't never seen you go down for the count."

"Thanks, for always making me feel better," I said.

"Shoot, that's my joy. You know I ain't never had no kids of my own. I got you and Brian, your mama, and your ridiculous uncle Ernie. Ya'll the ones I care about." She looked at my ankle. "You going be the prettiest bride I've ever seen," she said.

"Thanks, Aunt Freda," I said, giving her a hug. We started folding programs together. We had finished a huge stack when Tia's grandma Augustine came in with something that made me feel equally as special, my something *borrowed*.

"I brought something nice for you," she said, handing me a plain cloth bag. I opened it and took out a long wedding veil that was so sheer a gentle breeze could blow it away like a goose feather.

"It's beautiful," I said.

"Yes, I think so too, baby. I bought it for one my little girls. I had dreams of seeing her go down the aisle in it one day, but she didn't live long enough to wear it, and Tia wanted me to make her one of them fancy veils she saw in a magazine. Anyway, it's been sitting in my drawer for years. I had it cleaned the other day because I thought you might like to borrow it. I mean, I'd feel honored and blessed, if you did," Grandma Augustine said.

"You? I'm the one who is honored and blessed. Of course, I'll wear it," I said, placing it on my head.

She looked at me with her wrinkled face and beamed. "You look like a dream," she said.

"I feel like I'm in one," I told her.

"You are."

"Now, you just be smart and keep it that way. Be kind, and patient, and loving. Don't let nothing turn your marriage into a nightmare," Grandma Augustine said, taking the veil off for me.

"I won't," I said.

All three of us started folding programs, with me all happy, until I heard Mama and Brian's little cousin Demonee arguing downstairs. I rolled my eyes because I knew what it was about. This was our second rehearsal, and during the first one Demonee's escort, a cute, nerdy little friend of Brian's, kept following her around and trying to get her a drink or snack out of the vending machines in the basement. Everybody thought it was cute, except Demonee. It ticked her off, and she called him a little jerk. It hurt his feelings, so he left her alone, or so I thought he did. I guess he was back getting on her nerves again.

"He keeps grinning all stupid at me!" I heard her yelling at my mama.

"Don't be so difficult, little girl. He just likes you," Mama told her.

"I don't care. I don't like him and I ain't going down no aisle with him, and you can't make me," I heard Demonee say.

"Oh good grief," I mumbled. I shook my head and listened to them argue for another few minutes. Then Brian's dad yelled out.

"Demonee, I had them put you in this wedding so that

you would feel more like family and learn how to act in formal social situations. This wedding is difficult enough for us all, don't you make it any worse than it has to be!" he said.

This riled my mama big time and she said, "What the hell do you mean by that? What do you mean by difficult? It wouldn't be difficult, if your son woulda kept his hands off of my daughter!"

That's when I decided that it was time to deal with my something blue, the blue mood that was coming from Demonee and provoking the same negative feelings in the rest of my guests. A wedding was supposed to be a joyous occasion, and I didn't want her ugliness going into the ceremony the next day. I left the program folding to Grandma Augustine and my great-aunt Freda, and went running up the stairs. That's when I got my something *new*, Shell. She had somehow managed to come back with my man.

I was pissed. Since Shell had turned up on our doorstep, Brian had fixed just about everything in her house, and started painting the kitchen and bathrooms. I appreciated the cash that she and her family was giving Brian, but helping her was working my last nerve, and Brian knew it. I hadn't said anything too mean about her, but I huffed and rolled my eyes each time he told me that he was going over to her place. There was no way that he couldn't know how much she was seriously pissing me off. I pulled Brian into the girls' restroom to get him straight.

"Brian, what's up with you? What's that heifer doing at my wedding rehearsal?

"It's my rehearsal too Maxine, and she's here because I asked her to come in."

"For what?"

"Business."

"What kind of business?"

"She's waiting on me, that's all."

"Waiting, for what?" I asked, getting a bad feeling.

"Nothing, Maxine, don't trip," he said, shaking his head.

"*You* don't trip. What kind of business do you have with her the night before our wedding?" I asked.

"Work that's all," he said.

"Work? Brian, don't you dare tell me that you are about to go off and do some work for that girl right now. Are you crazy? We don't need money that bad," I snapped.

He looked annoyed and stressed. "Yes, we do, Maxine, or haven't you figured that out? Baby, we ain't got no kind of savings in the bank and we're going to have a stack of bills right after we move in."

"I know that," I said.

"Do you, Maxine? Because I don't know if you really thought all of this out."

"Of course I did. Why are going there again?" I snapped.

He pulled me into his arms, and we both calmed some. "Maxine, I'm not going anywhere. I'm trying to let you know that this isn't going to be easy. And what if you get pregnant for real? How we going to take care of a baby?"

"Brian, I'm not about to get pregnant," I said.

"You might, and how we gonna take care of a kid without any cash in the bank?"

"You're worrying too much. It's not going to happen. Don't be ridiculous," I said, waving the suggestion away with my hand.

"I'm not being ridiculous. I'm being practical. Shell's house needs a lot of work, and her family is paying me good money to help out."

"So what? Are you really telling me that you're going to help her, instead of staying at the dinner with me?" I asked.

"Maxine, I'll stay for a little while, but I got to make sure we get some bills paid. Shell's big sister is gonna drive us to the paint store to pick up some supplies. I need to go, since I'm doing the painting. You get that, don't you? I mean, baby, you understand that I need to do this right now?" he pleaded.

"Yeah, I guess I do, but I don't like it. Shell or Shelbee—whatever you call her—needs to find somebody else to help her."

"No, you just need to be cool. We doing what you want, Maxine. We getting married and we getting our own place. Just keep your eye on the prize, baby, and don't even think about anything else."

"She won't, if you stop giving her stuff to think about," Bonita said, stepping into the bathroom. As usual she had on a big T-shirt and a pair of cargo shorts. I couldn't wait for the wedding, so I could see her all girled-up for a change. "Look, I gotta go to the restroom. Ya'll need to do whatever ya'll doing outside," she said, heading to a stall.

A second later the restroom door opened again.

"Hey, everybody is out there wondering where ya'll at. What are ya'll doing in here?" Madona asked, stepping through the door as well, looking like a carbon copy of her sister.

"I'm trying to take care of some business, and they arguing about that Shell girl," Bonita called out from the stall.

"What?" Madona asked.

"You know that girl that keeps on needing Brian to do stuff."

"Oh that chick. Yeah, I saw her outside. Forget her. She ain't nothing," Madona said.

"Madona, stay out of this," Brian snapped.

"I'm not *in* this. I just don't like her that's all," Madona said and rolled her eyes.

"You don't even know her," Brian said.

"Please, I done seen her, and every time she been all over you. That's all I need to know about her. She likes to hang on other girls' men. She low class, and I can tell you that."

"Madona, shut up," Brian said.

"You shut up, Brian, and don't be talking to my sister like that," Bonita said, coming out of the stall. She rolled her eyes at Brian and went to wash her hands at the sink.

"You know what, Bonita. This is an A and B conversation, and both you and your sister can C your way out."

Bonita turned on the faucet and held her hands underneath a heavy stream of water, glaring at Brian like she wished she could turn the faucet in his direction and splash it in his face. "You know what, Brian, if I didn't care about my girl Maxine, I would cuss your think-he-all-that behind out, but I don't have time for your drama today."

"Me neither. Brian, you need to stop arguing with your fiancé," Madona said.

"And you need to get your own business and stay out of mine," Brian shot back.

"Maxine is my business. She my girl, so why don't you just stop arguing with her?"

This time Brian rolled *his* eyes. "We're not arguing, not anymore. Look, Maxine, everything I'm doing is for us and about us, and you know that. Now, baby, I love you, but I gotta go," Brian said.

"Whatever—do what you have to do," I said.

Brian rolled his eyes. "I'll see ya later," he said to me. Then he kissed me on the cheek and left.

"Girl, is Brian buggin' or what?" Bonita said.

"I don't want to talk about it. Let's just go do what we need to do," I said.

I was clearly pissed, but everybody was waiting on the CD, and the programs still needed to be finished before we went to dinner. Bonita was right. I didn't have time for nonsense.

We walked over to the church sanctuary, and I told myself that I would do what I had to do and not think about Shell. It really didn't work. I thought about her all evening. I liked her well enough. At school she seemed to pop up all the time, and was always funny and fun to chat with. The only thing I didn't like about her was the way she dressed, but a lot of girls went for the hoochie video-girl look. I couldn't hold it against her. She really was throwing some much-needed cash our way, and that was a good thing. I knew it was, but as I sat through most of the rehearsal dinner by myself, with all of my relatives constantly asking me why my man had gone off and left me, I couldn't help getting angry at her. As soon as I got home from the dinner, I called Brian and told him that I wasn't pleased. He was just getting home and he was tired and not in the mood for any drama.

"Maxine, I'm sorry about the dinner, but I told you what I had to do."

"And I told you what I needed you to do. Look, Brian, I've had to do everything for this wedding because you're always at Shell's house. That's bad enough, but you ditched me in front of all our friends and family to spend time with her."

"Maxine, what do you want me to do about that? I told you I had to get some painting done. The dinner is over now. What do you want me to do about it?"

"I want you to not get all nasty with me and apologize, because you know you were wrong."

"I was wrong? Maxine, you trippin'," he hollered. After that we got into a big fight.

We fought about any and everything we could think of and, when we were thoroughly exhausted, he angrily hung the phone up on me. I didn't know if there was even going to be a wedding the next day. He might not even show up. He might not even be there to go through with our dream.

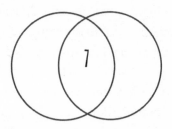

've been crying all morning. It is thirty minutes before my
wedding. I'm getting dressed and I'm not even sure if my
groom is going to show up. I don't know what I'll do if he
doesn't. Brian is the most special thing in my life.

I remember the day I fell for him, really fell for him. It
was in the sixth grade, on a hot summer afternoon. School
had let out because one of the fourth grade teachers had died
in a car accident, and all the other teachers wanted to go to
the funeral. Me and all my crew went back to my house. Soon
Brian and his friends were swapping X-Men trading cards in
my front yard, while me and my girlfriends were hanging
out in the street playing our favorite game, cheerleader. That
morning I had done something stupid. I put on a pair of
Mama's panties because I hadn't washed any of mine out.
They were nice undies, but way too big. Then it happened. I
went down for a split, and when I came up the loose underwear didn't come with me. They fell right around my ankles.

Quick as I could, I picked them up and ran in the house. I pulled a pair of shorts on underneath my khaki skirt. When I came back out, my girlfriends were really cool, they acted like nothing had happened. The boys were something different. They were acting stupid, laughing and pointing.

"Maxine, Maxine, the droopy drawers queen!" they teased. I was humiliated. I actually started crying. I stood there on my front steps bawling like a preschooler.

"Hey ya'll, shut up and leave Maxine alone!" Brian hollered at the boys. "Why ya'll acting like ya'll ain't seen drawers before. I guess ya'll mama's don't wear 'em," he said. The boys looked offended.

"Forget you, man. My mama wear drawers," Dre Royce, Brian's best friend, said.

"Well, why you laughing?" Brian asked.

Dre looked like he didn't know what to say. He hunched his shoulders and looked around at the other boys. For a minute nobody said nothing.

"Aw, we were just teasing," Dre said.

After that, the boys went back to trading cards. I dried up the tears and continued cheering with my friends. The whole time I couldn't take my eyes off Brian. We had been friends since we were old enough to walk, and we already had some kind of puppy love, but what I started feeling for him that day was much more than a kid's crush. He had stood up to his friends for me. Boys just didn't do that.

Mama came into my room, interrupting my thoughts. "Maxine, where the hell is Brian? I knew something like this was gonna happen."

"Mama, I don't know what you trippin' about, and don't

freak me out. Brian will be here, just start getting everybody else set up," I said, dabbing at my puffy eyes with a crumpled tissue.

"I'm trying to set you up with some common sense. Maxine, I'm telling you, you can't count on that boy. You already made a mistake, coming up pregnant. Don't make another by hooking up with this jerk," she said, shaking her finger at me.

"Mama, Brian is not a jerk, and you know it. I hate it when you call him that. It's not right."

"Not right! Maxine let me tell you what's right. Your being knocked up and having to get married at seventeen, me having to call my relatives and beg them for money, that's what ain't right. You know I hate begging folks for stuff. In fact, I don't like none of this."

"It's not for you to like, Mama. Why can't you see that? It's for me to like and Brian to like, cause we the ones who gonna have to live with it."

"Live with what? Maxine, look around you, Brian ain't even here."

"He will be," I said.

She rolled her eyes. "Maxine, losers ain't never around."

"Well, that's not true, cause your man, Andre, is right outside in the sanctuary," I said, pointing at the door.

"Maxine, this ain't got nothing to do with Andre."

"You wish that were true," I snapped.

"Look, Maxine, let me tell you something about my man," she said, pointing her finger at my face.

"What you gonna tell me, Mama? You gonna tell me about his ex, who keep showing at our house wanting to start fights. How many times has she been there since ya'll been together, Mama? Remember what happened two weeks after ya'll moved in together? Remember how she took a pipe and broke all the windows out in our house because Andre's child support check was late? If we woulda been home that pipe woulda probably been busting your head, or mine."

"Maxine, I ain't got nothing to do with that. I didn't do nothing to make that woman come over to our house."

"Yeah, you did. You took up with her no good babies' daddy."

"Maxine, I got a right to want somebody in my life!"

"You got somebody, Mama—me. You just can't ever seem to remember that."

"Whatever, Maxine. I'm not gonna argue with you today, but let me tell you what I can remember. I can remember where the church is on my daughter's wedding day, which is more than I can say for Brian."

"Brian will be here. Don't worry Mama. Just go make certain that the rest of the wedding party hasn't wandered off."

"Girl, if it wasn't your wedding day I would really get you straight, but I'm going. I'll go see what I can do about this mess," Mama said, as she left my dressing room in her pretty violet taffeta gown.

"Good, thank God," I said, adjusting my dress.

I was so glad to see Mama leave. She wasn't right about me not being able to count on Brian. He had shown me time and time again that he could be trusted, especially when it came to girls. I had never once seen him stray. Last summer some shorty was trying to push up on him. She wasn't a skank like Shell. She was an intelligent, gorgeous girl, who was doing an internship at Brian father's office. She was from Cuba, and she had legs that never stopped and long dark hair that never ended. She was around our age, so Brian's father invited her to a barbecue and pool party at their house. I was never really jealous of other females, but when I saw her come wiggling across the lawn in a tiny, tiny orange bikini I felt like a blimp in my halter top and shorts.

"Dang, baby got back and front and everything else," Brian said when he saw her.

I rolled my eyes over the comment, but I didn't feel disrespected or worried, until the girl started hanging all over him in the pool, and later when she kept asking him if he wanted her to get him some food and drinks from the kitchen. It pissed me off that she was trying to take care of my man, and I really was about to let her have it when Brian pulled me away from the party into the living room.

"Maxine, you don't need to trip over that girl. She looks good and all, but you're the only girl that I'm into, and you know that. Don't let her make you crazy. When the party is over, you're the one that I'm going to be hanging with, 'cause you know I got mad love for you, girl," he said, pulling me to him and giving me a kiss. The moment our lips touched, all the jealousy and doubt I was having disappeared. I felt even better when, instead of returning to the party, we grabbed some food and went to the park for our own little celebration.

The next day Brian told me that the intern had tried to give him her number, but he turned her down. He also told me that his father had invited her because he thought that Brian would see her in that swimsuit and that would be the end of our relationship. I felt sorry for the girl because Brian's father had used her, but I wasn't sorry that Brian hadn't taken the bait. Mama was wrong. Brian wasn't who she thought he was.

I walked to the window and looked out of it. "Please show up Brian," I whispered.

The singer Mama hired had already sung five solos, and the minister was complaining about having to perform another wedding right after ours, when Brian finally showed up looking hot in his white tux. I knew it was bad luck for the groom to see the bride in her dress before the ceremony, but I ran out into the hallway and fell into his arms anyway.

"I'm sorry. I didn't mean to make you mad. I just really wanted you to stay with me last night."

"Maxine, I told you where I was going and why. That should have been enough. I don't know why you had to come at me about it again," he said.

"I know, baby. I'm sorry. I know you were only trying to do right by us."

"Yes, I am. Look, Maxine, we got a whole church full of folks waiting, and I look pretty fly in this white tux," he said, turning from side to side. "Let's do this, girl. Let's go get married," he said, giving me a hug.

"Yeah, let's do it," I said, leading him off. We went arm in arm down the aisle, before the bridal party. I'm sure it looked strange to all our guests. We didn't care. We were in love and we were getting married!

"Are you sure you two are ready to get married now?" Sister Ashada asked, as we stepped up to the decorated altar.

"We're so ready," I said. She winked at me and began to

pray the opening prayer. I stared at the floor. It was happening. I was getting married. I couldn't believe it. It was like a beautiful dream.

"Let blessings of love, kindness, forgiveness, wealth, and wisdom rain each day into Maxine and Brian's life," Sister Ashada prayed. *Love* was all I really heard. After all it was all we needed. If you have love, everything else would naturally fall into place. Who didn't know that? That was always the problem with Mama and her men. She never really loved any of them. She loved that they paid the rent on time, took her out to clubs, and sometimes to nice dinners. She liked her men to be fine like Andre, the kind of dudes that other women sneak glances at when she and her man walked into Perry's 24 and 7 Beer Joint, but she never once told me that she loved any of them, not the deep love that makes you feel all ripped up when you man isn't by your side, the kind of love that me and Brian have. "Amen, Amen," I heard Great-aunt Freda and Tia's grandma Augustine say. They were way more into Sister Ashada's speech than I was. Don't get me wrong, I loved what the sister was saying, but all I could think about was me and Brian leaving for our honeymoon together. Brian's hand felt a little shaky in mine. I started caressing it to calm him down. There was no need to be nervous. We were definitely doing the right thing. I was so glad when we got to the end of our nuptials I nearly pulled Brian's arm out of the socket as we ran off down the aisle. "Girl, slow down. You gonna stumble and break your neck in that dress," Brian told me.

"I won' t stumble. I'm way too happy for that," I said.

"Yeah, I feel ya. I'm so glad you and me did this. You are definitely my favorite girl," Brian told me.

He told me that again when we went over to the multicultural center for the reception. It was the best thing I heard all evening, but there were other nice things.

"You look so beautiful," everybody kept saying to me. Sure, I knew they were only saying it because I had the dress and the veil, and they were getting a free plate of barbecued ribs and sausage from my workplace, Bobby's Rib Shack, but I ate up the compliments anyway. They were the same kind of comments Tia got on her big day, the kind any new bride would want to hear.

"Girl, this is really your day," my girl Bonita said.

"It sure is," her sister said, wiping a tiny spot of barbecue off of her lavender bridesmaid's dress.

"Girl, you know how it is. I got my man and a slammin' wedding. What more could I ask for?"

"I guess nothing. Ooh, I can't wait until I get me a husband too," Bonita said.

"Girl, you don't even have a boyfriend," her sister, Madona, reminded her.

"So, I can get one. You watch, I'm gonna get one—and pow! I'm gonna have my own wedding."

"Girl, your Mama ain't about to let you get married no time soon," I said.

"Yours did."

"No, I didn't. Maxine married herself off," Mama said, walking over to Bonita.

I cringed.

"Maxine married herself to Brian the minute she stepped

in my house with a big belly. Don't you be a fool and come up with one too," Mama told my girlfriend.

"Mama, this is not the time for that. Don't go there and ruin everything," I pleaded.

Mama kissed me on the cheek. "I'm cool, Maxine. I'm not gonna bring it up again. Enjoy your day, you and Brian supposed to be mingling and greeting. I'ma go get me some punch, ya'll just do what you need to do," she said.

"I appreciate that, Mama," I said. She nodded and walked away.

I looked around me. Where the heck was Brian? I didn't see him. I glanced at all the fancy decorated tables. The people seated at them were laughing and having a good time, without Brian. Where the heck did he go?

"Girls, I'll be back," I said to my friends. I picked up my dress tail and exited the conference room.

When I stepped outside the room, I didn't even bother going through the hallways of the multicultural center. It was after hours, so all the doors were locked, except for the reception hall doors. I went right through the main doors of the building, into the parking lot. Brian was there all right. He was talking to the one person I wished I hadn't invited, Shell. She wasn't originally on my list. I added her because my future husband thought it would be a friendly gesture. And even though she was wearing my nerves down, I agreed. Now I wasn't sure why. Instead of being inside with me, my man was in the parking lot chatting her up. To make matters worse, she had the nerve to wear a sexy white miniskirt and blouse set to my wedding. Everybody knows only the bride should be in white on her day. With Brian standing next to her in his white tux it looked like they were the ones who got married. I wasn't having that.

"Brian, what are you doing out here? I've been looking for you everywhere!" I said.

"Maxine, there was only two places for me to be, the bathroom or out here. I'm out here, what's the big deal?" Brian asked.

"The big deal is you supposed to be with me, and our room full of guests."

"A room full of guests that's eating up all the money your uncle gave us, and all the money my mom and dad chipped in. I'm not thinking about those folks. I'm thinking about the future. I'm out here trying to get hooked up with another job."

"Today, Brian? Are you serious?" I was fuming. "Work can wait. This is supposed to be a celebration!" I shouted just as a few last-minute guests pulled into the parking lot. I thought about toning it down, but I was too pissed.

"And I *am* celebrating. Shell's uncle is hiring me to help put up some fences at some rent houses he owns. The job pays real good, better than what I make at the card shop. I'm gonna take some vacation days and go with him to Dallas."

"What? When?" I asked.

"We gonna leave tomorrow," Shell answered.

"We who? What? Brian, what are you talking about? We about to start our honeymoon, in our own place. You can't take off," I said, not believing my ears.

He came over and playfully pulled me to him. I wasn't having that either. I pushed him away. "Brian, I'm serious. I don't want you to go putting up fences right now."

"Why not, Maxine? It's good money, and I thought ya'll needed some?" Shell butted in.

"What you think or don't think is not important here, Shell. I'm trying to talk to my husband, so keep your nose out!" I yelled.

Brian was out of his mind if he thought he was gonna leave me by myself and take off with Shell and her family.

"I didn't mean no harm, Maxine. I was just trying to help out, that's all," she said.

"Why don't you help yourself out of my marriage—and my business. I mean, I'm grateful for what you been doing for Brian, but he also has other responsibilities!" I told her.

"And I get that, Maxine!" Brian said.

"Do you? Because it seems to me that you would rather go build some stupid fences than be with your new wife."

"It's not like that at all," Shell said.

"I thought I told you to stay out of my affairs. I know you trashy, but are you also stupid?" I screamed.

"Maxine that was uncalled for," Brian said.

"No, what's uncalled for is her always finding something for you to do at the wrong time. Why can't her family hire a handy man?"

"They have one, me. Okay, Maxine, this is how it is," he said, in a stern voice. "We need money, they paying money. I'm getting in the car tomorrow morning and going to help out. That money will pay our bills and give us some cash to get our own crib fixed. I'm sorry if you don't like it, but don't take it out on me—or Shell. She's like an angel. I don't know what I would do without her help. Now, come on baby. Let's go mix and mingle, and let everybody know that we ain't single," he said, taking me by the arm.

I rolled my eyes.

"Come on, baby, don't be like that," he said, tugging me along.

"Okay," I said.

He led me back into the building, and Shell followed. A part of me felt like I should apologize to her, but mostly I felt like asking her to go away, and take her stupid family with her. I had a feeling that Brian would never get through working for her. As long as he was willing, there was always going to be something for him to repair, something for him to put together. I wanted to put something together too, me and Brian, without Shell.

"Maxine, my uncle say that them fences won't take no time to put up. He'll be back before you know it," Shell said.

I imagined a huge stack of heavy wooden fences falling off a truck and crushing her to pieces. It was a horrible, devilish thing for someone to think about a girl that was supposed to be an angel, but I didn't care.

"Maxine, be cool, just think about all the money I'm going to make," Brian whispered. I closed my eyes and tried to imagine stacks and stacks of money. It worked, but I kept seeing those huge heavy stacks falling off of a truck and crushing Shell to pieces. I closed my eyes, so I could keep seeing it again and again.

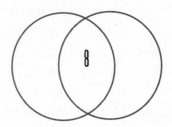

My new home is falling apart, emotionally and physically. Brian is never at home. He's always helping Shell and her family, and it's cutting into our couple time together. Every time I think we can be together as husband and wife, he's walking out of the door with a paint can or hammer. Our own house still needs work. The fence outside needs replacing, and the wasp nest over the door needs taking down. The wallpaper in our bathrooms is peeling, and our bedroom needs some of that paint he's using at Shell's place. When I bring all this up, all Brian says is that he will get around to the repairs when he can.

"Maxine, quit sweating me about that stuff. I'll get to it, when I get to it. You know I already got commitments."

"You're supposed to be committed to this house and me!" I yell.

"Maxine, I am committed. I just can't do everything."

"Then do one thing, Brian, and spend time with me."

"Maxine, I gotta go," he says, kissing me on the mouth, except lately he's been skipping the kisses.

Today, on my birthday, I went to Mama's after school and spoke to her about it, while she was cleaning the bathroom. "Already, Maxine, you already coming to me with a problem?" she asked, spraying the tub with foam cleaner. It clung to the sides for a second and started sliding down. I took a sponge out of her plastic pail and handed it to her.

"Mama, don't make this difficult for me," I said.

"Maxine, I'm not trying to make anything difficult. I just asked you if you have a problem already? You ain't been married but a little while, I didn't expect nothing to happen until after the baby was born," she said, sponging up the foam in the tub.

"I didn't expect no problems at all," I said.

"Well, you sure was fooling yourself. I know you married, but you still think like a child. A woman would have known a marriage thrown together because of a baby was going have more downs than ups."

"I am a woman, Mama," I snapped.

"No, you're a pregnant teenager playing house with a boy."

"If that's what you think, Mama, why did you even . . ." I started to say, but decided against it. I hadn't come for an argument. I wanted advice. "Brian is working all the time, that's all. All he does is work for Shell and her family. The only problem is we ain't spending no time together, that's what I'm dealing with."

"Dog gone, Maxine! What did you think was gonna happen?" Mama asked, angrily throwing the sponge in the pail. "How did you think ya'll was gonna live?"

"Off of the jobs we already had."

"Maxine, those little after-school jobs ain't gonna keep a house going, and that money you had left over from your wedding ain't gonna last for long. You guys had to have new furniture for your place and make repairs, plus bills every month. You know, I admire Brian. Can you believe that? I never have cared for that boy, but he's always tried to do right by you. He should be enjoying his graduation year, instead you done tied him up with a baby, a wife, and a new house."

"It's my year too, and I didn't tie him up. He wanted to be with me as much as I wanted to be with him."

"Physically yes, he's a young male, filled up all that testosterone. He wanted to hook up with you like any boy his age would, but you decided on something else."

"I didn't decide anything, Mama. I got pregnant!"

"Yes, you did, and as much as I don't like you being married, Brian took charge. He's working as hard as he can for your future. Let him do what he has to do."

"Whatever, Mama, fine, and I'll do what I have to do too," I said, storming out of the bathroom

"What's that? What you gonna do, Maxine?" she called after me. I didn't answer. She knew what I was going to do. I was going to do what any woman would. I was going to go get my man. It was something I should have done a long time ago. I slammed Mama's door shut and went to Shell's place.

When I got there, it didn't look like Brian had done all that much to Shell's place. If he was putting up fences for her family, why hadn't he put her fence up first? It was an old fence like ours, and half of it was falling to pieces. Loose boards were scattered all over the lawn. And what about the house? He was supposed to be painting inside and out. Only it sure didn't look like it, the outside hadn't even been touched. The blue paint was peeling, allowing the older, ugly gray paint to show beneath. When I walked up on the porch, I could see huge cracks in the concrete. Brian had told me he was helping fill those cracks. Clearly he hadn't gotten around to them. The work that he was supposed to be doing he hadn't even done, which meant it might take him several more weeks to do it. It pissed me off more. I wasn't going to take several more weeks of being by myself. I knocked on the door so hard I felt like my hands would go through the rotten wood. A second later a little girl and boy came to the door with juice boxes and bags of corn chips in their hands. I figured they must be younger siblings.

"What chu want?" the little girl asked.

"Where's your sister?" I asked.

"In her baby bed," the little boy said.

"Naw, your older sister, Shell."

"Shell ain't my sister. She my aunt," the little girl said and took a sip of her juice box.

"Yeah, her," I said.

"Shell, Shell, some girl out here looking for you!" the little boy yelled.

Both kids ran away from the door. I waited for Shell to emerge. I didn't know what I was going to say to her, I only knew I had to say something. How could I not? Me and Brian had everything planned, and here she comes. I didn't want to be mean to her, but I wanted her to stop taking up so much of Brian's time, our time.

I looked through the partially open door and considered walking inside. I had one foot in the door when Shell showed up. "Hey, Maxine, what's the deal?" she asked, stepping out on the porch. I noticed immediately that she had gained weight, not a lot, but her face was fuller, and her big boobs were straining against her tight cotton T-shirt.

"What are you doing here, Maxine?" she asked.

I hesitated for a second, thought about my words. "I don't know, Shell. I just felt like I should come by and say something. I mean, I like you, but this ain't right."

"What ain't right?" she asked.

"Brian, he over here all the time. All of his free time is spent here. He ain't doing nothing at our house, and he ain't spending no time with me."

"He's working, Maxine. Look at this place. Can't you see how much needs doing around here," she said, pointing to the peeling paint and cracked porch.

"I can see that, but what I don't see is how it's my problem, or my husband's."

"It's not a problem. The work just has to be done. My big sister say we got this place real cheap, but only because it needed a lot of work. I thought Brian could help out."

"He can, Shell, but not every day. Your sister needs to get a professional handyman or something, if it's this much work," I said, looking around.

"We ain't got much money to pay, that's why I asked your boyfriend."

"My husband," I corrected. And I shouldn't have had to do it. She was there when me and Brian got married. She knew we were legally married. Why was she disrespecting me like that?

"You know what, Shell. I'm not trying to get into nothing with you. I'm telling you that Brian ain't coming around here all the time no more, that's all," I said, walking down the steps.

"Did he say that?" she hollered.

"What?" I said, turning back.

"I asked, if Brian said he wasn't coming back?"

"It don't matter what he say. I'm telling you," I said.

She rolled her eyes. "Yeah, he told me you was like that. He said you always run everything."

"Excuse me?"

"Your *husband,* he told me that it always has to be your way."

"That's not true."

"That's what he told me," she said, shrugging her shoulders.

"No he didn't. He wouldn't say nothing like that," I snapped. Who was she to be telling me what my husband said?

"He said it, and you can believe that," she said.

"Shell, I don't need you to tell me what my husband thinks, so whatever he said or didn't say to you, you can keep to yourself," I said, starting to walk away again.

"You can't stop him from coming here!" she yelled.

Now I was pissed off. Was she out of her mind? I looked at that makeup pretty face of hers. She had turned all red again, and this time it wasn't an innocent blush. She was boiling.

"Are you for real? You ain't got nothing to do with my man. You don't tell me what I can say to him!" I said, flying up in her face.

"I don't have to tell you. I'm letting you know that you don't control him," she said, placing her hands on her hips.

"I control whatever I like!" I said.

"No, you don't. You don't control nothing, and you can't keep Brian away from me!" she yelled back.

"Shell, you ain't nobody for me to keep Brian away from. You don't even matter!" I hollered.

"I matter to Brian," she said.

"Yeah, I'm sure you think you do. Whatever, I'm done with this. Tell your sister she gonna have to find someone else."

"I'm not telling her nothing. If Brian don't want to come around here no more, he can tell me himself, but I know that ain't true."

"Yeah, right! I'll see you later, much later," I said, and I was trying to leave again.

"Yeah, you will, and besides you stupid anyway. Who goes around pretending they gonna have a baby?"

I stopped in my tracks.

Did she say what I thought she said? She couldn't have. That was a secret between me and Brian; I hadn't even told my girlfriends about it. I stormed back up to her. "You stay out of my business, Shell! What do you know about it?"

"I know your Mama and everybody else gonna figure out that you lying soon, because you can't pretend something like that forever."

"I don't have to pretend!"

"Yes, you do. You have to pretend, but guess what? I don't!" she said, and stormed off. She went in the house, slamming the door behind her.

I stood there speechless. What did she mean by *not having to pretend*? What could she possibly mean? And what did it have to do with me? Why should I care if she was going to have a baby? Girls had babies all the time. My high school was filled with girls plump with babies. There was nothing special about it. So what? Why on earth should I care? I started walking down the sidewalk, with every step my legs got shaky. With every step, I knew I had to care. Her face was fat and her shorts were tighter, that came to me now. It wasn't only her shirt. Those skanky little short shorts she liked to wear weren't fitting too good either. She had a bump, a small one. That was enough for me to care. Naw, she couldn't be. If she was, she had to have come to our hood that way. I trusted Brian. We had been together since we were little kids. I trusted him. We had just gotten married. He wouldn't do anything to hurt me. I headed down the sidewalk and felt tears in my eyes. I sucked them up. No, I didn't care that Shell was pregnant, because there was nothing to care about. Brian had simply spent the past few months fixing things at her house. He had told me that, and I believed it. I crossed the street and went a few blocks over to my place. When I saw my house, I started bawling. There was still so much work to be done, and Brian should be there working on it. Instead, it was crumbling to pieces.

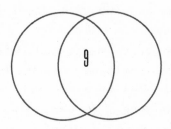

9

Me and Brian been arguing for three days, over Shell and her house. Actually, it's what I've been telling myself we're arguing over, but the truth is we're arguing over something neither one of us want to talk about. We're stepping around the ugly smell of this thing, like it's a puddle of puke on the bathroom floor. I'm so tired of arguing about what we are afraid to say. I want the truth to come out. I keep pushing and pushing Brian, hoping I'll push him so hard he'll burst open and his conscience will explode out. It hasn't happened yet. However, we've been together for so long, there's no way he can't know what I suspect. But, when it comes to Shell, he keeps playing it cool. He says he wants to go back over there because he's a man of his word, and it's the right thing to do.

"Maxine, let me finish what I started at that girl's house. Let me go do what I told that girl I would do," he said today after school.

"Her name is Shell, Brian. I know you know that. Why do you keep pretending that you don't even know her name?"

"I'm not."

"Then what's her name? You knew it three days ago. What's changed in three days?"

"Maxine, this is a dumb conversation," he said, walking into the bedroom.

I followed him in there. "I just want to know why you can't even say that girl's name to me. You acting like you scared to say it in this house. Why is that?"

"Maxine, why you keep starting stuff?"

"I'm not starting stuff!" I yelled.

"Yes you are, you always do! That's the one thing that I never liked about you," he angrily said. The words stung my face like salty water. I didn't even know where they were coming from.

"What did you say?" I asked.

"You heard me, Maxine. I ain't never liked the way you could start an argument out of nothing," he said, walking over to the closet and getting his black work slacks off the hanger.

"Well, why did you marry me?" I asked.

"I didn't marry you, you married me. Remember, you the one who come talking about going down the aisle with a big-ass white dress. I was fine with us being a couple. You the one who wanted to take it to the next level. You've always been like that. Whenever you not happy you always make crazy decisions and pull me into them. I knew the minute Tia got married you was gonna want to get married too. I knew you were gonna look over there and see how good she was feeling and try to see if you could feel that way too."

"So, what's wrong with that? Why shouldn't I be happy too, are you saying that you never wanted that? What are you talking about, Brian?"

"Maxine, I'm happy—or I was. I was happy the day I met you. You was the only girl that ever made me smile all day, every day. I was always feeling good with you."

"Was?" I noticed he hadn't said *are*, you are the only girl. He said *was*. I didn't know what to do with that. I sat down at the foot of my bed, collecting my thoughts. They came through confused and angry, with a thick coating of hurt. "Brian, what's going on here?" I asked.

"Nothing, Maxine, nothing at all," he said, taking off his jeans and putting on his slacks. He had said some of the ugliest things he had ever said to me, and he still wasn't going to tell me the truth. I couldn't stand another moment of it.

"Did you get that girl pregnant, Brian?" I asked. "Did you? I saw her face and how tight her clothes are fitting, and when I went to talk to her, she acted like I was trying to take her man away from her. Why would she act like that, Brian? Why?" I screamed.

He looked as if he didn't know what to say. He walked over to the dresser and got his black socks. I ran over and snatched them out of his hands. "Answer me, Brian. I know that girl is pregnant. I'm not stupid!"

He snatched his socks back. "Maxine, I don't want to argue with you about this right now," he said, sitting down on the bed to put his socks on. I was freaking, and he was sitting down to put on footwear. Was he even for real?

"Well, we are arguing about it, right now. Just tell me the truth, Brian."

"Maxine, you don't wanna know the truth. You don't even like the truth. You ain't never been able to handle it," he said.

"I can handle the truth when people tell it, but you been lying to me for months. Did you hook up with that girl the first day ya'll met? I can't believe you, Brian. You never done nothing like that before. What's wrong with you?"

"You know what's wrong, Maxine. You're what's wrong, you and my daddy, ya'll always telling me what to do."

"What are you talking about? What's this got to do with your daddy? I asked you if you wanted to be married and you said yes."

"Like I had a choice. I never did, Maxine. I don't think you understand that. You come walking into my bedroom with this crazy idea, and I didn't even have a chance to say nothing," he said, throwing his hands up.

"Yes you did. You said yes! You said it was a good idea!" The tears started to flow. I couldn't believe how he was talking to me. I hadn't forced him into marriage. He was acting like I pulled a gun on him or something. "You had a choice, Brian, and you chose me. What I don't understand is how you then went behind my back and chose Shell. How could you do that? How could you be so cruel?"

"Maxine, I'm not getting into that. Just leave it alone," he muttered.

"Leave it alone, hell! Brian, you owe me an explanation. Me and you been together for years, and now you gonna take up with some other girl. You owe me, Brian. I want to know why you would hurt me like this!"

"It just a thing, that's all," he said calmly, no screaming, no yelling.

"What's that mean, a thing?"

He shrugged his shoulders. "I don't know. I like her, that's all. She's nice."

"What, and I'm not? Brian, what the hell are you trying to say?"

"That's not what I said. Don't put words in my mouth," he said, reaching under the bed for his shoes.

"I'm not trying to put words in your mouth. I'm trying to understand that's all. We were gonna be doing our own thing in our own house, and you done went and ruined it all. I don't understand why, Brian. Make me understand," I sobbed.

He shrugged again. "There's nothing to understand. I didn't ruin it. You did, Maxine, you did. I tried to tell you that maybe we was doing things too quickly. I tried to tell you, but as usual you got your way," he said coldly.

"My way, Brian? This isn't my way. It's *our* way. I thought we agreed that it's the way we supposed to be because we love each other."

"I do love you, Maxine. I just don't want to be all tied up. I mean I could see it from the beginning. I knew it was gonna end up like this. The day that I got let go from the Redesign Center I should have told you that I wanted to call it quits. I should have tried to stop you before we ended up in this mess. I should have let you know that I wasn't feeling all this, but baby, it was just too hard for me to say no to you, and you know that. Anyway, I don't want to be a husband," he said, shaking his head.

I couldn't believe what he was saying.

"But you want to be a father? Ain't that gonna tie you down? Brian, you are either really trippin' or really dumb. What do you think you gonna have to do for Shell and that thing she having? She gonna want you to be a man. She gonna be looking for you to do something for her when that thing pops out. Don't you know that?"

"Maxine, my baby ain't no thing. And besides, I wasn't looking for what happened with Shell. I wasn't trying to be nobody's daddy. But I'll tell you this, Shell ain't like you. She don't be trying to get me to do what she wants me to do!"

"What I want you to do?"

"Yeah, Maxine, exactly what you want to do. Do you remember when you came back from helping take care of your aunt when we was little? You came back home after a long time, and you and your mama was acting all weird with each other."

"So."

"So, you decided that you wanted to just run away."

"Brian, what does that have to do with anything?"

"You said that your mama made you sick and you were gonna leave. And you wanted me to come with you. Do you remember that?" he asked.

"So what?"

"So, we stole some money from my father's desk and went running off like fools in the middle of the night. We didn't even know where we was going. It was too late to catch a bus, and we were terrified that somebody would see us if we was just walking down the street. It was pitch dark, and we decided to take off down the trail next to the bayou. We got lost in the pine and cypress trees and we was out there all night getting eaten up by mosquitoes and scared to death, until my daddy and some of the dudes he worked with found us. Can you recall that?"

"Of course I can."

"Well, Maxine, I never wanted to do that. I did that for you. We could have died that night. We could have fallen into the bayou and drowned or gotten bitten by a cottonmouth or rattler."

"I know that."

"You do now, but, baby, you the queen of having bad ideas, and I'm the king of going along with them, because I always feel like I have to take care of you. No matter what, I always do what is *best for you*. That's why I'm trying something else now, with Shell."

"Yeah, right. We'll see how long that lasts!" I yelled back. In all the time we were together, I don't remember being angry at Brian, not like this. We weren't perfect, we disagreed here and there, but I never felt like walking over to him and punching him in the face. That's the way I felt, like I wanted to hit him hard. I wanted to knock the stupid, hurtful words clean out of his mouth.

"It will turn out fine, Maxine. Shell don't put no pressure on me. She ain't like you. She's easy," he said, adjusting his shirt.

"Well, I know that trash is easy. You don't have to tell me that."

"That's not what I mean. I mean she don't need nothing from me, so don't even go there Maxine."

"Don't go where? Brian, don't try to defend that nasty heifer to me. And you know what? She may not need nothing from you, but you sure as hell need something from her. You need somewhere to stay, that's exactly what you need!" I said. I walked over to the closet and started pulling his clothing out, throwing them onto the bed. "Go stay with your trash on the side. I don't want you in my house!"

"Maxine, I ain't got to go nowhere. My daddy bought this house. It's my house too. You can't just kick me out," he said, trying to gather his things up.

"Fine, I'll leave, but I'll go tell your daddy exactly why I'm going!" I shouted. He looked stunned, then fear came to his face.

"Okay, Maxine. You want me out, I'm out," he said, picking up his clothes.

"Good, and don't even think about coming back!" I said.

"I won't! Why would I want to?"

"Go to hell, Brian," I said, and ran out of the bedroom. I went to the living room and threw myself on the sofa, sobbing. I was thinking about Brian and Shell, and our relationship, and suddenly I was thinking about having to go home. My marriage was completely falling apart, and all I could think is I was going to have to go back home, with my mama and Andre, or whatever guy she'd meet in a few months. That thought was coming through stronger than my feelings of hurt, pain, and betrayal. I didn't want to go home. I did not want to go home.

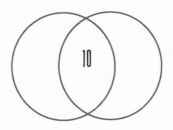

10

I told myself that I would never fool with men again after my husband died. Why not? It was my right as a woman to choose what I wanted to do with my life, and I didn't want a man in it," Great-aunt Freda told me this morning over breakfast. "I moved back home, and I got a job at a soda pop bottling company in a town nearby. I ran the machine that put the little metal tops on top of the bottle. All day long I would load it with grape tops, or lemon lime, or orange, or cola, or root beer, or whatever we was bottling that day. I made good money, but I was lonely and bored. I started going out, started dating the guy that ran the bottle labeling machine. The women at the plant all called him Big Money, which I later found out was meant to be a joke, because he never had any cash. That negro was broke as a gambler one hour after payday. He never had nothing, but I didn't mind. Because what he did have was a lot of charm, and a whole lot of something else that pleases a woman in another way."

"You mean he was good at making love."

She blushed. "Let's just say when he was around, this lady wasn't never singing the blues. I felt good with him. In fact, so good it was worth me paying for all the movies and restaurants we went to, and even the groceries when we didn't want to go out."

"Man," I said.

"That's right, and to make matters worse, I fell for him big-time," she said, putting sugar on her cornflakes. "I was crazy about him. I even thought I might get married for a second time after all, but it wasn't meant to be."

"Why not?"

"Well, one cold night when I was staying at his place I went into his drawer to get me a warm pair of socks and I just happened to find a checkbook. It wasn't any of my business, but I looked in it anyway. And guess what?"

"What?"

"Big Money really did have big money, nearly fifty thousand dollars. Can you believe that? He was holding out on me. Either somebody had left him a big check or he had been tucking cash away his whole life. I'm not sure which one it was, but I was hot. He had made a complete fool out of me. With him in my pocket, I wasn't able to keep a dime. I broke it off with him. I couldn't be with a man that I couldn't trust."

"Me either, that's why I kicked Brian out."

"I know that, baby, but you and Brian are more complicated than that. You been together forever. I was only with Big Money for a little while. It felt right for me to tell him to go to hell, but you telling Brian to go—I don't know, honey, it's just not the same."

"It is to me," I said, getting up from the table. I walked over to the stove and took out a sizzling tray of bacon. "Brian loves this stuff right out of the oven. He can eat it burning hot. I hope he's choking on some of it right now," I said, throwing the bacon in the sink.

"That's good food, don't throw it out, baby," Great-aunt Freda said.

"It's too late," I said, turning on the disposal. It whirred loudly, and the bacon disappeared down the drain.

"But not too late to save your marriage," she said.

"Don't go there, Aunt Freda, just don't go there," I said, staring to cry.

"Okay, I won't, baby," she said.

"How could he do me like that? How could he cheat on me with that nasty tramp?"

"I don't know that, baby. I don't know what makes some men do the things they do. No woman does. I do believe he loves you though. I'm firm in that belief."

"I'm glad you believe it. I'm not so sure anymore," I said.

I walked over and kissed her on the cheek. "I have to go Aunt Freda. I love you. I'm just not loving talking about this right now."

"I understand, baby," she said.

I left Great-aunt Freda in the kitchen and headed to my job at Bobby's Rib Shack. On my way, I stopped at Bonita and Madona's to tell them the bad news about my marriage. They were sitting out on the front porch in oversize shirts and cargo shorts when I walked up.

"Maxine, what's wrong with you?" Madona asked as I walked up the steps. I thought I could hold it all in, but I couldn't.

"Brian is gone," I said. "He been messing around with some girl at school, so I kicked him out."

"What? I know you lying, girl," Bonita said.

"No, I'm not. I threw him out a few days ago."

"I can't believe it," Madona said. She came over and she squeezed me tight.

"That bastard. I can't believe that he would do you like that," Bonita said. She came over and gave me a hug too. We stood there together in one big bunch until my tears dried up.

"I'm okay," I finally said, so they let me go.

"What are you gonna do, you got a baby on the way, and Brian done messed you up?" Madona asked.

"I don't have a baby on the way," I said, wiping my face with the back of my hand.

"Oh, Maxine, did you lose it? Some girl at our school lost her baby last year. She just went to the bathroom and it came out," Madona said.

I shook my head. "I didn't lose no baby. You can't tell nobody, but I was never pregnant in the first place," I said, feeling embarrassed to let the words come out.

"What? What are talking about?" Madona asked.

"I made the baby up," I said, starting to cry again. "Me and Brian, we just lied, so we could be together."

"For real?" both of the girls asked.

"Yeah, I had to do it, or Mama would of never let me move out of the house. You know how she is, and I couldn't stand it there with her no more, and all of her men. This month it's

Andre, next month it will be some other brother. I can't stand it. There's always some G in our house that I don't even know. I'm tired of all the player-daddy's who don't stay around long, and leave us struggling to pay their bills after they've left."

"So you made up a baby?"

"I didn't know what else to do."

"Dang, girl, what did your mama say when you told her?" Bonita asked.

"I haven't. She don't even know, and that's not even the worse thing."

"What is it?" they asked.

"The girl Brian hooked up with, she's pregn—" I started to say, but I couldn't get the words out. It was just too painful to say to my two girlfriends. I didn't want them to know what a stupid loser I was. I started bawling again. "I hate this. I really hate this. It's not fair. I didn't do anything wrong. All I did was love Brian. It's not fair," I said, busting into serious tears again.

"It's okay girl. Let it all out. Just let it go. We're here for you," they both said.

I cried on my girlfriends' shoulders until I had no choice but to leave and get to work. When I got to the rib shack with puffy eyes, I went straight through the back door, washed my hands, and started seasoning racks of pork ribs with Bobby's Special Cajun Seasoning. I was nearly finished with a huge bin of meat when Bobby came over and touched me on the shoulder. "Maxine, come outside with me, baby," he said, grabbing a couple of cold sodas from the cooler on his way out. We walked over to a bench next to the smoking pit and sat down. The billowing smoke and sizzling sound of the meat coming from the pit reminded me that I had only picked at my breakfast. I was still hungry. "Here you go," Bobby said, sliding a can of soda across the table to me. I popped the cap and waited for the hiss to stop before I took a drink.

"You know I love you, Maxine," Bobby said, stroking his graying Afro. "I been knowing you and your mama for years, and that's why I hired you. I don't usually like to hire teenagers. They ain't too reliable. They like to stay at home playing video games and talking on the cell phone when they supposed to be working."

"I don't," I said.

"Naw, you responsible. That's why I'm sorry I got to let you go."

"What? Why? I always do my job," I cried.

"You do more than your job, but I just can't afford to keep you on. People ain't eating out like they used to. Folks ain't got money to buy food somebody else done fixed."

"Yes they do. My mama does. She always does," I said desperately. I couldn't believe what I was hearing. I was being fired—fired—and I had bills to pay. How was I going to be able to handle things without a paycheck?

"Your mama *is* one of the few people that do, but it's not enough. Anyway, sweetie, I'm sorry, but I just can't keep you. He reached in his pocket and took out a wad of bills. I'm going to pay you through the month, because I know you and Brian just got married and got a bunch of bills."

"We do, please don't fire me," I pleaded.

"I'm sorry, Maxine. I know this hurts, but my other employees been with me longer and they all got family."

"I got family. Brian," I said.

"I know, but it's not the same, baby. You ain't got a house full of hungry kids, so it has to be you," he said, getting up and gently patting my head. "I'm sorry. I hope you find something soon," he said, placing the bills on the table. I took them without saying another word and walked away from the bench.

So many thoughts started to run through my head as I walked slowly down the street. What was I going to do for rent? I remember one time when Mama couldn't pay the rent because she was between men. The landlord came to our place every day for nearly two months and threatened to throw us out. Finally, after the third month, he did. I came home from school and found all of our stuff thrown out, or pretty much what was left of it. While we were away the neighborhood had helped itself to anything we had of value. The only thing left outside on the porch was some raggedy furniture that Mama had purchased from a garage sale, some photos of me and her during a lot nicer times, my broken toys that I hadn't played with since I was four, old clothes that didn't fit either one of us, a stack of unread newspapers, and my first grade report cards. That's all there was.

"Mama, they threw everything out. All of our good stuff is gone."

"I know that, Maxine. You ain't got to tell me what I already know."

I broke into tears. "Mama, what are we gonna do? Where are we gonna go?"

Mama looked around her. Several of our neighbors were standing in their screen doors staring at us, watching the shame of the situation that Mama had put us in.

"Maxine, dry those tears up. Can't you see these people

looking at us like we done done something wrong. Shoot, it ain't my fault that rent man threw us out. I didn't ask him to cause all this misery in my life. I would have paid the rent eventually. Let's go. I ain't gonna stay out here for these fools to make fun of me," Mama said.

I took the report cards and photos, and Mama moved us into a temporary shelter for women that same day. We stayed there for four months until we got kicked out because she couldn't find a job and they needed the space for someone else. After that, we crashed with several ladies Mama barely knew because she didn't want to tell our relatives that we didn't have a place to live. One of the ladies that we stayed with had a brother who thought Mama was cute. Mama starting hooking up with him, and the next thing I knew we were all moving into a house together.

As soon as we moved into our new place, I did my best to forget the crowded shelter and the room we shared with four other women and their little girls. I wanted to forget the left-over food that we got from the local food bank and clothing vouchers that we took to resale shops to get some used clothes, clothes that I eventually slept on the floor in when we had to crash at strangers' houses.

"Don't worry, we never gonna be without a place to stay again, Maxine," Mama said, as we were moving what little we had into the house with her new dude.

"Okay, Mama," I said, but I never believed it. I always knew that one day Mama would do something that would put us out on the streets again. I wasn't surprised at all when a few months later Mama's new man kicked us out for some sixteen-year-old girl he met driving the school bus. We ended up in a shelter again, but thank God we were only there a month until Mama found a job, and the government let us move into a little house.

Now it looks like I might be homeless again.

"What in the world am I gonna do for money? How am I going to stay in my house?" I said out loud. In a panic, I took out my cell and called Brian's dad's house. I was hurting and I needed Brian to know what was going on. The phone rang three times and the machine picked up.

"Please leave a message after the beep," a robotic voice said.

"This message is for Brian. Brian, Mr. Bobby just let me go from my job. How am I going to pay for all of this stuff by myself? You're supposed to help me out. You married me, so that's what you're supposed to do. You call me right now and tell me what you're gonna do. I mean it. I'm not going home to Mama because you screwed up. This ain't my fault. You better call me, Brian. You better help out!" I screamed into the phone.

I closed my cell and sat down on the curb to decide what to do next when the phone suddenly rang. I opened it expecting to hear Brian.

"Maxine, I'm on my way to your house right now, meet me there," Brian's dad said.

It took me by surprise. "Huh, what for?" I asked.

"I think you know. Meet me now."

"Yes sir," I said, and hung up the phone. I placed it in my skirt pocket and went to make my day worse, by having to deal with my father-in-law.

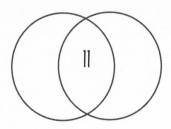

11

beat Brian's dad to my house and waited for him to show up. When I heard a knock on the door, I ran as quickly as I could to open it.

"Why'd you leave that message at my house? Surely you know Brian moved in with that stupid girl he got pregnant? Well, you need to know that I don't like it at all," he said, stepping through the door, in his sharp, brown business suit. I shut the door behind him.

"I won't beat around the bush," he said. "Maxine, you were never the future that I wanted for my son, but I don't like how things have turned out between the two of you. I honestly never saw this coming and I'm angry with Brian. I don't understand what he's doing with his life. He's let me down in ways that I can't even describe and he's let you down too. Yes, I found out that you aren't pregnant, but Brian still made a commitment. That's what marriage is, and he had no right to go outside of it and take up with another young lady."

"Ain't that the truth," I said, surprised that he was on my side.

"Yes, and with that said, I made a promise when I gave you and Brian this house. I told you that I would help with the expenses and do what I could to keep a roof over your head. I still intend to do that. Now, I know you don't want to go home, and I have a solution that will keep you in this home and keep your bills paid," he said.

"What is it?"

"Demonee."

"Excuse me?"

"Demonee."

"What? You mean Brian's screwed-up cousin that nearly ruined my wedding, Demonee?" I asked, with shock in my voice.

"Yes, she's presently staying with my mother, but my mother is having really bad problems with her diabetes, and it's hard for her to keep up with an unruly girl."

"Unruly? Try a hot mess."

"Yes, she's a handful, but she can be a good girl with someone who cares," he said. "But her mama can't take care of her. She has issues of her own, and Demonee is one of five girls she's trying to look after. It's sad really, so the whole family is trying to help out. I'd keep her myself, but you know I'm a bachelor, Maxine. Also, I'm away from home a great deal. Plus, I think it's better for a young girl to be around somebody she can relate to. Don't you?"

"Yes sir," I lied. I do believe that kids need somebody to relate to, but who could relate to Demonee?

"Anyway, she needs a place to stay and someone to look

after her. I thought since you had this little house you would be the perfect one to do it."

"Me?" I said.

"Yes, you. You can look after her, Maxine. I'll give you the money to fix up that little extra room for her, and I'll make certain that you are taken care of in other ways too."

"What does that mean?"

"Bills, mortgage, I'll pay it all, plus a little extra for groceries and wardrobe. I'll make certain that you don't want for anything."

"Still, Demonee. I don't know if I can do that," I said, shaking my head.

"You can do it, Maxine, or you can go home, and I don't think you want to do that," Brian's dad said in a stern voice.

"You don't know what I want," I said.

"Yes, I do. I always have. I knew it the first time I met you. You don't have any father to speak of, and your mother . . ."

"Don't say anything about my mama!" I said, raising my voice.

"Maxine, I don't have to tell you anything that you don't know. Besides, I didn't come here for that. I came to help. Will you accept my offer or not? If you do, you're going to have to keep your mouth shut. Nobody can know that Demonee is living here, or they'll take her away."

"Will that really be a bad thing?" I asked.

"Funny, but we really will have to keep it a secret. I have guardianship of her, so as far as anyone knows she'll be staying with me."

"But she won't. I'll have her," I said.

"Yes you will. It will be a small, but necessary lie that will benefit us all. So do you agree?"

"I ain't got much choice, do I? I mean, I don't want to get kicked out of this house," I said, looking around.

"No, you don't. But, Maxine, I know you can do this. You're a strong woman."

"I'm seventeen, I'm still just a girl," I said.

"Well, sometimes girls have to grow up quickly, and you put yourself on that path the minute you walked down the aisle. Anyway, we have a deal. I'll drop Demonee off in a few days. Here," he said, opening his wallet and taking out a bunch of bills. "This should be enough to pay your expenses awhile, and enough for you to start fixing up Demonee's room. Thanks for doing this, Maxine. I know this isn't your choice, but I think it will work out for everyone."

"Yes sir," I said, taking the money.

I opened the door again, and he stepped out. I breathed a sigh of relief and sat down on my couch. This wasn't what I wanted when I was having Tia's grandma Augustine make me a white dress. I wanted Brian and me to live together in our house and have a great life, not me and Demonee. The money in my hand suddenly felt heavy, like it was weighing me down. Or maybe it was just me weighing myself down, with Demonee, with my failed marriage, and with Brian's daddy who liked to control everything. Still, with Brian's father's help I wasn't going to have to go home to my mama. I kept my mind focused on that.

Don't get me wrong. I love Mama, but I don't understand her. She really never ever puts my feelings first. One Mother's Day me and Uncle Ernie threw a party for her, and invited our family members and some folks from her work. The last person that showed up from her job was a fine sister, who looked like she could be some type of supermodel. Of course, every dude in the place immediately started to hit on her. She couldn't turn around without somebody offering her something to eat or drink, or asking her if she wanted to dance. I didn't pay it no mind, but Mama did, because one of the dudes that was all over the supermodel sister was a dude that Mama was crushing on. They weren't going out or anything. Mama just liked him, but that was enough to set her off. Anyway, when the party was over, I thought that Mama was going to come and thank me and Uncle Ernie for giving her a nice surprise. Instead, she lit into us about inviting some woman that was trying to steal her man. Uncle Ernie got mad and told her to get out of his face, but I just ran to my room and soaked my pillow with tears. When I came out of my room hours later, I apologized to Mama for inviting the woman, because I was the one who had gone to Mama's job on her off day and invited everyone over. She accepted it, but didn't offer one of her own.

"Maxine, the next time you and Ernest want to have something like that for me, you ask me who I want to have over to my house. Don't be going to my job and inviting people that I don't even like."

"Yes ma'am," I said, but I knew that no matter what, I would never ever plan a party for her again. It seems like there was always going to be an issue with Mama, her men, and me, and I was always the one that was going to end up being hurt.

There was nothing else to think about. I put the money in my purse that Brian's dad gave me and went to see how I could fix up Demonee's space.

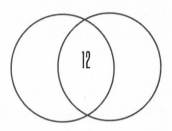

12

T hings had moved quickly, and with Demonee coming, there was no way that I could hide what was going on in my house. Eventually Mama was going to drop by my place and wonder where Brian was and why the heck Demonee was in my guest room. It was time to give her a call. She'd be pissed when I told her everything that had been happening, but it was better that she found it out from me. Mama is clearly not good with the kind of surprise that doesn't come in a decorated box. She was going to hit the ceiling when she found out about the switch in my household, and I would rather she did it over the phone.

It took me almost fifteen minutes to find Mama's new cell number tucked underneath some shorts in my dresser drawer. I dialed her number and suddenly wished that she wouldn't answer. The phone rang nearly eight times before she picked it up.

"Hey, Mama, what's up?" I asked.

"You tell me, Maxine. I got a call from school about you skipping. They say you done missed all kinds of days. Don't be no fool girl. You better not mess up. You need to graduate school and get a diploma. Why you been missing so much time anyway? Your honeymoon been over. You better get your mind in the right place and get back to school."

"I will, Mama. Quit nagging at me. I didn't even call for that," I said.

"I'm not nagging, I'm parenting. You got to think about your baby's future. She or he ain't gonna have much of one if you ain't got the education to get a job. What are you gonna do, spend your entire life working part-time at the rib shack?"

"No, Mama. I can't do that," I said.

"Look, what's up with you? I ain't heard from you in days. You know I still got a phone, don't you?" she said.

"Mama, don't be that way. I got something to tell you," I said.

"Well, what is it? Spit it out."

"Mama, I lost my job," I said.

"What? How come, how could Bobby let you go, and you got a baby on the way? I thought I knew him. What kind of bastard is he?"

"He's not, and I'm not," I blurted out.

"Maxine, what are you talking about?"

"I'm not, Mama. I mean, I never was. I'm not pregnant. I'm not gonna have your grandchild."

"What? Did you make a mistake? Did you miscarry?"

"No, Mama. I was never gonna have a child."

"Maxine, are you for real? What the hell are you talking about young lady?"

"Ain't no baby, Mama. I lied. I got Brian's cousin to get me some fake test results. She was the one pregnant, not me."

"What! Are you crazy? Now I know you didn't make up no baby and lie to me. Why in the devil would you do something like that? Have you lost your mind? Tell me why in the world you would do something like that!"

"I don't know, Mama," I cried.

"Well, I don't either, Maxine. You can't lie about something like that, it's gonna come out sooner or later. What were you gonna say when you didn't start to show?" Mama asked.

"I don't know. I didn't think that far."

"No, you didn't think at all. I can't believe this. Of all the dumb things to do. I been buying stuff for a baby, saving up what little money I got to help out with some daycare or something, and you and Brian been acting like some stupid kids and lying. I knew I couldn't trust that boy. He was just trying to get you all alone, so I couldn't keep him straight about messing around with you. I can't believe he put you up to this!" she yelled, so loud I nearly dropped the phone.

"He didn't put me up to anything. I wanted this—I wanted to be married."

"That don't make no sense, Maxine. You put Brian on the phone right now. I want to tell his black behind off!"

"He ain't here, Mama. He ain't even here! Mama he got another girl. You know that girl Shell that we was arguing about, she about to have a baby for him," I cried.

"What? You can't be telling me the truth, Maxine."

"I am, Mama, and I don't know when. She already showing, so he probably was messing around with her before she even showed up at my house that day."

"Probably? Hell yeah, he was messing with that little heifer. I told you, Maxine, didn't I tell you? That boy is just like his mama and daddy. He thinks that he can treat people any kind of way. Where is he at? I'm gonna find him and kick his behind," Mama said, sounding like she was ready to jump through the phone. I couldn't have that. There was enough trouble between me and Brian without her getting into the middle of it.

"You're not gonna find nobody, Mama. This ain't got nothing to do with you."

"Like hell, it don't. Maxine, how you gonna live? You got to bring your behind home with me. That's more money on my grocery bill. So, it is my business."

"No, it's not, and I'm not coming home."

"What do you mean you not coming home? How are you gonna live? Who gonna pay your bills?"

"Brian's dad."

"Brian's dad? What the hell do you mean by that? What kind of man wants to take care of a seventeen-year-old girl? What does he think he's up to?" she said.

"Nothing, Mama. He's just helping out."

"For free, for nothing?"

"No, it's not that. Look, Mama, you can't tell anybody, but I'm keeping Demonee. Her mama threw her out and her grandmother can't take care of her."

"How is that your problem?"

"It's not, Mama, but somebody got to take care of her."

"Let her uncle do it."

"Brian's dad ain't never at home."

"So that leaves you to take care of they family's mess?"

"It's not a mess. Demonee stays here, and Brian's dad pays for everything. I get to stay in my house."

"I don't like this. You need to bring your butt home, but I'm gonna let it go for now—for now—Maxine. I'm not cool with this, but for now I'm letting it go, just for now. Do you understand me?"

"I understand. I gotta run, Mama," I said.

I hung up the phone and grabbed my purse to leave my house, because there was somebody else that I needed to tell the bad news. I knew that my best friend Tia had a camera on her computer, so I was off to the library to make a video conference call to her. I had asked the librarian the day before if I could do it, and she told me that she would show me how. The truth is, making the call to Tia was something that I did not want to do. I didn't want to give her the details of how my marriage had failed.

I love Tia, but I didn't want her to be sorry for me, her dumped girlfriend. But I didn't have a choice. Best friends don't keep secrets from each other, at least not for long. No matter how much it hurt. I was going to have to tell her how Brian had ruined everything and broken my heart.

I walked out of the house and locked the door behind me. As soon as I hit the sidewalk, I heard someone call my name and I turned around. It was my crazy, but loveable, Uncle Ernie. He was racing up the sidewalk dragging one of his little girls behind him. I rolled my eyes when I saw him. I knew he was coming to ask me to keep one of his kids. He was my favorite uncle, but I wasn't in the mood to watch *Dora the Explorer* or change smelly diapers.

"Hey, Maxine, wait up. You running like they got a sale

on weaves down at the beauty store," Uncle Ernie said, hurrying toward me.

"Be quiet. I don't even wear a weave," I said, and actually laughed.

"I need to," he said, patting his short hair. "Them young sisters in the club love a brother with a big Afro."

"They don't have weaves for old brothers whose hair just won't grow," I said.

"Aww, Maxine, don't be that way. Don't be trying to make a brother feel like he getting ready for the nursing home."

"Getting?" I said.

"Aww, shoot, forget you girl. I ain't even thinking about you," Uncle Ernie said, and laughed.

"You're funny," his little girl Bethany said.

"She thinks she is," Uncle Ernie said to her. "Look, Maxine, you got to help a brother out tonight. Bethany's mama done dropped her off at my house this morning and told me she can't come get her until tomorrow."

"So," I said.

"So," Bethany said, and giggled.

"So, tonight is half-price night at Obsidian Queens."

"Obsidian Queens, that place where them women be running around with nothing on? I'm not seeing how that's my problem."

"They have swimsuits. Ain't nobody running around naked."

"Whatever, I still don't see how it's my problem. I don't have any four-year-olds," I said.

"Aww, come on, Maxine. Don't do your uncle like that. It's Friday night, a brother got to get his weekend on."

"Get his weekend on," Bethany echoed, and stuck her thumb in her mouth. I looked down at her and shook my head. She had a new pair of bright white Jordans on and a cute sunflower yellow dress that I knew had come out of some fancy baby store. Uncle Ernie always makes certain that his kids are taken care of financially. It's the physical part that he has problems with. Great-aunt Freda says that he fathered his first baby when he was just fifteen.

"It didn't give him much time to learn what true fatherhood is, and I guess he still hasn't quite figured it out," she once told me. Something about that makes me sad for Uncle Ernie and his kids. It makes it difficult for me to turn him down.

"Okay, I'll keep her," I said.

He grabbed me and kissed me on the cheek.

I pulled away. "You ain't got to do all that," I said.

"Okay, okay, I'm just trying to say thanks."

"You can thank me by paying me," I said, holding out my hand.

"Aww, come on, Maxine. You know I got to spend my money at the club. I'll get you next time. You know I'm good for it," he said.

"Yeah, right. Okay, whatever. Drop her off before you leave."

"I will," he said.

"Cool," I said, and started to walk off.

"Wait a minute. I'll walk with you," he said.

On my way to the library, I realized that I was happy that Uncle Ernie and Bethany had come along. Uncle Ernie always has some kind of crazy funny story to tell, and as we walked he had me laughing my head off about Bethany's mama trying to squeeze her ample rump into a pair of jeans that Kate Moss couldn't get on.

"Girl, I heard all kinds of hollering so I ran into the dressing room."

"Why? What was wrong? Was Bethany's mom yelling?" I asked.

"Naw girl, she wasn't saying nothing. That hollering for help was coming from the seams in them jeans she had on," he said, and doubled over with laughter.

"You need to quit," I said.

"Naw, she need to quit eating them Lays potato chips and Hostess Ding Dongs."

"You're a fool."

"You're a foo, Daddy," Bethany said.

"Ya'll wouldn't love me if I wasn't," Uncle Ernie said, as we walked into the library parking lot.

We looked around at all the empty parking spaces.

"Shoot, don't nobody read no more?" Uncle Ernie asked.

"I do, I wead," Bethany said.

"Oh you do? Well your papa gonna take you in here and find you a book," Uncle Ernie said as we walked through the glass double doors.

I followed him, curious to see if he knew where the children's book section was. I wasn't surprised when he walked past the rows of colorfully illustrated books right into the adult fiction section. "Let's see what we got here," he said, searching through the books on one of the long shelves.

I snickered and sat down at a computer with a video camera

attached. I logged in and watched Uncle Ernie going from shelf to shelf with poor little Bethany in tow.

"Uncle Ernie, you're in the wrong place," I started to whisper when someone caught my eye. I saw a girl walk past the doorway, a light girl, with a skin-tight T-shirt and a pair of shorts that barely covered her rear end. I knew without getting up that it was Shell.

"What the hell is she doing here?" I asked.

"Who, what?" Uncle Ernie asked, walking over to my computer.

"That girl who just walked in. What is she doing here? She probably can't even read."

"Who, what? What girl?" Uncle Ernie asked, walking to the door. He peeped out and came back with a puzzled look on his face. "You talking about that bright girl?" he asked.

"Yeah her," I said.

"What, you don't like her?"

"It's complicated," I said.

"What that's mean? Man, ya'll young people always got some issues with somebody. That girl is all right," Uncle Ernie said.

"You know her?" I asked.

"I dated her mother some."

"What mother? It's just her and her sister," I said, adjusting the camera on top of my monitor.

"I mean back in the day, a long time ago. I dated her mama when they lived here before."

"Before? What before?"

"Back in the day, when they used to live here."

"They never lived here," I said.

"Yeah, they did. I know. 'Cause like I said, I used to date her mama. She was one fine woman. I took her out for a while. They lived six or seven streets from here."

"You're wrong. They didn't live in our neighborhood. I would have known. Shell would have been in my school," I said, starting to feel strange.

"Not a long time ago. That's when they was bussing, trying to put ya'll hardheaded black kids in with them hardheaded Latino kids on the other side of town."

"Ain't nobody's head hard, and you're wrong, because I wasn't bussed nowhere."

"No, you weren't, but she was. They divided this neighborhood up by streets. Some of ya'll stayed here, and some of ya'll went someplace else. You probably too young to remember that, but I know because my little boy, James, was one of the kids that was bussed. Anyway, to get back to my point, I know that girl lived here. I used to pick her mama up from work. She cleaned houses for a living. In fact, she used to clean for your mother-in-law some."

"What? No way. That can't be, Uncle Ernie. I never saw her mama at Brian's mom's house. His mama's maid was from Ecuador. She wasn't black."

"Naw, she wasn't, but that girl Shell's mama did work for your mother-in-law. She and two other ladies cleaned them little rent houses that your mother-in-law used to own down by the railroad. You mother-in-law hired her to help fix up things when new tenants moved in or out. Plus, she worked for your mother-in-law at her house for a little while too. She took care of the household when your mother-in-law's permanent maid went back home. I remember, because her permanent maid's daughter was sick or something and she left to look after her.

Well, when her maid tried to get back in the United States, there was something wrong with her papers. She had to stay over there for a really long time until they figured everything out. At least that's what Shell's mama, Sha'ree told me."

"That never happened," I said.

"Yeah, it did, baby. You probably don't remember because that was when you wasn't living with your mama. You weren't even in the neighborhood, and they moved away before you came back. Sha'ree got a job cleaning for a hotel in Dallas. I sure did miss her. We didn't date long, but we had some good times."

"Uncle Ernie, what the hell are you talking about?" I shouted. Every eye in the library turned on me. I got up from my seat and rushed out of the room into the next section.

"Maxine, what is wrong with you?" Uncle Ernie asked, running after me with Bethany.

I stopped in the children's section and collapsed into one of the little chairs.

Uncle Ernie sat across from me and pulled Bethany into his lap. "Maxine, what is going on?" he asked.

"He's known her as long as he's known me. He's known her as long as he's known me! I didn't know that. I thought maybe he had met her a little while ago in Dallas, but he probably knew her back when we were young. She's known my husband as long as me."

"Maxine, what are you talking about? Are you okay?" Uncle Ernie asked.

My head was spinning. I had to get outside and get some air. "I gotta go, Uncle."

"What? I thought you was gonna get on the computer."

"Not today. I gotta get out of here," I said, hurrying

through the library. I rushed into the hallway and went the opposite direction of Shell, hoping that she hadn't caught a glimpse of me. I went through the double doors of the library with my heart racing like crazy in my chest. All I could think about was getting away from Shell, away from what I had just heard.

In my mind, I had always had the advantage over Shell because I've known Brian his entire life. But he could have known Shell just as long as he knew me. Of course he did. He met her at his mother's house. Parents always take their little kids to work, when school's out, on holidays, they always do. God, it hurt so much to think of Brian spending time with her when we were just kids, playing games with her in the backyard, chasing her around the room. And it was all because I wasn't there for him, because my mama had picked some loser over me. And she wondered why I would do everything I could to get away from her for good? I just wanted to stand in the middle of the parking lot and scream. I started down the steps of the building when once again I heard someone call me. I looked across the parking lot and saw a girl with a scowl on her pretty brown face coming toward me. Demonee. She walked up the steps looking like she wanted to knock the hell out of me, or maybe even the whole world.

"My uncle dropped me off at your house, but you wasn't there. Some lady across the street said she saw you come over here, so I came to find you," she said in an icy tone.

"Well, here I am," I said, in a not-so-nice tone myself.

"I don't want to live with you. I just want you to know that."

"Well that makes two of us, because I don't want to live

with you either, but sometimes we got to do what we got to do."

"So, I still don't have to like it. I don't even like you. You ain't my mama. You ain't nobody, nothing," she said.

I gulped when she said that, and did everything I could to hold the tears back. How did she know that it was exactly how I felt, like nothing, like I didn't matter to anyone? I had just seen the girl that my husband was shacked up with and pregnant for, and I felt like nothing.

"I don't want to live with you. I wanna live with my mama," she said, and started to cry.

I wanted to scream at her and tell her that I didn't care where she lived, but my heart went out to her. I understood her tears. There we were, both of us, standing there wanting what we couldn't have. She wanted to go back home and live with a mother who obviously couldn't or wouldn't care for her, and I wanted to go home and live with Brian who obviously couldn't or wouldn't care for just me. Great-aunt Freda would say that we were two potatoes boiling in the same pot. The only thing left for us was to be completely drained and mashed. I didn't want that. It wasn't fair for either one of us to be squashed into mush by the people that we love.

"Demonee, you ain't got nowhere else to go and neither do I, so why don't we just go home and see how we can live in my little house without killing each other. I fixed your room up real pretty," I said.

Her face brightened a bit. "For real, I got my own room?" she asked, wiping away her tears.

"Yeah, you wanna come see it?"

She shrugged her shoulders. I figured that was the best

answer I was going to get, so we took off and headed for my place.

"Do you like to read?" I asked, hoping that I could get some kind of conversation started.

"Naw, and I don't like libraries, so don't think you gonna make me come back here," she said.

"I won't. I'm not coming here either," I said, thinking of Shell roaming around the library. She was probably going from shelf to shelf looking for baby books. The whole thing made me want to throw up. "Trust me, Demonee, neither one of us will be back here. Let's go see you room," I said, leading her back toward my house. She walked away with me reluctantly, but reluctantly was all I needed for a new start.

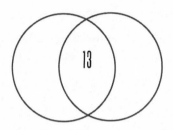

13

When we moved in, Brian put up his favorite two posters, one of Jennifer Lopez and the other of Beyoncé. Neither one of the women had on much clothing, and I never liked staring at them while I was lounging on our sofa. Today I finally said goodbye to the barely dressed divas. I didn't yank them down and rip them to shreds. It was almost ceremonial the way I tenderly took them off the wall and folded them, before tossing them in the trashcan outside. I don't know why I did it that way, except tearing them to shreds would have been the angry thing to do, and I'm tried of being angry. I don't have the time for it anyway, not with all I have to do with Demonee.

Demonee has been here for two weeks, but it seems more like two months. The house is filled with her. When I get up for a drink of water at night, I stumble over her sandals on the living room floor, and her toothbrush is now next to mine in the plastic cup on my bathroom sink. The news program that I like to watch each morning before I take off to school has now been replaced with shows like *Hannah Montana* and

Degrassi, and when I do a load of laundry, I have to check and see if she has anything that she wants to toss in before I start the wash cycle. The house that used to be mine and Brian's is now mine and Demonee's. I thought this would happen gradually, but she entered like a flash flood and immediately started washing away the life that I had with my husband. To make things worse, the day she moved in I swear she was hiding a huge box full of trouble in her *That's So Raven* backpack. As soon as she stepped into the house, every bit of space was filled up with bad spirits. Let's just say I understand why her name is Demonee. Now every day is a fight to try and get her to do what she's supposed to do and act like a child her age ought to act. I hate the drama of it, but it keeps my mind off of Brian.

"That was dumb. Why did you throw them posters away?" Demonee said.

"I needed to."

"Shoot. I coulda traded them at the CD store for something," she said, while she was out in the yard playing catch with Coffee Bean, my neighbor's chocolate lab puppy that loves to wander into my yard.

"Demonee, stop worrying about my business and go get dressed for school," I said, putting the lid back on the can.

"Fine, whatever. I'm just telling you how dumb you are," she said, rolling her eyes and going back in the house.

I rolled my eyes too. I picked up Coffee Bean and took him, tail wagging, back to my neighbor's place. I liked dogs, but the truth is when I was a little younger than Demonee I wanted a brown bunny. Mr. Harlan, who raised bunny rabbits and chickens down by the tracks, was selling them. The bunnies were only twenty bucks. They were large and fluffy and could hop around your house, or sit in your lap while you were watching TV. That sounded great to me, and I wanted one more than a little kid wants a bike without training wheels. I talked about the bunny every day for nearly three weeks until Mama finally promised that she would get one for my birthday at the end of the month. Well, the end of the month came, and so did my birthday, but no bunny. Instead, I got two cheap stuffed animals from the dollar store. I was already out of my stuffed-toys years, so they were the last thing that I wanted. But when I asked Mama why she broke her promise, she told me that she had to spend her money on a new blouse, so she could look good on a date with a guy she was seeing.

"Maxine, I'm sorry, but I had to get me a new top."

"What? Why?" I asked.

"Because I just did. Baby, it's not easy when you got a kid. Men don't like to walk into responsibility. I have to work a lot harder to get what I want. I have to look like something the men can't pass up. I know it's unfair, but sometimes I have to put me first."

I didn't have a problem with the *sometimes*. It was the *always* that bothered me, and set me to crying for most of that day.

The next morning when I woke up, I found Brian standing outside my window with a big fluffy bunny. It was white with black spots, and not brown, but it was still perfect to me. I opened the window and let him in, and we played with the bunny all morning. When Mama came in and saw it, she grumbled about Brian trying to show her up. I didn't care one bit. Because unlike her, I had gotten what I wanted *from my boyfriend*, and I didn't have to hurt someone I loved to get it.

I dropped the dog off in my neighbor's yard and headed back home. When I got back, I cleaned up the living room some, then I went to check on Miss Thing. I knew I was in for another dramatic episode when I spotted her outfit. The skirt barely covered her behind, and you could see clean through the top. She looked like a younger version of Shell. There was no way I was gonna let Demonee go out of the house like that. Her school had a dress code, and I didn't need any extra drama in my life because of her breaking it. The last thing I needed was the school to call her uncle at work and tell him that he had to come pick her up, because she wasn't dressed decent.

"Girl, now you know you ain't going nowhere in that outfit," I said, standing in her doorway.

"You don't tell me what to do. You ain't my mama!" she flared back.

"I didn't say I was your mama. I said you ain't going nowhere in what you got on," I said calmly. She rolled her eyes up to Jesus.

"Why not? I seen you go out in things like this," she said.

"No, you haven't. Besides, I'm grown. I can wear what I want."

"You ain't grown," she said. "You ain't but seventeen, that ain't even an adult."

"I been married and I'm living in my own house. My mama don't have to wash my clothes no more. That makes me grown," I snapped.

"Whatever," she said, rolling her eyes back up to the Savior. It made me want to go over and snatch that outfit right off of her pint-sized behind. It's what my mama would have done to me, if I talked noise like that.

"Ain't no whatever," I said. "You ain't going nowhere

with all your assets on display. Every two-bit dog in town will be barking at the front door. Anyway, you know they ain't gonna let you in school like that. It's just gonna cause trouble. Dang, Demonee, why you always got to be this way?"

"I ain't being no way. You the one trippin'. Why you got to be in my business?" she said stepping over to her dresser. She picked up a can of temporary color and sprayed it on her long bangs, turning her hair bright blue.

"They gonna say something to you about that too," I mumbled.

"So, let 'em say what they want."

"They'll do more than that. They'll call your uncle and tell him to come and take your butt home."

"Good," she said. "At least he'll have to spend some time with me. He told my grandma he would take care of me."

"He is taking care of you. Why you think you staying here with me?" I asked.

"'Cause he don't want me. Nobody does. I hate them all," she said, sounding like she was about to cry. I felt like crying with her, over Brian, over the life I thought we would have. There were so many tears I could have shed over that. There wasn't time to do that though. There was so much more that I needed to worry about.

I sighed and went over to her twin-sized bed. I sat down on it. "Look, Demonee, just give a sister a break and change into something nice. If you do that we can both get to school," I said softly. She rolled her eyes again and started yanking everything off. I watched her strip herself down to a stretch-lace training bra, and briefs that had little orange bows on them. I was reminded that she was still nothing but a little slip of a girl. She needed to be home with her mama, not stuck in the house squabbling with me. She yanked one of her bottom dresser drawers open and came out with a soft mauve peasant blouse and mid-length mauve skirt that would set off her copper brown skin. She was pretty in pink on the outside, and red hot with anger underneath.

"You look good in that, girl," I said, getting up from her bed.

"Whatever, I'm still wearing this blue in my hair, unless you think you can make me take it out," she challenged, with her hands on her hips.

"Look, do what you want, little girl. Just go get your breakfast and take your behind to school. I ain't got time for you," I said.

"Don't nobody have time for me," she mumbled.

With that she slipped on a pair of yellow flip-flops and rushed into the dining room. I went to my own room to get dressed. While I was putting my clothes on, I heard her slam the front door and breathed a sigh of relief. I was free at last. I slid my feet into my own flip-flops and left the house.

I breathed another sigh of relief when I hit the street. I was going to have a whole day of peace to myself. I wasn't actually going to school, like I said. Truth is, I don't go to regular school anymore. Because I missed way too many of my classes, my school kicked me out. I now go to an alternative school, with the twins, and I don't mind it. I don't have to see Shell or Brian, and I can stay focused on getting my life back together. Things are simple at my school. There's no time to get sidetracked. We don't have sports or anything like that. All we do is basic skills, science, and business programs. Most of the time I'm so bored

I want to run screaming out of the old building we have classes in. I want to, but I don't. After losing my job, and having to depend on Brian's dad, I now know that I need to have a good education. I want to make certain that I get a diploma. If I work real hard I may never need another Brian's dad in my life. So I'm in school each time the doors open, except today. I'm free today, because my school is having parent-teacher conference day. Mama is my legal guardian, so they sent her a note about the conferences. When I went to see her a while back, I told her she could go if she wanted to, and she said she would think about it. She knows that I don't want her all up in my business now that I'm on my own.

"If I ain't got nothing better to do, I'll go over there and see what's going on, even though you ain't living with me no more. I'll go, 'cause I don't want you messing up any more of your life. You gonna finish school," she said.

"I know I'ma finish. Don't worry, and if you go over there talking to them teachers don't say anything dumb," I told her.

"You the one dumb, Maxine," she said, coming out of the bathroom in her bright red slip. "You the one up and lied so you could marry that silly Brian boy, and then up and let his daddy push that fast little cousin of Brian's off on you. I don't know what you were thinking. I should make you bring your tail back in this house with me."

"All right, Mama, can we not revisit that same zoo? I already seen all the animals in there. Just give it a rest. I'm taking care of myself, and I ain't asking you for nothing. You ought to at least feel good about that."

"I don't feel good about nothing. The only thing I would feel good about is you coming home, but I know you ain't got sense enough to do that."

"Let's not go there, Mama. See you later," I said. And I meant much, much later. What Mama thinks doesn't matter. She doesn't run my life anymore. She was never that good at it anyway.

So, I let Mama decide what she was going to do about the conferences. Me, I was going to see Bonita and Madona. I had told them a few weeks ago about Demonee moving in and Brian's dad paying the rent. They didn't give me a hard time about it, because they know how much I need the money.

I cut across the street and went into Kelly Ville projects, in the best mood I had been in since Brian moved out. As I came up the sidewalk, I nearly ran into a group of old men carrying folding card tables out to the empty basketball court so they could play dominoes.

"Where you going, pretty gal?" a bony white-haired man asked me.

"Somewhere you can't go," I said, giggling. All of the men laughed. I grinned and continued on.

I got to the last apartment on row G of the Kelly Ville complex and knocked. While I was waiting for somebody to turn up, I sat down in the wooden rocker on the porch. I heard the sound of house slippers slapping the hardwood floor, and a second later the door pushed open. Madona was standing there with serious bed head wearing a pair of short pink pajamas with white clouds all over them. Underneath, her stocky brown legs were white with ash. She looked like she could use a glob of Vaseline.

"Maxine, what are you doing here so early?" she asked.

"Wishing that I brought you some lotion to put on them ashy legs," I said.

"I got something to put on my legs, pants," she said, laughing.

"Well, you need to get them on quick."

"Maxine, don't even trip. I could braid that hair on your legs. When the last time you shaved?" she asked and laughed.

I thought about the answer. The last time I shaved was with Brian's razor. I was never very good at buying my own.

"I always shaved when Brian got through with the Bic," I said.

She looked regretful. "I'm sorry, I didn't mean to remind you of your no good ex. Come on girl," she said, walking back through the house. I followed her through their stylish living room. The twin's mother works as personal assistant to a nice doctor out in River Oaks. Each time the doctor gets something new in her house she gives them the barely used old stuff. Their entire place is filled with kick-ass furnishing.

We passed through the dining room and went to her bedroom in the back of the house. As soon as she opened the door, I got a shock. Something was up with Bonita. She didn't look nothing at all like the Bonita I knew. Shoot, girlfriend had finally started paying attention to the fashions in her teen mags. Instead of the tomboyish big cotton shirts and cargo pants she and her sister usually wear, she had on a short black tank and a pair of skin tight stretch jeans. All kinds of blond streaks were working in her dark brown hair, which she had actually taken a curling iron to. And even I was jealous of her makeup job. With cool purple eye shadow and sparkly red lip gloss, she had managed to kick her Plain Jane looks up a big ole notch.

"Dang!" was all I could say.

"Hey, Maxine. What's up, girl?" she asked, walking over to her dresser mirror.

"Hey girl, what's up with you?" I asked.

"Nothing, I'm just trying to look good for my new boyfriend," she said.

"What new boyfriend?" I asked.

"Some boy she met on the Internet."

"I didn't meet him on there. I just been talking to him over the computer, and he is fine," Bonita said.

"Well good for you. I hope he fine, and nice too," I said.

"He likes me for me, what could be nicer than that?"

"Nothing, I guess."

"Anyway, what's the deal girl? Is that little girl you living with still trippin'? What about Brian, you heard from him?"

"Naw, I haven't heard from Brian. And right now I don't even want to talk to his sorry behind. I took his posters down today. I thought I was gonna cry while I was doing it, but I didn't. I don't know, it just felt like I was handling my business. As for Demonee, she's trippin' *herself* out. She ain't doing nothing but bringing trouble down on her own head."

"I remember how she was at the wedding. I kept hoping you would send her tail home. She was getting on my nerves. Here we was trying to have a special day and all that little heifer was doing was ruining it," Bonita said.

"No lie to that," her sister said.

"Well, Demonee is a mess, and a pain. I don't like dealing with her, but we do what we got to do, and right now I got to do this. Don't ask me why. It just makes things better."

"For who?" Bonita asked.

"Me and Demonee, I guess. We both need a place to stay, and I need the cash."

"How come Brian don't help you out?" Bonita asked. "He your husband. He still got responsibilities, even though he don't live with you."

"We ain't tight like that no more, and he got other responsibilities," I said vaguely. I still couldn't bring myself to tell the girls the truth about Shell and the baby.

"Responsibilities—you his responsibility. I'll bet you wish ya'll was all in love again," Madona said.

I thought about it for a minute. "Madona, things get real complicated when you talking about being married and living together. I didn't know that. I wish I had before we went down the aisle. Anyway, I didn't come over here for all that. I came over here to catch up with my girls. So what's the deal? Who is this new brother you trying to get with?" I asked.

"Girl, his name is Billy . . . ," Bonita started. Right then my cell in my pocket rang.

"Shoot," I said, pulling it out. I pushed the talk button.

"Maxine, I thought we had an understanding!" Brian's daddy barked into the phone.

"We do, what's up, sir?" I asked.

"Demonee, that's what's up. I just got a call from the school about her."

"What? What about, sir?" I asked, feeling my temperature go up.

"I don't know," he said. "The vice principal said that she wanted to talk to me in person."

"Oh crap."

"Yeah, oh crap," he said. "Now look here, Maxine, we had an agreement. We agreed that you would watch out for Demonee and I would pay your expenses."

"I know, sir," I said.

"Do you? Because part of watching out for her means that I don't get disturbed on my damn job for her nonsense. Do you understand me, Maxine?"

"Yes sir, I understand perfectly," I said obediently.

"Yes, well you better, or you can take your behind home and live with your mother. I don't give a damn, but I'm not going to be paying for you to stay in that house and having to deal with my stupid disobedient little niece too. Do you understand me?"

"Yes sir," I said.

"Good, now I called over to your school and I know you don't have classes today, so you go take care of this."

"How do I do that?"

"You're going to have to figure it out. I have an extremely important meeting that I can't get out of. I'll meet you at your house as soon as I can."

"Yes sir, I'll fix things, sir," I said. I put my phone away and turned to the girls. "I'm sorry. I gotta bounce," I said.

"Right now? How come? You just got here," Bonita said.

"I know, but it's something up with Demonee."

"What's up?" Bonita asked.

"I don't know, but I gotta go. I'll see ya'll later," I said.

"We'll be here!" Madona yelled, as I was heading for the bedroom door.

I rushed from the house and made my way to Demonee. What the heck had she done? Everything in me told me that I really, really didn't want to know. I headed on down the street wishing that I had never met Brian or his dumb family.

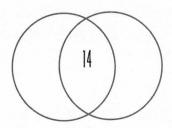

14

ran into Demonee a few blocks before I got to the house. She came toward me with a big grin on her face, as if nothing was going on.

I walked up to her and got in her face.

"Girl, what's wrong with you? You're going to ruin everything. What the heck did you do?" I asked. The grinned disappeared from her face.

"It wasn't my fault. That school is just trippin'. I hate how stupid everybody is," she said.

"How stupid everyone is! Demonee, what the heck did you do? What in the world is going on?"

"Nothing, I just have to stay home for a while."

"Stay what? What do you mean stay home?"

"It ain't no big deal, just five days I gotta stay home," she said.

No big deal! Five days, that's how long Demonee's little behind can't go back to school, and when she does go back she's going to have to apologize to Mr. Matthews, the security guard. He was the one that she cursed out because he caught her and a classmate on the gym roof with two boys. The boys ran when Mr. Matthews opened the door, leaving the girls to take all the blame. Mr. Matthews also said that there was a strong smell of weed in the air, and he saw Demonee's friend hand something to one of the boys before he took off.

"How could you be so dumb? You're going to mess us both up. Your uncle is going to be seriously pissed," I said.

"So, I don't care," she said.

"You better care, because your uncle is gonna be like a raging bull on us as soon as we walk in the door," I told her, shaking my head.

And was he ever. When we got home he was waiting there to hear what I had to say. I barely got the tale out before he was roaring like an angry beast.

"Who do you think you are, little girl? Where do you get off skipping class to mess with some drug thug, and then cursing out the one person that's trying to stop you from doing it?" Brian's dad yelled. Demonee didn't seem phased. She held her ground, didn't let the fact that Brian's dad spends all his free time coaching a local semi-pro football team get to her. I've seen Brian's dad out on the field bossing around dudes that looked like they could pick up an SUV and toss it forty yards. He yells and throws a fit on them, and they act like they're too scared to even open up their mouths. Having him in her face should have rattled Demonee, but not girlfriend. She stood there with her blue bangs hanging in her face, looking like she could throw an SUV several yards too.

"I wasn't messing around with no drug thug. My friend

plays JV basketball for our school, if you wanna know," she said, in a matter-of-fact way.

"Well, good for him, but that doesn't mean anything. Sports players get busted for drugs all the time. Believe me, I ought to know. Managing sports is what I do."

"Yeah right, I guess you talking about that little team you try to coach," Demonee said sarcastically. "I'll bet all them losers use drugs."

"Dang, touch down," I mumbled to myself. I couldn't believe she said that. Brian's dad couldn't either. His light brown face turned poinsettia red.

"Excuse me? Let me tell you something, young child. You will not be disrespectful to me," he said, pointing a finger in Demonee's face. "You will not talk to me like *you* tell me what to do. You think it matters that your friend plays sports. That just makes it worse. I know what sports players are like. That boy is probably after only one thing, and Lord knows an incorrigible, defiant girl like you might just be fool enough to give it to him. That's why you should have been somewhere studying your math, instead of skipping class and ruining your reputation with some idiot."

"My friend ain't no idiot! You don't even know what you're talking about," Demonee hollered, looking as if her huge dark eyes were gonna come out of her face.

"Oh, I don't, I don't," Brian's dad said. Then he stroked his short black beard and got quiet.

I held my breath. I knew what was coming. He was about to let loose the calm smack down, no yelling, no screaming. He was just going to say the thing that would cut her the deepest. I had seen him do it two or three times with Brian.

"Let me tell you something, young lady," he said after a few moments, "I don't have time for this. Do you understand me? You will not take up my time with this. It's irrelevant. You are irrelevant. Now I agreed to take care of your expenses because my mother asked me to. I put you in this house and I got a female to look after you," he said pointing to me. "All this I did because my mother asked me to do something for your little ungrateful behind. But I won't have my life interrupted. I won't be called from my job for nonsense. You can't *and don't* have that kind of affect over my life, nor anyone else's. That's why you're here, because you don't affect anybody's life, not mine, nor your grandmother's or your mother's. That's why your mother threw you out," he said in a matter-of-fact way.

"She didn't throw me out," Demonee said, defiantly, but she looked as if Brian's dad had just kicked her in the stomach.

"Then why are you here? Why can't you go back home? Don't fool yourself, little girl," he said. "You're here because your own mother didn't want you in her house, and we both know that."

"That's not true. You go to hell!" Demonee yelled, and took off for her room.

"Demonee, you get back here!" I shouted after her. The door slammed so loud I thought it would break off the hinges.

"Take care of this, Maxine!" Brian's dad raged. "She's my niece, and I do care about her, but I'm the last stop for her. I can't keep saving a child that doesn't want to be saved. You don't know how many times I've already had to deal with her drama this year. You let her know that I won't be bothered with her nonsense, or you can go back to where you came from, and she can go into the system, and I mean that," he said.

"Yes sir, whatever you say."

"Don't whatever-you-say-sir me. Look, I'm trying to do the best I can for everyone. I didn't want to fool with Demonee, but it all fell on me. So I'm trying to do what I can for her. All I'm doing is trying to be responsible for a kid that nobody in this world wants, and I don't have to tell you that."

"No, you don't. I understand. You ain't her daddy or her mama, so why should you have to deal with what she puts down? I'll get on her, I promise."

"You do that," he said. He took a white handkerchief from the inside pocket of his suit and dabbed at his sweaty forehead as he walked to the front door. When he went out of it, I locked the door behind him.

As soon as I tried the knob to make certain the door latch actually caught, I headed for Demonee's room, but something stopped me. I didn't know what to say to her, not really. Demonee had messed up, true that. Brian's dad certainly had a right to get on her about her actions. What if she got pregnant fooling around with some stupid boy, when she should be in class? Or what if she flunked out of her courses and got left back? Once that happened, it would be hard as hell to catch up. I knew a girl that happened to. She got left back and couldn't get on grade level again, so the next year she got left back once more. She was bigger than everybody in our grade. Rita was her name, but the kids called her "That big dumb girl." Lord knows Demonee stripped my nerves raw, but I still didn't want something like that to happen to her. That was reason enough for me to go and get on her about her ways, like I promised her uncle I would. Only, man, what Brian's dad had said was harsh, but so true. Demonee was being passed around like stale leftovers that nobody wanted to eat. She was just a plate scrape from ending up in the garbage disposal. If it wasn't for Brian's dad, that's exactly where she would be. He was the only thing that was keeping her from being completely thrown away. So as much as I didn't want to make her feel worse than she was feeling, I had to hip her to the fact that it wouldn't be a good idea for her to keep pushing his buttons and end up being out on the streets.

I headed to her room to tell her just that. I stopped when I heard her sobbing through the door. I knew how awful it was to have someone say the worst thing they could say to you. Before I let Brian go, he really laid me low when he told me that Shell was finer than me. It hurt that he liked her fair skin and bigger boobs, and of course her size. Before she got pregnant she could probably wear a size six, while I usually needed a twelve or a fourteen. That bothered me most of all. I remember standing in the mirror the morning after Brian left, looking at my small chest and chunky figure. I thought I was the ugliest thing in the world. I'll bet Demonee was hurting like that too. I decided that I wouldn't throw a fit on her no matter what. I would talk plain to her and try to make her understand why her uncle had every right to set her straight.

"Demonee, come open this door," I said. All I heard was sobs.

"Demonee, get over here and open up this door, right now." More sobs, then the latch clicked and the door opened. She greeted me all snotty faced, with tearstains all over her pink outfit.

"What you want, Maxine? Why you yelling outside my door?" she asked in the normal funky way.

"I ain't yelling. I was simply trying to get you to open up."

"Why?"

"I just want to talk to you," I said, pushing past her into the room. I glanced at her bed. Her flowered pillowcase was soaking wet. "Demonee, what you doing in here crying like you a two-year-old?" I asked. She stomped over to the bed in her flip-flops and threw herself on it.

"I ain't crying. Go away, Maxine," she said.

"Girl, I ain't going nowhere. What's the matter with you? Why you always making trouble?" I asked.

"I ain't making no trouble."

"You getting kicked out of school, messing around with some sorry boy, and doing drugs."

"I ain't messing around with no sorry boy, and I ain't doing drugs. My friend ain't even like that."

"Ain't even like what? Girl, you screwing up big time. You 'bout to fall off a cliff and don't know it. Why you wanna go getting your uncle mad like that?"

"Forget him. He don't mean nothing to me. I hate his ass," she said, bringing all kinds of anger to her wet face.

I wagged my finger at her. "Don't use that kind of language up in here, Demonee," I said. "I ain't cursing at you. Don't curse at me."

"I ain't cursing at you either. You the one in my face. Go away and leave me alone, Maxine," she said.

"I'll go when I get you straight. Look, girl, Brian's daddy is harsh. I'm not saying that he ain't, but girl you got to start acting like you got some sense."

"I got some sense, and he ain't had no right to talk to me like that," she said, wiping her snotty nose with the back of her hand.

I took a little more pity on her and softened my tone. "Look, Demonee, I know you don't like it, but he got every right. He the one buying the drawers you wear. You ain't got nothing. Your uncle is the one putting food in your mouth—and mine too. He the one paying the bills and stuff around here. Or did you forget that?"

"So, that don't mean he can lie on me and say lies about my mama."

"Your mama ain't here, Demonee. And I'm sorry about that, but it's just you and me, and your uncle. Your uncle, who ain't got no time to be leaving his job to come and see about you."

"I didn't ask him to leave his job," she said, crossing her arms in front of her chest.

"Naw, you didn't. You just up on the roof, making out with some thugs instead of going to class."

"I told you, I wasn't messing around with nobody. That was my friend Destiny. She was the one all over her boyfriend. Me and my friend was just talking, and we wasn't doing no drugs," she said with an angry scowl on her face.

I threw my hands up in the air. "All right, all right, I give," I said. "I ain't gonna argue with you all day. I'm just telling your little behind that you shoulda been in your class."

"I don't wanna be in class," she said.

"So, I don't either, but I go every day. That's what you do when you in school, Demonee. You go to class."

"I don't wanna go. I hate math."

"Who doesn't? Look, Demonee, you gonna be adding and

subtracting crap for a long time, so get over it and quit acting a fool before your uncle puts both of us out."

"I don't care what he does."

"You better care. Where you gonna go if he stops taking care of you? You gonna go stay with that little boy you was kissing with?"

"I told you I wasn't kissing no boy!" she shouted.

"Look, whatever, just quit cutting the fool, Demonee. Whatever you and your friend is doing you better be doing it in that math class."

"Forget you, Maxine. You ain't my mama. You don't run me," she said, angrily throwing her monkey pillow on the floor. I picked it up and chucked it back at her.

"I'm not trying to run you. I'm trying to keep you out of the system. But I'm finished talking though. You do what you wanna do, Demonee. Go on and ruin your life, if that's the way you like to roll." She threw her pillow down again. I didn't bother picking it off the floor. I left her room, slamming her door behind me.

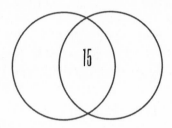

15

Sunday morning I called Bonita's and Madona's place to see what they were up to. I knew they would be home. They are churchgoers, but the Pentecost church they go to has services on Saturday afternoons, so Sundays they usually spend the day cleaning their place. I figured they would welcome a break. I rang them and asked if they wanted to meet me at Mama Florene's for breakfast. Madona said she would come, but Bonita was out, so it would only be the two of us. I was a little disappointed when I heard that. I wanted to hang out with both of them. I thought that after we ate we could go down to the park. On Sunday there usually isn't a bunch of dudes down there just waiting to hit on you. We could have spent some time together under the shade of the live oak trees, just hanging out and talking girl talk.

"Shoot, well, I guess it's Bonita's loss. I'll see you at the restaurant," I said to Madona.

* * *

I made it to the restaurant a few minutes before Madona, and waited out front for her to turn up. When she did come, she looked pretty gloomy. The corners of her mouth were all turned down. Even though I didn't want to ruin our time together by dealing with more troubles, I asked her what was up.

"Maxine, you don't believe in spells, do you? I mean, don't believe they work?" she asked.

"What? Of course not. Girl, you know I don't have time for that junk."

She frowned. "It ain't junk, all kinds of folks around here is doing it," she said.

"Yeah, old folks who ain't got nothing better to do." Aunt Freda believes in that stuff, and my friend Tia's grandma is seriously into that mess. Last year none of the tomatoes in her garden turned ripe, and she swore it was because some demon had walked through her rows at night and put a hex on them.

"Sometimes—I mean—if there was a spell, something that could put you and Brian back, would you use it? Would you try it and see if it would work?"

"What me and Brian is going through can't be fixed overnight, especially not with voodoo."

"But if it could? If you and him could just be together again, and all you had to do was bury some chicken bones in your backyard or sprinkle a handful of salt into a river at midnight, would you do it?"

"Maybe, I don't know. Look, Madona, right now I don't even know what I would do with Brian if he came back. I mean, how would I just be living with him and ignoring that he left me for another girl?"

"Shoot girl, that ain't nothing. He ain't gonna stay with

that hoochie. You and him been together forever. You were his first everything. My mama say that people don't never forget they first love," Madona said.

"And what if I wasn't? I mean, what if he fell for her first?"

"How could he? Ya'll been knowing each other just about your whole life."

"Yeah, but things are different."

"How? I don't understand."

"Neither do I," I said, not wanting to get into a long heavy conversation about Shell and how long Brian had been knowing her. It was too much for me to deal with, and I had come to breakfast to just hang out and forget about all that.

"Why we talking about spells anyway?" I asked.

"I'm worried, and I'm just trying to think of something that can help."

"Help what?"

"Bonita and her new boyfriend. She sneaked out the window late last night to be with him."

"Sneaked out?"

"Yeah, and it's not the first time either."

"For real, that's messed up. She gonna end up in a lot of trouble doing that," I said.

"I know, that's why I'm reading this dumb book," she said, pulling a small red book out of her jeans pockets. "My cousin sent it to me from New Orleans. There's supposed to be a spell in here to keep things hidden. I thought maybe I could use it on my mama, so she won't find out what my sister is doing. I'm pretty desperate."

"You must be, but girl that ain't gonna work. Your mama gonna find out if Bonita keeps slipping around, and ain't nothing you can do about it. Besides, remember that crazy spell that you guys had me do with ya'll last year? Remember when we took them dang pigs feet and flung them in the bayou? Remember how we was doing all that chanting and stuff because we was trying to lose weight? When the last time you could squeeze your big butt into anything that wasn't plus-sized?"

"I see your point, but I'm only trying to look out for my sister, like you trying to look out for Demonee."

I rolled my eyes. "Demonee. That's an issue I don't even want to discuss. Look, we both love Bonita. We'll figure something out. Let's go get something to eat," I said. We entered the crowded restaurant, squeezing our way through several booths packed with hungry-looking black folks, until we stopped at a little card table sitting beside the refrigerator.

"Let's hurry up and order something to eat," Madona said. "I'm so hungry I could eat a package of frozen sausage right out of the freezer. I wouldn't even need to thaw it out."

"Me either," I said. I checked my skirt pocket to make sure I had some cash on me. I felt a few crumpled one-dollar bills, just enough to buy three strips of bacon and some French toast. I waved for Mel the waitress to come over and get our order.

"You know what you want already?" Madona asked.

"Don't you?" I asked, then I waved for Mel again.

As soon as I got my order, I gobbled my toast down so fast the pats of cold butter on top of the stack didn't even get a chance to melt. Then I stuffed my face with the bacon and wiped my mouth with the napkin. The whole time I was doing that, Madona was filling me in on her sister, and I was reluctantly talking about Demonee. We both agreed that girls could act really stupid when they first hook up with guys and that Demonee and Bonita needed to concentrate more on school and less on their new crushes.

"My sister acts like this is the first boy she ever dated," Madona said, shaking her head.

"It probably is the first boy for Demonee, that's what worries me," I said, snatching a piece of sausage off of her plate.

"Dang, oh man, you not gonna believe this," Madona suddenly said.

"What?" I asked.

She pointed to the takeout counter upfront. "Ain't that Shell?"

"Crap, I can't believe it," I muttered. There was Shell, up at the counter buying herself some breakfast. It was the second worst thing I could imagine. The first would have been if Brian was with her.

"Let's go," I said, pulling my money out of my skirt pocket to pay the bill.

"I'm not through. Don't tell me you gonna let that cow scare you off?" Madona asked.

"Nobody scares me off. I just don't need the drama. I came here to chill, not get more stress."

"All right, I hear you. I'm coming," Madona said, pulling her money out too. We left enough cash on the table to pay the bill and a nice tip.

"Let's go out the back door. I don't even want to look at her," I said.

We put our napkins on the table and walked through the restaurant and out of the back door. Once we got in the alley, we headed back around to the front of the building, so we could hit our street. When we got near the front door, Shell came stepping out. She was bigger now. She had a real bump pushing out beneath her low-cut T-shirt. It made me nauseous. I started walking more quickly.

"Where you off to, Maxine?" she hollered after me. I wasn't gonna stop, but I noticed that Madona had quit moving.

"What's it to you?" she asked Shell. I caught her by the arm.

"Madona, let's go," I said.

"Why you got to go?" Shell asked.

"We ain't got to do nothing, nasty heifer," Madona said.

"Madona, I told you, I don't want this. Let's go back home and watch some TV or something," I said.

"Where you been hiding, Maxine? I ain't seen you around school," Shell said.

"She don't go to your school no more. She left because she didn't want to look at your sorry behind," Madona said. Then she noticed Shell's belly. "Maxine, is she, is she . . . ?" Madona asked.

"Forget you. I don't even know who you are," Shell said, rolling her eyes.

Madona's eyes snapped away from her belly. "You don't need to know who I am. All you need to know is I don't like you messing around with my friend, skank," she told Shell.

"I'm not messing with your friend," Shell said.

"No, you messing with my husband," I told her.

"Yeah, well it ain't my fault that he would rather be with me. You shouldn't of tried to make him do stuff that he didn't want to do."

"I never made Brian do anything. Is that what he told you,

that I made him do stuff? Like what, say he loved me, marry me? Is that the kind of stuff that I made him do?" I asked.

"Yeah, that's the kind of stuff you did, and it's not even what he wanted."

"So what does he want? He want to stay there with you in that raggedy shack you call a house, and have some little stupid baby?" I asked.

"Yeah, that's what he want. And you know why, cause I ain't making him do it."

"Good for you. I hope ya'll will be very happy. Come on, Madona," I said. We both took off, and Shell came walking after us.

"Me and Brian will be happy. I always make him feel good, while all you do is try to get him to do what you want. I told him that last year, when he was telling me he had a girlfriend and all. I told him that he was better off with me. I told him, and I was right. 'Cause the next thing I know, you was trying get him to marry you. I told him not to do it. I knew he wasn't gonna like it at all," Shell said.

"What did you say?" I asked.

"I said I told him that he wasn't gonna like being married to you at all."

"You don't know what he likes. Why don't you go on about your business, tramp," Madona growled.

"I'm going. I'm going. By the way, Brian said he left some stuff at your house that he needs," Shell said.

"Tell Brian that he can come get whatever he wants, as long as he don't bring your skanky tail with him," I said.

"Whatever," Shell said, walking away.

Madona stood there glaring at Shell like she wanted to go

kick her butt. She probably would have too, if Shell wasn't pregnant. She probably would have whipped her tail good.

All I could think about was what Shell had said, that she had told Brian not to marry me last year. Last year when Brian wasn't supposed to know her, last year when I was supposed to be his one and only. How could I think that he didn't know Shell when she mysteriously turned up on my doorstep? God! How could I have been so stupid?

"Maxine, what's going on? Is that baby Brian's? Why didn't you tell me and Bonita? You mean that trash running around with your man's baby? You not gonna let her get away with something like that are you? You ought to go after her and set her straight for real," Madona said.

I shook my head. "I'm the one who needed to be gotten straight, and she just did it," I said.

"Maxine, don't believe anything she says. She can't take anything from you."

"She didn't, he went willingly. I just didn't know it."

I took my cell phone out and rang Brian's number. To my surprise, he picked up.

"Hello, Maxine," he said.

I couldn't utter a word. I just stood there listening to the soft whisper of his breath.

Madona snatched the phone out of my hands and put the speaker on. "Your trashy girlfriend say that you left some crap at Maxine's house."

"I don't know what you're talking about. I got everything I need," Brian said. "I didn't leave nothing behind."

"Yes you did, and Maxine says that you can come get it or you can shove it up your . . ."

"What? Girl, you are for real trippin'! You need to stay out of my business. I told you I didn't leave nothing behind," Brian said, cutting her off.

"Like hell you didn't, what about your w—"

I knew the next word was wife. I snatched the phone from Madona's hand.

"Brian, just tell your girlfriend or whatever she is to stay away from me," I said.

"Maxine, I don't even know what you are talking about!" Brian shouted.

"All you need to know is that I don't want her in my face, now or ever!" I said, and hung up the phone.

"Why did you do that? I was about to go off on that fool," Madona said.

"He's not worth it, and, Madona, I need to not deal with this right now."

"Well, when you gonna deal with it? You gonna let Brian get away with playing you like this? You gonna let him let his nasty girlfriend talk trash in your face? Shoot, I don't even have a man, but I know that you can't just let them get away with just anything. Girl, you too soft sometimes."

"I'm soft? Madona, you like baby dolls."

"I like them because there ain't no complications with them. I just dress them pretty and set them on the shelf."

"It's not that easy with guys, Madona. You can't just put them on the shelf when you don't want to be bothered with them."

"Why not? That's what Brian did to you, well ain't it?"

She had a point. "Yeah, I guess it is," I said.

"Well, do something about it. Find him and kick his butt,

or shoot, at least go back to your house and burn up whatever he left there. Girl, destroy it all, you know, like Angela Bassett did in *Waiting to Exhale*. I saw that on TV the other night."

"That's TV, Madona. It don't work like that in the real world. I can't go burning Brian's stuff up."

"Why not? He done burned up your whole life."

"Not yet. I'm still here, Madona."

"Look, whatever. I still want to kick somebody's butt. Are you sure you don't want to go after Miss Thing and give her what she deserves?" she asked, pointing to Shell.

"She's already got my lying, cheating ex. It's exactly what she deserves. Let's go home," I said, walking away. Madona followed without saying anything more about Shell, and I was glad. I didn't even want to think about her and my man, or was he really her man? Only she knew. Perhaps I was the one that got in between them many years ago? For the first time it really sunk in that I might be the girl on the side, and Shell was the one that he had given his whole heart to. Maybe it was me that took him from her, and she had just shown up at my house that day to claim what was clearly her own.

"I wish Bonita would stop being so stupid about boys," Madona said.

"I wish we all would, girl," I told her. "I wish all of us girls would stop being fools."

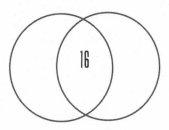

16

t was actually an overcast day, but to me the sun seemed to dance across the sidewalk as I walked Demonee back to school this morning. For five long days she had been stuck in the house, mostly watching TV and getting on my nerves. "I'm bored. When you gonna fix something to eat?" she asked, each day when I got home from school.

"Why didn't you fix something to eat? You been home all day?" I asked.

"I don't know how to cook nothing," she said.

Ain't that the truth. She doesn't know how to cook or clean good, or do too much of anything. I guess nobody ever took the time to teach her. Me and Mama don't get along too well, but she taught me how to take care of myself. I started cooking dinner when I was barely out of elementary school, and I was doing laundry, vacuuming, and making beds long before that. When me and Brian moved in together, there was no doubt in my mind that I could take care of everything that needed to be taken care of in my house. Not Demonee. She's in middle school and she can barely do anything. She still needs to learn so much, inside and outside of the house.

I dropped her off at the main gate of her school.

"Demonee, please don't screw this up. If you mess this up, it's gonna be bad for everybody. Handle your business in the office, and then go to your homeroom." I said.

"We don't have homeroom. We have advisory," she said, rolling her eyes. I ignored the comment.

"Demonee, I'm on your side, and I know how you feel, but you can't—"

"Nobody knows how I feel about nothing," she said, heading into the gate.

"You know who used to walk me to school every morning? Brian," I said. "Long before we was married he was walking me."

"So?"

"So, one time he got sick with some weird flu, and I don't mean kind of sick. He got so sick he was up all night puking the lining of his stomach out. When I went by his house in the morning, I didn't know if I should kiss him or call 911. He told me he was too ill to go to school that day, so I told him to rest and that I would stop by when I got out of my classes, but you know what? I wasn't even down his porch steps when I heard him calling me, telling me he was going to walk me to school. He kept insisting, and I eventually dragged his crazy sick behind back to his bedroom."

"I don't understand. Maxine, what are you trying to say?" Demonee asked.

"I'm trying to tell you that things change, and sometimes folks let you down. Now I walk myself to school, but I still get there." I grabbed her by the arm and held her there for a few moments. "Demonee, I know how it feels to be let down by the people you trust. You feel like nobody in the world gives a rat's behind about you. I know, because I been dumped time and time again by my mama, and my husband just kicked me to the curb and took up with another girl. So, I know how you feel, and it ain't fair. But, Demonee, you gotta start looking at your situation. Be smart, do what you need to do to help *take care of yourself*. Right now that means not fooling around in school and not doing anything to piss your uncle off."

"I gotta go in, Maxine," she said.

I let her go, and she went through the gate. I crossed the street to go to my own school. There was nothing more that I could do for her. It was her game, and she had to decide which moves to make in it. All I could do is hope that she had the common sense to make the right play.

My new alternative school starts a lot later than my old school, so I got to my own school a whole thirty minutes before the bell rang. I waited in the courtyard for Madona. I knew that Bonita wouldn't be with her because lately all she's been doing is hanging around with her new boyfriend, Billy. It's weird, really. I would be happy that Bonita has a new boyfriend who likes her, if he wasn't making her do all kinds of things that she normally wouldn't do. Besides sneaking out on a constant basis, and ditching her sister, she's started skipping class. Last week it was Algebra II on Wednesday and English on Friday. "Girl, you are messing up bad," I told her, when she came walking over to me in the hall on Friday afternoon.

"No, I'm not," she said. "What's the big deal? I just skipped a couple of times. Besides, I just stopped over here to ask you about Brian. Madona told me that she wanted to beat that girl Shell's behind the other day. I can't believe you let her get all up in your face."

"It wasn't like that. She was just someplace that she didn't need to be, and I was just trying to get back to my house. I didn't even want to think about that little skank. I mean, every time I think of her I just want to slap her face off."

"When is her baby due?" she asked.

"I don't know and I don't wanna know," I said.

"I wouldn't either. Why didn't you say something about it?"

"I tried, but I couldn't. I didn't even want to deal with it."

"I know, but me and Madona are your girls. You should have said something."

"I know, I'm sorry."

"It's okay," she said. "I guess I wouldn't want to say anything either. But if I was you I would call over to her house and cuss Brian out, tell him to keep that heifer out of your face."

"You do it for me. I'd just be way too pissed to get the words out," I said.

"Don't ask me to, cause you know I will. I'll tell that bastard off."

"Go to class, Bonita," I said, "and don't be late."

"I'm getting there," she said.

"I know, but I want you to be there for real. If you miss too many classes, girl, ain't no way you can make them up."

"Maxine, you know I'm going to handle mine," she said.

"Are you, Bonita? Because right now I don't know, girl-friend."

"I'm cool, Maxine. You ain't got to ride me, just remember some of the stupid stuff you did with Brian. You missed a lot of school too."

"And look where it got me. I'm starting everything again. If I had to do it all over, I would have taken my behind to class instead of sitting at home playing housewife."

"I ain't nobody's wife, Maxine. Billy is just my man, and I like being with him."

"Well then be with him after school or something. Don't keep blowing all your classes off. Go to class, girl. Okay?" I pleaded.

"Don't worry, I'm on my way, girlfriend," she said, and walked off.

I waited in the courtyard for about fifteen minutes. When Madona didn't show up, I decided to go in early to my Market-ing class. My teacher, Ms. Kregan, is really cool. She always lets us log on and check our e-mail before we start working on our projects for the day. As soon as I got in, I took my seat and started up my account. A message from Tia popped up in my inbox. The subject line said click on this. I opened the e-mail and saw a video file. I clicked on it, and Tia popped up in a cute blue tube top.

"Guess who just got a video camera? I been seriously missing you, Miss Maxi. Girl, give me a call or write me an e-mail. By the way, check this out," she said, pointing. The video screen cut jerkily to a huge mural filled with a watercolor of an inviting beach scene. A handsome African-American family were smiling and laughing around a well-spread picnic table right next to a beautiful green-blue ocean. There was food everywhere and clear glasses full to the brim with what looked like fruit punch, or maybe soda. I couldn't really tell what it was. The point is the glasses and the people were overflowing with happiness, like Tia. I envied her even more than ever. She was so excited to be showing me that her husband had created something beautiful and special. What had mine created? His work of art was a broken home and a baby with another woman. Why couldn't I have Tia's life? After I found out about Brian knowing Shell for so long, I was too afraid to call her. I didn't want Tia to hear how much hurt was in my voice, but there was something about the painting, and the happiness it was bringing to her and her marriage, that made me want to call her. That kind of happiness wouldn't be shattered just because she got a bad call from her girlfriend.

I turned off the computer and went outside to phone my best friend. It took only a couple of seconds for Tia to pick up. "Hey, girl. I been missing you something bad too and I really need to talk to you," I said, as soon as I heard the sound of her voice.

"What is it, girl?" Tia asked.

"Brian's been cheating on me, and I had to throw him out," I cried. For a long time she said nothing as if she hadn't heard a word I said.

"I don't think I heard you, girl. Did you say that Brian was cheating?"

"Yeah, you heard me. He been cheating with some skanky girl at our school."

"Who? I know you kidding. Brian? Brian is cheating?"

"Yeah, he's been messing around with some girl."

"What girl? Brian? That ain't even like him."

"That's what I thought, but I don't know, some girl just showed up at our house one day."

"At your house, you mean your new place?"

"Yeah, she showed up, asking if he could come help her and her sister move some stuff. I didn't know her, but I gave in, 'cause we needed the money and all. The next thing I know he was with her."

"I don't believe it! I just don't even believe it!" Tia said.

"Believe it."

"Well, why, what is she like? Why he fooling around with her?"

"I don't know. She's kinda cute, but trashy. She's always dressing hoochie."

"Hoochie? Girl, Brian don't even like girls like that."

"He does now."

She got quiet, like she was trying to get her mind fixed on what I had said. "Do you want me to come down there, girl?" she asked after a bit. "Doo-witty just finished working on the painting that I showed you. He'll get paid soon. I can use my rent money and the little money we got hidden in the icebox to come see you."

"Naw, don't do that. You can't spend your rent money on me. How are you gonna pay your rent next month? I just wanted you to know what's going on because I been so miserable. Tia, Brian done knocked that girl up."

"When? How?"

"It don't matter. I just needed to tell you. I just needed you to know how bad I been feeling," I said between sobs.

"Don't cry, Maxi. I'm going to come down. I don't care how I have to swing the money. I'm gonna come," she said.

"I don't want you to do that. You can't afford it right now, and it ain't gonna change things. I just wanted to let you know. Please don't think I'm stupid."

"Why would I think that?" she asked.

"Tia, there was no baby. I wasn't pregnant. I just made it up, so me and Brian could get married. I wanted to marry him bad. I wanted to be just like you and Doo-witty, living in your own place and happy."

"I know. I know," she said.

"I wasn't trying to lie or nothing. I just wanted to be out of my house. You know how Mama is. I just wanted to get away, so I made up a baby. Now, I come to find out that Brian done went and made a baby for real."

"I'm coming down, Maxi," she said.

"Naw, you can't. You need to keep that money for your expenses. Plus, you remember you said that you wanted to start saving money for college. You still want to go, don't you?"

"Yeah, you know I do."

"Then don't go throwing your money away on me. Plus, I don't want you coming down here feeling what I'm feeling. I don't need you to feel terrible too. I just needed you to know, that's all. I gotta go to class. I'll call you tonight and tell you all the details."

"I'll be here," she said quietly. "You know you my girl. I'll always be here for you."

"I love you," I said, and hung up.

*　*　*

❦ 165 ❦

Thirty minutes later I was feeling much better about things when my phone rang right in the middle of my Marketing class. I asked to go to the bathroom and answered it.

"Are you the older cousin of Demonee Blis?" a female voice asked.

"Yes ma'am," I lied.

"This is Ms. Fitzpatrick from Demonee's junior high school. We're calling you because we were told by Demonee that her uncle was out of town on business, and she's temporarily staying with you."

"Yes, ma'am, that's true."

"Good. We would like you to know that Demonee will be returning home this morning. Her suspension has been extended, and when she returns, she will need to have her uncle with her."

"Great," I muttered under my breath. Aloud I said, "Yes ma'am, but I don't understand. Didn't she apologize to the janitor? She told me she would when she left this morning. She told me she was ready to go back to school. What's going on? Why did she get into trouble again?"

"I can't answer that for you, Miss. You'll have to get the information from Demonee or you can speak to Principal Chang. He's in a meeting right now, but I'll set up an appointment for you as soon as he gets out.

"Naw, that's okay. I can find out from Demonee, and her uncle can straighten her out when he gets back." With that I clicked off the phone and went back to class. When the bell rang, I took off for home, bringing anger with each step. I found Demonee there at the house, sitting on the front steps playing with Coffee Bean.

"Take him home right now and get back here, girl!" I said.

"I didn't do nothing wrong!" she yelled at me, and then stomped off with the puppy. When she came back, I was all over her. Oh how I yelled, especially when I learned what she had been sent home for. She threw a book. She actually threw her math book at her teacher. She went to her math class to find out what she missed the week before and ended up throwing a book at her teacher, Ms. Hopkins. If Ms. Hopkins hadn't moved out of the way, the book would have hit her square in the face, and Demonee would have been in big trouble—or bigger trouble. She was in a lot now. What she did usually gets you put out of school completely. There are all kinds of kids at my alternative center who are there for stuff like that. Some of them are even on probation because their schools have pressed charges. Demonee was lucky. Her teacher stood up for her.

Demonee tried to explain. "My teacher, Ms. Hopkins, told the principal that it was her fault, and it was. She shouldn't have been yelling at me and telling me that my math grades sucked. All I did was tell her that math was stupid. She didn't have to clown me in front of the whole class. Anyway, she said that she probably should have phrased things differently or something like that. So Principal Chang just extended my suspension. What's the big deal? It's not like I got kicked out or something."

"Demonee, do you know how lucky you are that your teacher didn't let you go down for acting a fool like that?" I asked.

"I wasn't acting a fool, and forget that heifer, Ms. Hopkins.

She didn't have no business getting in my face. I hate her," she said.

I felt like slapping her face as purple as her T-shirt. "No, you don't. You don't hate nobody. You just don't like her telling you what to do, and so what? That's her job. Five days a week she gets to stand in that classroom for an hour and tell you what to do," I said.

"I don't want her telling me what to do. I hate her."

"You don't even know her. She's just your teacher."

"I know her and hate her. She's always making people do stuff," she said, stomping past me up the steps. I stopped myself from yanking her back by the silly braid she had clipped on the back of her head, but I let her go. She stomped into the living room and clicked on the TV. A soap opera flickered on to a love scene, a blond chick with five pounds of makeup was taking it all off for some guy with a beard. I turned the TV off.

"What did you turn that off for? I was watching it," she snapped.

"I don't care what you was watching. You better quit trippin' girl. All you got to do is go to school and do what you're told. We all have to do it. Your math teacher ain't there for you to like. She's there for you to learn from," I said, sounding way too much like my mother.

"I don't want to learn nothing from her. I don't want to be in her class. Me and my friend hate her," she said, screwing up her face again.

I rolled my eyes up to the ceiling. "Oh, there it is. It's always got to come back to that little boy you hanging with. Look, girl, you gonna fool around and get screwed up for real over that boy. You let him handle his own business, and take care of yours. You gonna mess around and end up in juvie or something over that little boy, and then ain't nobody gonna want to be bothered with you."

"I'm not gonna end up nowhere!"

"Yeah, I know. That's what I'm trying to tell you!" I hollered.

She crossed her arms and poked her lip out about a mile. I wished I could smack it back in. Then something came over me, and I realized again that she was just a kid that nobody but me seemed to care about. How could I forget that? She was sitting there in her shirt and shorts, which were covered with puppy slobber and fur. She was just a girl, a little thrown-away girl. I couldn't help but feel a little sorry for her. How couldn't I? I was a thrown-away wife.

I sat down on the floor next to her. "Demonee, I know it don't seem fair and school is definitely a pain, but you just have to deal—you and your little friend. Ya'll only got to put up with Ms. Hopkins one hour out of the day, and after that, you doing your own thing. Now, I'm sorry that you don't want to be in her class, but she's the only teacher that works with the poor math students. That's why you in there, cause you needed to catch up on all your math."

"I know that. I still hate her," she said.

"Okay, but you still have to deal with her. It's as simple as that." I sighed. It was like talking to the wall. "Okay, Demonee, I see we ain't getting nowhere with this. But look, girl, your uncle is gonna have a dang cow when he finds out you been put out of school again."

"So," she said again—and got quiet. I took her silence to mean that she didn't care. I was about to remind her how we both might end up out on the street when worry came to her face, and she spoke again.

"Do you have to tell him? I don't want you to tell him. I don't want him to be mad again," she said, in a voice that made her sound like the little kid she was.

"Demonee, he's gonna find out. There's no way I can keep this a secret. He's gonna find out, and there's gonna be hell to pay."

"He doesn't have to. Can't you do something about it, Maxine," she pleaded. "I don't want to go to no home."

"You should have thought about that before you acted like an idiot," I said, but I softened my voice some when I saw her legs trembling next to me. She talked a lot of crap, but underneath she had to be terrified of what might go down. I knew how that felt too. When Brian left, I felt scared and helpless. I was sitting all alone in the house by myself, pondering how I was gonna end up.

"I'll see if I can fix this mess. Just go to your room, Demonee. I got to get back to school," I said. She left the sofa and went to her room.

I sighed. I couldn't believe that she had thrown a book at a teacher, though I had come close to doing that on at least one occasion. I went to the kitchen and drank a glass of milk. I downed it quickly, and after mulling things over a bit, I came up with a plan to keep Brian's dad off our backs and get Demonee in school again. It was a very simple plan, but it was hard for me to deal with because it involved my ex Brian. See, the weird thing is Brian sounds exactly like his dad on the phone. Several times I've called Brian's dad's house and started talking all sexy to him on the phone, thinking that he was Brian, only to discover different. "Maxine, this is not Brian," his dad would say. I would feel all embarrassed and break out into giggles. I figured that I could use that to our advantage. I could get Brian to call the school as his father and make things right. All he had to say is that he was going to be out of town for a while and ask them to let Demonee back in, so that she wouldn't miss school while he was on the road. I figured it would work, because what school would want a kid to miss so much time that they couldn't catch up? Sure they wouldn't like it, but would they really say that Demonee couldn't return, if they knew her guardian was gonna be out of town for something like a month? If Brian called them and pleaded her case, the school was sure to give in. Then me and Demonee could go back to our lives and I could pray that nothing else awful or stupid came my way. I hollered at Demonee that I was leaving and then took off for school—Brian's school—praying that he would do this one important thing for me.

I got to Brian's school just as the third-period bell rang. I didn't bother going to the main office. The office personnel all knew me. They wouldn't dare let me go see my ex during school time. Instead I went directly to where I knew Brian would be, the culinary school behind the gym. Brian's third-period class is a baking class. It is actually a class that we signed up for together, because I wanted to get more cooking skills. Brian isn't really into the class, but when we broke up it was way too late for him to switch his schedule around. He was still in there making hot loaves of wheat bread and strawberry croissants, even though he would probably rather be spending his time in Auto Mechanics or Woodshop.

I leaned against the wall in front of the school and hoped that none of the kids I used to hang with spotted me on their way to class. I didn't want to have to explain to them why I was there. I just wanted to speak to Brian. I was thoroughly elated when I saw him walking alone toward me. It occurred to me that he could have been with his girlfriend, and that could have caused some serious drama, drama that would have got me kicked off campus. He saw me and quickly walked up.

"Maxine, what are you doing here?" he asked. I was speechless—I didn't even know what to say. I hadn't seen him in so long. All I wanted to do was take him in, his freshly shaven face, his high-top sneakers, even his smell. How could a girl not respond to how her man smells? He smelled like coconut oil. It was in the sheen spray that he always liked to spray on his fro. It was the smell that I smelled each morning when he was doing his hair. It took me back to him standing in the mirror in the bathroom doing his thing, while I stepped on and off the digital bathroom scale, hoping that my weight would change each time the numbers stopped moving again.

"I need your help. It's Demonee. You know she's staying with me, right? I know your daddy told you."

"Yeah, he told me."

"Well, she's in trouble."

"Ain't no big surprise there. Demonee's whole family is trash. They don't do nothing but cause other folks problems. If you had any sense, you would let my daddy kick her to the curb. I don't even know why you took her in," he said.

"Don't you? Brian don't go there with me. You know exactly why Demonee is in my house, our house. She's there because I don't have a choice. She's there because of you."

He looked uncomfortable when I said that, like he wanted to be somewhere else.

"Maxine, we don't need to get all into that again. I gotta go to class, and you supposed to be at school."

"Well, I'm not. I'm here. I'm here trying to do something for your cousin, and me."

"Maxine, what are you talking about? What do you need me to do?"

"Help me out, and Demonee. She did something stupid as hell. She threw a book at her teacher. The school says that she can't come back until your father brings her."

"So."

"So, I can't let that happen. He's taking care of me and Demonee, only because I agreed to look after her and keep her out of trouble. She already got kicked out once before for skipping, and he jumped all down my throat. If he finds out about this, he's going to take it out on both of us. You gotta help me out with this. This is all your fault. You gotta make it right," I said.

He looked unhappy when I said that too, but also a little angry. "Maxine, I don't have to do nothing but be black and die," he said sarcastically.

"Come on, Brian. Just help me out—you owe me this. You know you do," I said.

"Maxine, you put me out, do you remember? I'm not really the reason why you stuck with that girl."

"You can believe that if you want to," I snapped. "Look, Brian, I just need you to call the school. You sound just like your daddy on the phone. Just call them and say that you will be out of town for a month or something. Ask them if they will let Demonee back in without you, so that she doesn't get behind in school. That's all I want you to do. Can I count on you to do it? Because I know that I can't count on you for anything else. I found that out by marrying you."

"Maxine, don't start that, not if you want my help," he snapped back.

"It's not just for me. I'm asking you to help your own flesh and blood. That's all I want."

"Fine," he said, taking out his cell. "Is Principal Chang still the principal over there?" he asked.

"Yes, do you remember the school's number?"

He nodded, and punched in the numbers. "Hello, this is the uncle of Demonee Blis, and I'm calling about an incident that she was involved in today. I was hoping that I could have a few words with Principal Chang," he said, exactly like his father would have.

"Just one moment," I heard a voice say over the speaker phone.

I held my breath and hoped that he had also picked up some of his father's other techniques.

"This is Principal Chang. What can I do for you, sir?" I heard after a few more seconds.

"Yes, Principal. I'm Demonee's uncle."

"Yes, I remember you. You're the lawyer. I believe we met at parents' night."

"No, sir, I'm in marketing, and I was out of town. Anyway, I just want to say that I am extremely sorry about Demonee's poor behavior. I don't condone it at all."

"Neither do I, which is exactly why I sent her back home."

"Of course, sir, I totally understand that, but Demonee has been through a great deal, and I'm afraid her actions sometimes reflect the unsuitable living situation that she has been reared in. However, I do feel that overall she's a great kid, and I believe that with a lot of love and attention she can become a wonderful young lady. She just needs structure and guidance."

"That's exactly what she needs, but she also needs discipline. She needs to know that we have rules and regulations in our school to protect both our students *and our teachers*. Her behavior was potentially dangerous and way out of line. She could have really hurt her teacher or even one of the other students."

"I know that, sir. I know that what she did was way over the top. I know that she needs discipline to go along with the structure and the guidance. That's why I'm respectfully asking you to give her a break just this once, and allow her back into school. I'm going to be out of the country for at least a month, and I really don't want her to miss that much of her schoolwork while I'm away. I know right now it's hard to believe, but I honestly feel that school provides her with all of the things that we are speaking about. I think staying away from her studies for too long will be a real disaster for her. Won't you please reconsider, and let her come back in a shorter amount of time?" Brian asked.

The principal hesitated for a bit. "I don't usually change my mind about problem students, but I'll agree to a one week suspension, and that's only because her teacher, Ms. Hopkins, spoke up for her. If deep down she's a good student, she's going to have to prove it."

"She will. Thank you, sir. I'll tell her that she can come back next week, and make certain that she is there with a new attitude."

"She had better, because I won't be giving her any more chances. By the way, I'll look forward to seeing you at our next PTSA meeting. We are going to implement some major changes to our school next year, and we could use someone with marketing skills to help get the news out to some of our less attentive parents."

"I'll be there," Brian said.

"Thank you. Have a good day, sir," Principal Chang said.

"You too," Brian said, and hung up the phone.

I wanted to kiss him. I really did, until I realized that he had just fooled the principal as easily as he had fooled me, about Shell and God knows what else.

"Thanks," I said.

"You're welcome. Now, are we done with this? Because I have to go to my next period."

"So do I," I said.

"Good, and Maxine, don't come around to my class no more. If Shell sees you, it's just gonna be a thing, and don't none of us want that."

"You think I care what Shell wants, I mean do you really? You know what? Just go, Brian," I said.

"I'm going. Ain't no more that I can do anyway. Bye," he said, walking away.

I waved, but didn't say anything. I stood there confused. I didn't know if I should call him back and give him a good cursing out, or tell him how much I wanted him back. In the end, I decided that it was best to leave well enough alone. I left the campus and went back to my own life, the one that he didn't seem to want any part of.

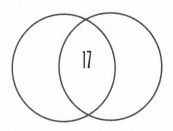

17

The sweet smell of lemon poppy seed muffins filled the air this morning. I fixed them because they are De-monee's favorite breakfast meal, and I wanted to get her off to a great start as she returned to school again. She's been way too long at the house, and it was time for homegirl to get up and get out. With that in mind, I threw together something I knew she would like. Then I went to her room to make certain that she got her tail out of bed on time. I tossed a handful of stuffed animals at her fuzzy head while she was sawing some serious logs. "Let's go, Miss Thing. It's time to go back to junior high."

"So what? I go to school all the time," she said drowsily.

"Girl, just get your butt out of bed and get dressed," I said. I waited for her to crawl out from beneath the covers. When she was out, I pulled her room together, like I used to do after Brian got up. I fluffed the pillows, made the bed, picked some clothes up off the floor, and went back to the kitchen.

As soon as Demonee got ready for school and finished wolfing down three hot muffins and a scrambled egg, I grabbed her backpack and we headed off to her school. On the way, I told her to keep her mouth shut and not tell any of her friends how we had gotten over on the principal. If Brian hadn't come to our rescue, it would have been a total disaster. I would've had to tell Brian's dad everything, and a nuclear explosion would have gone off. We would've gotten it from both sides, from his dad and Demonee's principal. Honestly, I couldn't believe that the principal gave in like that. He seemed pretty hard-core in his discipline of Demonee. See, nowadays most kids get in-school suspension. They sit in a classroom by themselves all day and do their schoolwork. They are not allowed to participate in any school activities, like pep rallies or dances, and they can't eat lunch with their friends. For most kids that's a big-time punishment. That's why principals give it. But the principal kicked Demonee completely out of school twice, so I'm thinking that she must seriously get on his last nerve.

I know that Brian could care less about Demonee, but I can't do anything about that. I just thank God that he made the call. He kept his promise to me, I just wish he would have kept the one he made for our marriage.

When we got to school, I waited in the schoolyard while Demonee checked in. As she went through the double doors that led to the administrative offices with her head held high, I thought she was either pretty brave or pretty foolish. It wasn't easy going to the principal's or even V.P.'s office for anything.

Back when I was in junior high, I had been a guest there a few times. The last time I was there, I was taking up for my friend Tia, after some boy kept calling her a slut. I tried to make him stop, and we got into a fight. We both ended up in the principal's office, and in a real mess. I wouldn't want to go through that ever again. I had to admire Demonee walking into that office, like it didn't bother her one bit.

When Demonee didn't come back from the office right away, I walked into the school, praying that she hadn't gotten herself into another drama. God knows how I was gonna pull it off if she screwed up again. I went down the hall some, toward the office, so I could hear if somebody was yelling at her. All I heard was normal office sounds, the squeaky wheels of a chair rolling around, the constant tap of a keyboard, and desk drawers being banged shut. Demonee came out of the office with a genuine smile on her face. It tripped me out for a minute, Demonee with a smile—I didn't see it often, and I smiled back.

"Everything cool?" I asked.

"Yeah, I just have to go to class," she said.

"You gonna have a lot to catch up on. You missed a lot of days."

"I know *that*, Maxine," she said.

I sighed, but I wasn't about to ruin the mood I was in.

"Forget it, I'm sorry. Just go to class. I'll see you later," I said.

"Whatever," she told me and took off in the opposite direction.

"Why do I bother?" I mumbled. I checked my watch. I had a while until my school started. I figured I should go thank Ms. Hopkins, Demonee's math teacher, for not letting the principal kick Demonee out. No teachers at my school would have done that. Somebody had to tell her how nice it was. I rushed to her classroom, so I could talk to her before the kids got in.

Man, I felt uncomfortable when I entered the math wing. I don't know why. Maybe it was because I hadn't done it in a while. I passed what used to be Mrs. Shakria's class and remembered working problems on her blackboard. She would stand right next to you while you tried to make sense out of whatever the heck she had thrown up on there. I do admit, sometimes I needed her help and it was cool to have her standing there—sometimes. Mostly all she did was freak a sister out. And homework, girlfriend never stopped giving it. Page after page, chapter after chapter. When I was in her class, I stayed up all night doing her assignments. Shoot, I know why Demonee was bugging over Ms. Hopkins. Ms. Hopkins gives a lot of homework too. Demonee comes home with pages and pages of worksheets that she has to do. Still, that didn't give Demonee a reason to throw things at her. What the heck was Demonee thinking?

A foot or so from Ms. Hopkins class I stopped and got my story together. I was Demonee's older cousin and, if she asked, I was around twenty. I could easily pull older ages off. I never had much of a baby face. When I was around Demonee's age, I looked the age I am now. I walked to her doorway and looked inside. She was at the blackboard erasing some neatly drawn problems, looking just like the kids in my hood described her. They said she was the professional type. She never came to work in jeans. She liked to roll out in a nice skirt and jacket, like the businesswomen downtown. The kids said the way she talked was always professional too. She broke it down to you in good diction, instead of slang. Her hair was like the older usher ladies in church. She didn't go for any of the new weaves or all those crazy colors. She did it up in a neat ball. Like I said before, as far as I knew most of the kids liked her. They said she was generous with the A's, and was always available for extra tutoring after school. Man, except for all the homework, I wished she was my math teacher too. I didn't even know what an A looked like.

I went into Ms. Hopkins's room. To my surprise, I hadn't beat all the students in. There was a girl in there, a pretty little cheerleader type about Demonee's age, with shoulder-length glossy black hair and thick black lashes. She was sitting at a desk with her way-too-shapely legs crossed, holding a conversation with Ms. Hopkins.

"That's all I could sell, Ms. Hopkins," the girl said, throwing three catalogs onto her desk. "The kids ain't buying nothing. Nobody ain't buying nothing. My mama say the economy is bad, so people ain't throwing away they cash."

Ms. Hopkins sighed. "I understand that, Petal, but you've had the merchandise catalogs for a month and you've sold only two items. The other students have tried really hard and sold so much more. This is a very important project, and will help out some very needy people. I need everyone who signed up to do their best."

"I am doing my best but, shoot, I got other things to do too, like all that school work you keep giving us."

"Giving you work is my job. I have to make certain that you can pass your state exams and be prepared for the future."

The girl rolled her eyes. "Okay, whatever. I don't have time for this. Later." She got up and hurried to the door. She was in such a rush that she didn't see me. She bumped into me pretty hard, and dropped the catalogs she was carrying. I lost my balance, and I caught hold of the molding on the doorway.

"Dang, you need to be a little more careful, girl," I said.

She snatched her catalogs up without saying a word.

"Excuse me would be nice," I told her.

"Yeah, it would. Why don't you say it?" she snapped.

I was shocked. "Because you ran into me. And when you do that you supposed to say *you're* sorry."

"I would if I was. Besides, you the one blocking the door."

"Excuse me, little girl!" I said.

"See, I knew you knew how to say it," she said, and walked off.

Little rude heifer, was she trippin' or what? I rolled my eyes at her back and stepped inside.

Ms. Hopkins walked up to the door. "I'm sorry about that. That little girl has some issues. She can be so charming when she wants to be, but when she doesn't, you'd better watch out. Anyway, may I help you?" she asked.

"Yes, ma'am. I'm Demonee's older cousin," I said. "She's staying with me right now."

"Oh yes, Principal Chang told me that Demonee's uncle was out of town again and you were watching her for a while."

"Yes, ma'am. Her uncle is away on business. She's staying with me until he gets back."

"That's good. You'd be surprised at how many children Demonee's age get left all alone when their parents have to be away. But wait, don't I know you? Didn't you used to attend here?" she asked.

"I did a long time ago."

"Oh, well, I probably don't know you. I'm just starting my third year here, but it seems as if I've already worked with a decade of students. It's hard for me to recall them all, but every once in a while I see a face and it triggers a memory. Anyway, did you like going here?" she asked.

"It was okay, but I didn't have a cool teacher like you. That's why I'm here. I had to walk Demonee to school today, and her uncle wanted me to thank you for helping Demonee out. It was a real nice thing to do. I mean, most teachers would have let her get into big trouble, even if they had a choice not to."

"Well, Demonee is a problem child, but I feel like the problem can be corrected as long as someone cares about her. She deserves a chance. Don't you think?" she asked.

"Yes, ma'am, she does. Well, I better go," I said.

"Please tell your uncle he can come by anytime."

"I will," I said, and exited her room.

I walked through the hallway wondering if Demonee knew how lucky she was. She had a good teacher, one who really cared. I had never had a teacher like that. I hoped and prayed that Demonee didn't find a way to mess the whole thing up.

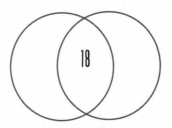

18

ven though I've changed my address at the post office, some of my mail still goes to my mama's house. Today she called me over to pick it up. I decided to take Demonee with me, so that we could grab something to eat on the way over. We stopped at Wangs and Thangs and picked up some hot wings before we went to the house. When we got there with our greasy wing bags, Mama was sitting on the porch with the mail.

"Ya'll didn't bring me nothing?" she said.

"I figured you already cooked," I told her.

"You figure a lot of things, Maxine, and half the time ain't none of them right," Mama said.

I sighed and handed Demonee my wing bag. Then I took the mail from Mama's hand and thumbed through it. It was mostly just junk mail, a couple of advertisements for a teen fashion website, some grocery store flyers, a New York art catalog that Tia had signed me up for, and an ad for a new lottery game. "You called me for this?" I said.

She reached over and pulled out a thin brochure from the stack I had in my hand and gave it back to me. I opened it and saw that it was advertisement for class rings.

"What's that?" Demonee asked.

"Nothing," I said, closing the brochure.

Mama took the brochure and opened it again. "Your old school sent this. What do you want me to do about it?" she asked. "You went to that school for three years. You wanna get a ring or not?"

"Mama, I ain't got no money for that and you don't either. Besides, I don't even know when I'm going to graduate."

"I do—this year. I'm not having no do-overs in my house because you wanted to shack up with that boy."

"I wasn't shacking up with Brian, and you know it, Mama," I said.

"Well, you might as well have been, for as much as you got out of it. Now he off with some other girl, and you spending all your time playing babysitter."

"I'm not a baby," Demonee snapped.

"This is grown folks talk, you stay out of it," Mama said.

Demonee rolled her eyes, but she didn't back talk. She knew better. Mama will only put up with so much. She's not Brian's dad, but if Demonee really pissed her off, she might find herself flying backward off the porch.

"Mama, don't start nothing," I said.

"I'm not trying to start anything. I'm trying to do something for you!" Mama said.

"Do what?" I heard Andre's deep voice say. I looked up and saw him standing at the screen door with his muscles bulging out of a black jersey with the sleeves cut off, and his long legs sporting a big red pair of baggy shorts. Great, it was all I needed. I was hoping that I could pick up my mail while he was out shooting his usual game of afternoon hoops but, of course, I wouldn't be that lucky.

Mama took the ring brochure and folded her hands over it in her lap.

"Do what?" Andre asked again. "Maxine, you coming around here begging for stuff? I thought you was supposed to be married. I thought your man was supposed to be taking care of you?"

"My man does take care of me."

"Yeah, you and that other girl. What's her name? It's Shell, ain't it? Your mama say he been taking real good care of her too," Andre said.

"You don't know what you talking about," I said.

"Yeah, I know. That little boy that you think is better than everybody else just proved to you that he ain't no different than any other dude out there."

"Brian loves me," I said.

"Yeah, and he sure knows how to show it. Look, Maxine, if you here begging for a handout you can hang it up. You said you wanna be a woman, so go be a woman. You married now, and married folks handle they own business."

"How do you know? You ain't never married nobody!" I yelled.

"It don't matter, little girl. I can still handle my own."

"Whatever," I said.

"Yeah, whatever. And let me tell you something else, Miss Think-you-know-everything. You been played. See, you was so busy lying to get what you wanted, it never even occurred to you that that boy you was with was an even bigger liar than you are. He played you straight up. Now he running around with his *real* baby mama."

"Go to hell," I said.

"You go first," he said, " 'cause you sure ain't coming back here. Shoot, I ain't got no time for this mess. I'm going and find my lucky Nikes, so I can get out to the court. See ya later, married woman," he said.

I glared at him.

"Don't you give her a damn thing," he said to Mama. "I work too hard for the money that I bring into this house. Let her man pull his money out of his pocket and take care of her. Send her back to him, wherever he at," he said, and walked away from the door.

"Mama, why did you tell him my business?" I asked. I felt like going after him and strangling him with the shoestrings of those Nikes, and afterward I could go after Mama for once again not standing up for me.

"Don't worry about him. This is between you and me."

"No, Mama, it's between the three of us. Why can't you ever figure that out?"

"Like you figured out that Brian was good for nothing?"

"What do you want from me, Mama?" I asked.

"I want to buy you that ring," she said.

"What for? Mama, if I don't graduate you just stuck with a ring with the wrong year, plus I don't even go to the same school anymore. I'll be graduating from someplace different. The ring won't mean nothing."

"It will mean something to me, Maxine. I was looking forward to seeing that ring on your finger this year. Andre don't know it, but I've been saving up my money for it. It was something that I was waiting on. Now you done went and messed things up."

"I messed things up? Just me alone."

"I didn't say that. The fault was mostly your husband's. Anyway, I'm just saying that I was planning on something and now my plans are all screwed up."

"I know that feeling. You don't know how much I know that feeling. And then I got to stand here and listen to your stupid man talk smack to me."

"He ain't stupid, and it's some truth in what he says. We both know that. Besides, Maxine, ain't none of this really up for discussion. I'm your mother, and you don't get to tell me what to do. I'm not okay with anything that is going on with your life right now, especially with you taking care of this girl because her family won't do it. I have a good mind to call over to Child Protective Services and tell them what is going on in your house."

"If you do that, Mama, you'll be screwing things up for everybody. Don't do that please?" I pleaded.

She rolled her eyes. "Maxine, I'll do what I think is best for you, and you know it," she said.

"Yeah, I know, even if it ain't right."

"Little girl, don't make me mad," she threatened.

"Whatever, Mama. All I know is it's dinnertime and I got to get Demonee home, because we both got homework to do," I said. "Do whatever makes you feel better. I wear a size nine. Let's go home and eat, Demonee," I said, walking away from the porch.

"Call me when you want to fix the disaster that you done

got yourself in. Call me when you get tired of playing mama," Mama called after me and Demonee.

"Call me when you learn how," I mumbled under my breath.

I wasn't going to spend my time arguing about that ring that I didn't even want. There was only one time in my life that I really wanted a ring, and she ruined it for me. Years ago Mama and I got into it over a promise ring that Brian gave me when I was around thirteen. It was only a silver ring with a fake diamond in it, but when Mama saw it, she threw a fit.

"Maxine, I know you don't think I'm gonna let you walk around with that thing like you about to be married," Mama told me.

"It's just a promise ring, Mama," I said.

"And what did you promise him, Maxine?" she asked, with a pissed-off look on her face.

"I promised to give him my love, Mama."

"And that's all you better be giving him. I better not hear you giving him anything else. In fact, you give me that thing. I don't even want it on your finger. Take it off right now."

I shook my head and she grabbed for it.

"Mama, don't take it. Brian gave it to me," I said, yanking my hand back.

"Fine, you keep it, but you watch yourself. You getting too grown for me, Maxine. You ain't promised to nobody and you tell that boy Brian I said so."

"Fine, I'll tell him, Mama," I said. Of course I didn't. I loved me some Brian, and there wasn't nothing wrong about the ring, because it meant something to him and me. It was just like her to never truly understand what I really needed and wanted.

"Would your Mama really call CPS because she mad at you?" Demonee asked.

"I don't know what she'll do. I never have," I said.

Demonee and I decided to take a shortcut through Peaceful Rest Cemetery, so that we could get home earlier and eat while the wings were still hot. It sounded like a good plan to me, but Demonee started eating her wings as soon as we passed the first grave site. She chewed the meat off and threw the bones down all over the place.

"Demonee, keep them bones in your bag," I told her.

"Why, they ain't going nowhere but on the ground?" she said, and tossed another one like she didn't care.

I stopped and picked the bone up. I wrapped it in a napkin and threw it in my bag.

"What did you do that for?" she asked.

"Because it was the right thing to do, and I've had enough of people doing the wrong thing around me."

"Maxine, you always making a big deal out of nothing."

"Am I?" I said. I grabbed her arm and made her follow me to the back of the cemetery. When we got there, I pointed to a grave that hadn't been there long. "You see that?" I said, pointing to the grave. "It's somebody's child. That's why you should keep your bones in the bags. How would you like it if somebody threw thrash on your child's grave?"

She didn't even look at the grave. "I ain't throwed no trash," she said, defensively.

"Anything that you would put out on garbage day is trash, Demonee."

❧ 190 ❧

"Whatever," she said, taking another wing out of her bag. She was about to put it in her mouth when she actually glanced at the child's stone. She noticed the words etched into the red granite.

"It says her mama thought she was a perfect daughter, a perfect niece, and a perfect child."

"Yeah," I said.

"How old was she?"

"Two."

She looked stunned. "She wasn't but two? Well, how her mama know all that about her? How her mama know she was perfect? Maybe she was gonna grow up to be somebody her mama didn't even like. Maybe she wasn't gonna be perfect at all."

"Nobody is perfect, Demonee."

"Then why her mama say that?"

"Because to her she was."

She turned sad. "I wish I was perfect to my mama, but I do things that she don't like. Me and her don't always agree on stuff. She real certain about everything, but me, I don't know."

"Don't know about what?" I asked.

She hunched her shoulders. "I don't know, whatever. I don't always feel the way I should about stuff. I feel different sometimes. My mama say the way I feel ain't right. I should feel things the way she does."

"That sometimes happens, Demonee. Me and Mama don't always understand things the same way. It's just a mother-daughter thing. Your mama gonna always think she knows best, even when she doesn't."

"Is that why you don't want that ring your mama wants to buy you?" Demonee asked.

"Something like that. The ring is more for her than me," I said.

"Oh, like my mama and my little sister Akina's disability check. If it don't come on time, my mama always call somebody over at the disability office and throw a fit. She tell them that Akina got to have it so she can get her asthma inhaler, but when it comes, mama go right out and buy herself some new clothes and dope. When Akina's inhaler runs out, Mama begs the people at the free clinic to give her one for nothing."

"It's not exactly like that," I said. "Let's just say that me and Mama don't always agree, but it's okay, sometimes."

"Really?"

"Really."

She thought about it a second. "Whatever," she said. "I don't care what nobody thinks. Why should I? Don't nobody care about me. I'm going home." She started through the cemetery. I followed after her. She opened her bag again and took out a wing. Before we reached the cemetery gate, she had eaten all the meat away, but she didn't toss the bone out. I took it as a good sign. Maybe she was learning some respect, learning that you didn't spread trash just because things weren't exactly going your way. I wish that Mama could learn it. I wish she could learn when I really needed a hug, and not to be dumped on.

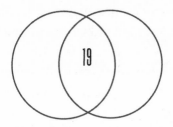

19

The phone rang bright and early this morning. I answered it, thinking that it was Madona, wanting to tell me once again that Bonita had skipped class or ditched her at lunch, or something like that. She had been calling me with Bonita updates for days. I was all ready to have a conversation about how her sister was trippin', but instead I heard the voice of my other good friend, Tia, on the phone.

"Hey girl, what's up?" I asked.

She immediately started telling me how much fun she and her husband were having in New York. I listened to her for a long time, pretending that I was there with her and Doo-witty, and also wishing that there was some way she could return home and be with me. I missed Tia. Things were so much better when she was here. We could hang together and play tunes, or just spend time dishing and gossiping about things at school. I can't do that now. The twins are going through their own drama. Plus, most of the time I'm depressed and mad at Brian, and worried about Demonee.

"Last night me and Doo-witty were invited to a great lit-tle art gallery in Midtown. They are going to show some of his paintings, and everybody in New York will be able to see them. Isn't that wonderful?" Tia asked.

"Ooh girl, you must be proud. I know how wonderful I would feel if I had a husband that was all special like that."

"I know, I'm so proud of Doo-witty, and he's been taking speech therapy too. His speech is getting better. He doesn't stutter so much now. We're both really happy about that."

"And I'm happy for you and him. It's not a good thing when you're tumbling all over your words. You know my cousin Juanita. That girl can barely get a sentence out without tripping over it. And it's worse when she gets nervous. You can barely understand a word she says."

"Yeah, I know. I'm glad that Doo-witty was never that bad. Well, that's enough about me. What's the deal with you and your ex?"

"My ex is my ex, and I plan on keeping him that way."

"Don't you miss him?"

"I do, I was just laying here thinking about how Brian used to be snoring all night. It probably would have bothered a lot of women, but it never bothered me. I liked hearing the noise, because I knew he was here with me. I miss being all close like that, but girlfriend that already seems like it was a long time ago."

"Does it really?"

"Most of the time. Then sometimes it seems like Brian isn't gone at all. I can still feel him in the house. I walk in the bedroom and I swear there is a dent in my pillow that looks like the one his big ole head used to make."

"Maybe it's his spirit."

"He ain't dead, girl," I said, and laughed.

"Naw, my grandma Augustine says that sometimes live folks have spirits too. They leave them behind when they don't want to go away from a place."

"You don't really believe that, do you?"

"Naw, I'm just talking. I miss you being with Brian. Ya'll was really happy."

"Maybe," I said.

"Yeah, maybe," she repeated.

We both stopped talking. I couldn't hear anything but the soft whisper of her breath in the receiver.

"It's really hard, isn't it?" she finally said.

"Yeah, it's hard. Every day it's hard."

"I know, are you sure you don't want me to try and come out?"

"Naw, it won't make much difference. We'll both just be sitting here depressed."

"Okay, well, I gotta go girlfriend. You know you my girl. Stay cool, stay sweet."

"You too," I said. I hung up the phone and rolled over in the bed. From the kitchen I heard Demonee toss her oatmeal bowl in the sink.

"Demonee, don't leave no mess in that kitchen this morning. I ain't about to clean up behind you," I hollered out.

"I'm gone, Maxine," she hollered and slammed the back door. I sighed and got up. I guess I was going to be washing the breakfast dishes again. Truth is, I could have run in and gotten on her behind before she went out of the door, only I didn't care. As long as she was going to school without starting

World War III, I was cool with having to bust the suds. All I wanted was peace. I went to the bathroom to get dressed for my own school day.

After the best bubble bath in the world, I slipped into a nice pair of slacks and a soft mint green peasant blouse and went into the kitchen. Sticky oatmeal was all over the range top and the sink was piled high with crusty dishes. I put on one of the aprons Great-aunt Freda sent me last Christmas and got to work. I had the sink filled up with water when a knock sounded on the front door. I turned off the water and went to answer it.

"Dang, I was just fixin' to get my sink cleaned out!" I said. I walked over to the door and flung it open, expecting to see Madona. My heart leaped. Can you believe it? Women always say that on TV and you don't believe them. But guess what? It's true. My heart leaped when I saw Brian. That's the only way I can describe it. I hadn't seen him since that day at school and I just couldn't help it. All the love that I had for him deep down came boiling up to the surface. Then I noticed he was wearing the same black and white Rockets T-shirt that he used to put on when he went to work at Shell's house.

"Speak of the Devil and he will appear. What do *you* want?" I asked, putting my arm up to block the door.

"I want to be somewhere else, Maxine. I think you know that," he said.

"So why you here then?" I asked. He looked at my arm on the door frame.

"Girl, you better let me in here," he said, pushing past me. I rolled my eyes and walked back into the living room.

"Don't be coming in here like you own something, 'cause you know you don't," I said.

"I'm not. I'm—" he said, looking around. He noticed the bare walls. "Hey, where is my Jennifer Lopez and Beyoncé posters?" he asked.

"In the trash where they belong. I didn't want to look at them half-naked heifers every time I came into my living room."

"Well, why didn't you give them back to me?"

"Why didn't you take them with you?"

"I would have, if I had known you was gonna chuck them out."

"No, I carefully tossed them away. I chucked you out. There's a difference."

"Okay, look, whatever. I didn't come over here for that, Maxine," he said, getting all serious. "We got trouble."

"I know that, or do you think I somehow forgot about your girlfriend?"

"Naw, I didn't think anything like that. Besides, it ain't the trouble I'm talking about," he said.

"What is it then?"

"Yesterday I was at Daddy's house and a letter came from Demonee's school. I took it out of the box and I hid it until I could get a look."

"What did it say?"

"Something about a list," he said, shaking his head. "Apparently because of Demonee's low grades and behavior problems, they put her on a special list of kids that may eventually drop out."

"Is that all? They don't have to worry about that. I would never let her do that," I said.

"I know, but that ain't the thing. It turns out all the parents of the kids on that list are being asked to come to what they call a retention-and-support powwow. The parents have to make an appointment at the main office, and all of their teachers will be at the powwow."

My heart leaped again, but this time it wasn't from seeing Brian. "Oh crap! Dang, I thought we would have more time than this. Your dad is gonna find out about Demonee getting kicked out of school for sure. Dang, I knew he might find out, only I was hoping that it wouldn't be until the end of the year. Then maybe he would cut us some slack, because it would be all over and done with."

"Yeah, well we don't always get what we want, Maxine. And you know how mad Dad can get over nothing. When he finds out we put something over on him, he's gonna go through the roof. Man, I don't know why I let you pull me into this mess. I don't need no trouble with my daddy, Maxine. He been trippin' ever since we broke up. He doesn't like Shell."

"Me neither—that tramp! I can't believe you left me for her," I said.

"Don't start that, Maxine. You told me to go. I don't even have time for that today. You just gonna have to do something about this situation you caused."

I frowned. "I didn't cause no situation. I was trying to prevent one," I said.

He walked over to the sofa and sat down in a huff. "Maxine, you done screwed us all up over that little stupid cousin of mine. She ain't worth none of this. She ain't gonna do nothing but keep causing trouble. She can't help it. Her whole family is like that."

I rolled my eyes. "They your family too. Besides, I heard that before," I said. I went to the sofa and sat down too.

"Well you obviously didn't hear it good enough, Maxine." His voice softened a bit. "Look, Maxine, I know you been trying to keep this place since I left. I get that, what I don't get is you doing all this stuff for a girl that don't even treat you right. Since Demonee been here she been in trouble for skipping class, throwing things at her teacher, cussing folks out, stealing."

"Stealing? What do you mean?"

"Mr. Diamond said that she took a T-shirt from his store."

"I don't know nothing about a T-shirt."

"Well, he does. He told me that Demonee came in with one of her little girlfriends one day. He said they were the only ones in the store at the time, and when they left two of his *That's So Raven* T-shirts were missing."

"Did he see Demonee take a shirt?" I asked.

"No, but did he have to? She's my cousin, Maxine. I know her. Do you really think that it's the first time that I've heard something like that about her?"

"No, I know she ain't no saint, or nothing close to it," I said.

"Anyway, my point is, you can't do nothing for Demonee. She's just going to bring you more trouble. You need to let her go on and go to a foster home. Maybe she'll find somebody to treat her nice. It would be good if she had some mothering. Don't you think?"

"I had some mothering. It wasn't good for me," I said.

"What are you talking about, Maxine?"

I hesitated for a second, collected my thoughts. "Something

that happened a long time ago. Remember when I went to stay with Aunt Brenda for a year to help her out around the house after she had a heart attack?" I asked.

"Yeah, I remember that. I hated that you were gone. I was glad when you got back."

"Were you really?" I asked, remembering what Uncle Ernie told me about Shell.

"Of course, why you wanna ask something like that?" he asked.

"It don't matter. Anyway, I missed you too, but that ain't really what happened. I didn't go and stay with my aunt."

"Yeah, I know, you don't have to tell me," he said, in a sad voice. "I know that was the year your mama let you be turned over to the state because she didn't want to lose her boyfriend."

"I never told you that. How did you find out about it?"

"I didn't find out. My dad did. You know how he is with his little connections. He told me a long time ago. He said your mom's boyfriend was hitting you, but she wouldn't get rid of him because he was paying the rent."

"Something like that, except she also really thought she was in love with that dude. Anyway, one day he beat me with a shoe so bad I could barely sit down for the pain, so I told my teacher. Everything blew up, and you know that I eventually ended up in foster care, until Mama stopped being a fool."

"Yeah."

"What you don't know is how it feels to be living with somebody that ain't even related to you 'cause your own family didn't put you first. And they didn't, Brian. Not a one of them offered to come and get me when Mama kicked me out.

I kept waiting for someone to come and save me, but my own family treated me like I didn't matter. Nobody showed up at the court, or my foster home. I stayed there at that home with folks I didn't even know. I slept in their bed and ate their food. They weren't mean people, but I knew every day that they didn't want me. I wasn't their child. They had older children that they treated way better than me, always bought them new toys and games, fixed them a hot breakfast before they went to school each morning, helped them with their schoolwork, made certain that they always had clean nice clothes to go to school in. I didn't. All I had was what I left home with, and I went to school dirty a lot because my foster mother wouldn't wash my clothes, or let me use the washer to clean them myself. I knew every day that I was just some kid that the state paid them to keep."

"I'm sorry about that. I'm sorry about what happened to you."

"I know, but it doesn't change things. Brian, I know how Demonee feels when she wakes up each morning and sees me instead of her own blood kin. I know because I was just like her."

"Not exactly, you never got into the trouble that she gets into."

"Because I had you. When I came back home, I knew that I had you. Plus, I was way too scared. After I came home, I was worried for a long time that Mama would send me back. In fact, Brian, it's only been recently that I stopped feeling that way. When I turned seventeen, I figured that I was too old to go back into foster care if my mama chose some dude over me."

"I didn't know that," he said, reaching out and touching my hand.

I moved it away. "It doesn't matter, Brian. My point is, not a single person in Demonee's family wants to be responsible for her, wants to rescue her. I know exactly how that feels."

"So you're rescuing her?" he asked.

"I guess so. I don't know. All I know is nobody in my family was willing to do it for me. Can you understand what I'm saying?" I asked. I looked over at his watch. Time had slipped by quickly. "I gotta go, Brian. I don't know what I'm gonna do about this, but I can't be late today. My teachers are already on me about leaving early a few times for Demonee's drama. Just keep that letter away from your dad. I'll figure something out, and I'll make sure you don't get into a pickle with me."

He hunched his shoulder. "Aww, it's okay. I'm always in trouble over something anyway. I can take whatever my daddy dishes out," he said.

"Really?" I asked.

"Yeah, I can do it for you," he said.

"Thanks," I said, a little shocked that he would still say something like that to me.

"I better bounce," he said, getting up from the sofa. I had forgotten how tall he was. When we were together, his daddy was always trying to get him to play basketball or run track, because he had lots of height and long legs. Brian never went along with it. He said he might get hit with a basketball in the face, or trip on the track and knock his teeth out. Of course, those things would probably never happen, and Brian knew it.

It was just his way of letting his dad know that he wasn't going to do what he wanted him to do.

"I'll see you later," he said, heading for the door, but he turned around. "Why didn't you ever tell me about the foster home, Maxine? I knew, but you never really came out and said anything."

"It was my pain, Brian. Something that I had to live with, and I didn't want you to live with it too."

"Yeah, I get that, but I knew about it, so I lived the pain anyway."

"I didn't know," I said.

"You're really strong, Maxine, way stronger than me. You don't always fight back, but you do know how to survive. That's the one thing that I always loved most about you," he said, and went out the door.

I waited until he walked out of the yard. I went out on the porch, a bit wobbly in the knees. After all he put me through, he was still the only one that I wanted to be with. How could that be? How could I still be so stuck on a guy that didn't even know how to treat me? Why didn't I jump on him about Shell and how long he had been with her? Why did I just go all gooey inside? I wanted to work everything out in my head, but I had to keep my thoughts focused on the thing that I needed to deal with right now: Demonee. I needed to think of a way to keep her uncle from going to that meeting at school. I couldn't fix my situation. Maybe I could fix hers.

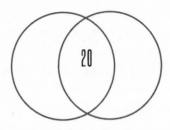

20

Before the meeting Brian's dad was supposed to attend, I called the school and pretended to be a parent. It's a good thing that I did. I found out the meeting wasn't even going to be held at school. It was going to be held in a conference room at the district offices.

"There are going to be advisors and speakers there, but the teachers may or may not be attending. It's up to them to decide whether or not they need to come. From what I was told by the principal, this is more or less a meeting to decide how to best structure the students' workday in order to help them reach their full potential. The advisors on hand will have copies of each students' records and know how to create and individual plan for them," the principal's secretary told me on the phone.

As soon as I hung up the phone, I realized there was a little hope that I could keep Demonee and the rest of us out of trouble. If the teachers didn't have to go to the meeting, I figured most of them wouldn't come to it. But I had to know for sure. I especially had to know about Ms. Hopkins, Demonee's math teacher. I was worried about her, mostly because I didn't know if she had actually met Demonee's uncle. I didn't know if he had spoken to her that day he went up to the school. Then there was Demonee's French teacher. Demonee's uncle had mentioned her a couple of times. He hadn't met her but he admired her because she knew a lot of languages and gave up a chance to be an interpreter just to teach. Those were the two teachers that I was concerned with. However, at some point Demonee's uncle could have met one or all of her teachers. I had to know for certain if any of them were planning to show up.

According to Demonee, her teachers wouldn't know her uncle's handwriting from a hole in the wall, and I was counting on that. After I did my Marketing homework one night, I stayed up and typed a note to her teachers and signed something close to her uncle's signature on the bottom. In the note, I told them how sorry I was about Demonee's poor grades and behavior, and asked them if they were going to attend the meeting. It took a few days for them to respond, but eventually they all sent notes back with Demonee. Four of them said that they really thought Demonee could be a good student with lots of help, and two of them said they thought she could do better if she simply tried harder. Ms. Hopkins said that she really wanted to be there, but she had another meeting to attend at the same time. So, the only one out of the group that actually said she would attend was Ms. Fleur, Demonee's new French teacher. This didn't surprise me because Demonee had told me that her class was the only one that she was flat-out failing. It was good news to us though, because it meant that I had only one teacher to worry about.

When I found out Ms. Fleur was the only teacher coming, I called in a favor from my Uncle Ernie. I figured he owed me for all the time I spent changing diapers and reading bedtime stories to his kids. I rang him up and asked him to go to Demonee's meeting as her uncle. He didn't like it one bit, but he came by the house anyway. I told him everything I could about Demonee. If he was going to play her uncle, he had to know the right things to say.

"Maxine, I don't know about this little scheme. I'll do it if you want me to, but if any of them people find out that I barely even know that child, somebody gonna be in all kinds of trouble. They sho' gonna call her real uncle's house and ask him what the devil is going on," he said, while we were going over stuff at the kitchen table.

"Ain't nobody gonna call nobody, if you just be cool and do what you supposed to do. All you got to do is sit in the meeting and listen."

"I'm listening now, and I'm telling you, girl, this is a bad idea," he said.

"It's the only one I can think of."

"It's gonna fall apart, Maxine," he said, shaking his head. "Something is gonna go wrong. I'm gonna screw it up."

"No you won't," I said, and just to make sure, I went along.

We got to the powwow a little late because Uncle Ernie didn't pick me up on time. There was already a group of folks lined up to speak. One after the other, professional-looking men and women strolled up to a wooden podium and gave a speech about why teens drop out. Uncle Ernie must have thought most of the speeches were boring. He threw his head back in the middle of one of them and started snoring away. I poked him hard in the ribs. He startled awake. "What's going on? Why you pushing on me?" he asked, wiping slobber off of his face before it trickled onto his starched, beige shirt.

"Shhh! They trying to talk about something important."

"What, trying to keep kids in school? Shoot, I can tell 'em how to do that. Just put 'em in the military if they don't wanna go to school. After they get through running around in the Middle East with bullets flying over they head, they'll be happy to take they behind back to school. I know I would." He pointed up at the podium, where a thin blond guy was talking. "Shoot, these white folks don't know nothing about dealing with no kids. I'd have the law going around from house to house signing these knuckleheads up for boot camp, girls and boys. I'd put a gun in they hand if they don't wanna carry a book," he said.

"And they'd probably shoot you with it," I said.

He chuckled. "Maxine, you always did crack me up." He leaned his head back in his chair and tried to sleep again. I poked him once more.

"All right, all right, dang, give me some peace, girl," he said.

"Peace in Heaven."

"Not for me. Shoot, the way I do things the Devil might not even let me in Hell. At least that's what my last girlfriend told me," he said, and laughed.

I couldn't help but giggle too.

"Shhh! I'm trying to hear something to help my son," said

a sister that looked like a cross between an orangutan and a werewolf.

"No she didn't. She need to quit trippin' with a kid as ugly as her son got to be, he don't need to be in school. He need to be in the Houston Zoo," Uncle Ernie whispered.

I put my hand over my mouth to keep the giggles in, but some slipped out.

"Quiet!" the lady hissed.

Uncle Ernie made a funny face at her. She turned back around in her seat. I was glad. I didn't need her drawing too much attention our way. When the final speaker got up, he pointed to a row of folding tables in the back that had letters of the alphabet taped to them.

"Those are the advisors assigned to your children," he said, gesturing to the intelligent-looking people sitting behind the tables. "You may now go over and speak with them. There are three for each group. Just go to the table with the letter that corresponds to your child's last name, and they will be happy to help you out."

"Maxine, what's Demonee's last name?" Uncle Ernie whispered.

"Blis, it's Demonee Blis," I whispered back.

He doubled over with laughter. "Aww naw, hell naw. I know you lying," he said, slapping his knees.

I smacked him on the back. "Come on, Uncle Ernie. Damn, don't be blowing this for me," I said.

He stopped laughing and straightened up. "Ooh, ooh, girl, you 'bout to make me bust my sides wide open. Don't even think about telling me nothing like that again," he said, wiping tears out of his eyes. "I know ain't nobody put *Bliss* on the end of monster baby's name."

"It's Blis, spelled with just one *s*, and I know it don't fit her, but that's her name," I said. I glanced over at the tables. All the other parents were already at them. There was a line of worried-looking mothers and fathers sitting on a bench next to the A–C table.

"Look at all them folks over there," Uncle Ernie said, pointing to the A–C group. He spotted the ugly woman, sitting on the bench waiting for her turn. "I shoulda known she would be over there. *A* for ape. That's her and her son. She sho' in the right place," he said, laughing again.

"All right, all right, let's just go see about Demonee," I said. We started over when I tensed up. "Aw man, what a nightmare!" I cried.

"What, what is it?" Uncle Ernie asked. I just kept staring at the door, staring at the problem I should have known all along was gonna walk in. Ms. Hopkins, Demonee's math teacher. There she was coming in the door, in a two-piece dark blue suit, with what appeared to be a leather-bound grade book in her hand. I decided it was best to give the whole thing up. I had to get Uncle Ernie out of there and figure out what to do later.

"Uncle, we got to go," I whispered.

"What? I thought we was gonna talk to somebody," he said.

"Not today. We gotta bounce," I said. We turned to get the heck out.

"Please, have a seat, sir," a large lady with glasses suddenly called out.

"Uh, oh uh, okay," Uncle Ernie said.

"Uncle, don't," I whispered. He walked over to the lady's table and sat down anyway. I took an empty seat next to him, looking like I could yank out all the hairs in his short fro. The lady advisor looked at me all weird.

"Oh, uh, this is my niece," Uncle Ernie said.

"Hi," I mumbled and straightened up my face.

"Nice to meet you, now who are you here for?" the lady asked.

"Demonee, her name is Demonee Blis. I'm her, uh, her uncle," Uncle Ernie stammered.

Of course, the moment she heard Demonee's name, Ms. Hopkins waved and started over. "I'm here for Demonee Blis too," she told the advisor.

"Wonderful, please sit down," the woman said. Ms. Hopkins pulled up a seat next to Uncle Ernie.

"Now we can begin. I'm Mrs. Knightly, and this is Demonee's uncle and his niece," the woman said. I caught my breath and waited for Ms. Hopkins to respond. In my mind I heard her say, "There must be some mistake. I met Demonee's uncle at the start of school. This gentleman isn't him." That's what I waited for. I just knew she was gonna knock the whole building down on us.

"Oh, hello. I know we've spoken on the phone a couple of times about your niece. It's very nice to meet you," she said, holding her hand out to Uncle. He shook it with a relieved look on his face.

"Uh yeah, me too," he mumbled. I said nothing. It was as if every cat in Texas had my tongue. I didn't know what to say. All I could do is thank God that Ms. Hopkins hadn't met Demonee's real uncle.

"Well, shall we start?" Mrs. Knightly asked.

Ms. Hopkins smiled. "Whenever you like," she said.

"Yeah, let's get it over with," Uncle Ernie said.

I kicked him under the table. He gave me a mean look. I

totally didn't care. All I cared about was not getting caught. I sat happily and quietly through the rest of the meeting, while Demonee's fake uncle and Ms. Hopkins talked to the lady that was gonna help Demonee stay on track and stay in school.

When I got back home, I called Brian and told him that Demonee was taken care of and we were off the hook. When I hung up the phone, I went and told Demonee. She was in her room, lying on her bed in her goldfish-print bathrobe, listening to her portable CD player. I turned it down and told her how everything went. She grinned for just a second, like any kid would after you just pulled them out of the fire.

"Okay, cool, thanks for letting me know," she said.

"Aren't you going to say thank you?"

"For what? You and that dumb ole uncle of yours didn't do that just for me. You was taking care of yourself, and Brian. Ya'll woulda been in trouble just like me," she said.

It made me mad, and I snapped at her. "Maybe we would have, but you're the only one that would have ended up in a foster home or something, and you know it. So don't be such a smart-ass about it. It's you that we were taking care of tonight, and don't you forget!" I yelled. She rolled her eyes up to Jesus, then common sense came over her.

"Look, whatever, thanks for helping me out," she said.

I sighed. "You're welcome," I said, and left the room.

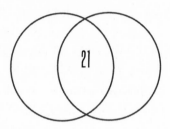

21

This afternoon I spent way too much time weaving white nylon sunflowers into my hair and painting my nails and toes antique white. I did it for Great-aunt Freda. She was having a little get together at her assisted-living home this afternoon, and I wanted to wear her favorite color, so I did it all up in white. Besides the flowers and polish, I put on a pretty white sundress. When I left my bedroom and walked out to the living room, Demonee was sprawled out on the sofa, eating a bowl of popcorn and watching a video of some rappers that I hadn't seen before. She had the sound on mute and was bopping her head to music she couldn't even hear. I wasn't having it. There was way too much that she could and should be doing around the house.

"Why don't you get your butt up and go clean that junky room I told you to straighten up yesterday. I can smell them musty gym clothes you left on the floor the minute I walk in the house," I said to her.

She glared at me, like she wanted to back talk, but she didn't argue. She went straight to her room and got to work.

I grinned. She's been doing what I ask a lot more often these days, because she knows she owes me big-time. I'm really enjoying not having to constantly fight with her. Plus, today I don't want to do anything that might put me in a bad mood. It's Great-aunt Freda's day. I just want to enjoy spending time with her.

I finished off Demonee's popcorn and picked up the phone to give Mama a call. I hadn't spoken to her since the conversation about the ring and, to be honest, I really didn't want to get into it with her. I just needed to know if she was going to drop by and see Great-aunt Freda on her special day. She and Mama weren't as close anymore, but it still bothered her when Mama didn't come around to visit. I dialed Mama's cell number and waited for her to answer.

"Hello?" she said, after the third ring.

"Hey, it's Maxine. I just want to know if you are going to come to Great-aunt Freda's thing today?" I asked.

"I told her last week that I would. Me and Andre are on our way right now."

"Okay," I said, and started to click the phone off.

"Have you heard from Brian?" she asked, before I could hang up.

"No, I haven't seen him," I lied.

"Well, ain't no big surprise there. I guess that means you still playing mama."

"I guess it does," I said.

"Maxine, don't take that tone with me. You know that I can pull the plug on all of this at any time. Don't get smart with me. Don't blame me for what Brian did."

"What you did too," I said.

"Excuse me?"

"What you did too, Mama."

"Maxine, what the hell are you talking about?"

"Did you know that Shell's mama used to work for Brian's mom, and that's probably where Shell met Brian? Did you know that she worked for Brian's mom while I was away? Remember when I was away, Mama? Remember when I wasn't living at home?"

"Maxine, I remember that, and I told you you ain't got to keep throwing it in my face. How was I supposed to know about Shell's mama? I don't even know who she is!"

"She's the mother of a girl that's gonna have a baby for my husband. That's who she is," I said. "Look, Mama, I don't want to talk about this no more. I ain't heard from Brian, and I probably won't. I'll see you at Aunt Freda's," I said, and hung up the phone. I wasn't going to spoil my good mood by arguing with her about my ex. I went to the kitchen and washed my hands in the kitchen sink. When I was through with that, I hollered at Demonee again.

"Demonee, I want that room clean by the time I get back here, and when you finish with that you can straighten up the living room too."

Seems like I barely had time to read the huge cardboard advertisements at the top of the bus before it stopped a block from the complex Great-aunt Freda lived in. I got off the bus and immediately spotted white balloons tied to the cedar trees in front of her unit, and a picnic table decorated with a white lace tablecloth. When I got closer I noticed there was a straw picnic basket on the table and a two-liter bottle of RC. I walked over and picked up the bottle.

"Be careful with that. I'm breaking out the hard stuff today," I heard Great-aunt Freda say.

I looked over at the screen door and grinned.

She opened the door and greeted me. "You ain't seen a fat man riding by selling watermelons off a truck? 'Cause, that's a sure sign that rain is on the way," she said, coming out in a beautiful white suit and white pumps and, of course, her favorite white Sunday hat.

"Why?" I asked, taking her by the hand to help her down the steps. Recently she's been having a few problems with stuff like stairs, but at seventy-five she still takes a mile walk each day.

"Why, I don't know. You just have to add it all together, the fat man, the watermelon, and the truck."

"How?"

"Well a truck is something that brings things, a watermelon is something filled with water, and a fat man is something heavy. If you put it all together, you get a heavy amount of water being brought in."

"I don't get it."

"It's an old saying. Folks back home used to say all kinds of stuff like that."

"Oh, like when it rains from a clear sky, that means that the Devil is whipping his wife."

"Yeah, like that."

"My social studies teacher calls those folk sayings."

"Well, I guess that's true, 'cause all the folks that I grew up with say them," she said. She eased her frail frame down in one of the folding chairs, and I sat across from her. I peeked in the picnic basket. There was a plate of fried chicken covered with plastic wrap. Some mini sweet potato pies, a bowl of German potato salad, and a saucer of fried green tomatoes. Everything but the salad was hot. I could tell because the plastic was foggy.

"Yum! Hey, where's everybody else at?" I asked.

"Your Mama already been here and gone."

"Mama been here already? I thought she was gonna stay awhile."

"Me too. That's why I was waiting to fix the food, but she come by here with that new man she living with. She said they had a family gathering at his mama's house to go to. They gobbled up two or three of them little sweet potato pies with some Blue Bell ice cream and left. Before that your uncle Ernie and one of his women showed up here. They had a couple of kids with 'em, so I made some Kool-Aid and let them eat chicken wings and potato salad. Them kids ate like they didn't know food existed until I gave them a taste."

"That don't surprise me. You know them girls Uncle Ernie hook up with like to spend all their money on weaves and nails. It wouldn't shock me if they kids miss a meal sometimes."

"Yeah, well, at least they let they mama bring them by for a while. Not too many kids want to come see an old lady these days—adults either I guess. Your mama and uncle couldn't wait to get up out of here."

"Yeah, well, you know how Mama is. She don't never like to stay anywhere too long, and Uncle Ernie got to finish up his date quick with one girlfriend, so he can get to another one.

You know how he is too. I sometimes wonder, what them women see in him?"

"Promise, that's what they see in him. He can be a straight-up clown sometimes, but he always giving them women money for they kids. I'm sure they all believe that one day he gonna be the one they settle down with. Then they'll have his money *and him*. It's promise, promise that one day he'll give them the life they want."

"Well good luck with that," I said, taking the plastic off the tomatoes. I grabbed one up.

"Give me one of them too," she said. I put mine on a plastic plate and picked up a another one. Before I gave it to her, I broke it in half.

"Maxine, what you doing?" she asked, taking it from me with her fingers. "I don't need you to break nothing up for me. I can eat just like you. I still got my own teeth," she said and flashed her row of thirty-twos.

"Sorry."

She grinned and patted her heavily wrinkled cheeks. "I may not have a lot of choppers, but I can still do just what everybody else do," she said.

"I know," I said. "I'm just stupid sometimes." She threw half of the tomato into her mouth and chewed it up.

"Maxine, you ain't stupid. I ain't never known you to be stupid in my life. When you married Brian, I thought that was premature, but not stupid, because I know that you loved Brian. And, shoot, you and him have always been like the kids that I never had, so I love him too. No matter what, I still love him, even though his father needs to quit wearing his drawers so tight and mellow out."

"Ain't that the truth. It's all I can do to keep him off of me and Demonee."

She tossed the other half of the tomato into her mouth and gobbled it up. "Yeah, I know. Your Uncle Ernie told me there was some trouble," she said, after she finished.

"He did. Damn, Uncle Ernie got a big mouth. I told him not to go blab stuff to everybody."

"He wasn't blabbing. He told me he had seen you a little while ago, and I asked him how you was doing. That's when he told me what was going on, 'cause he knew he couldn't lie to me. When he finished, I told him not to tell nobody else. He won't, cause he know I'll fry him up like a pan of these tomatoes if he do anything to hurt my grand-niece."

"Good, I don't need no more trouble. I got all I can handle right now."

"Why, why you even bothering with that little girl?" she asked.

I shrugged. "I don't know, cause if I don't, I don't think anybody else will."

"You really believe that? I mean do you really think Brian's daddy would let her go into a home, when he can do better for her?" she asked, taking the greasy plastic off the fried chicken.

"Why not? You know Mama did. She let me go like I was a puppy she was putting up in a kennel. Naw, it was even worse than that. You have to pay to keep a puppy in a kennel, so you care how they get treated. Mama didn't care what happened to me, as long as she could have things her way. You know she only came by to see me three times while I was in foster care, and each time it was right before I was supposed to take off to school. She would spend about fifteen minutes with me before the school bus came, pretending to be all motherly, and telling me that she was sorry I was still at a home. But as soon as that big yellow bus pulled up to the corner, she would dash out of the house and back to the person she really cared about."

"I know. That was bad business that happened between you and your mama. Every day I wished that I had been in a position to take you in, but I was in and out of the hospital with my thyroid and other things. They wouldn't have let me keep you."

"I know. It wasn't your fault."

"No, it was you mama's. She has a lot of them, and her biggest one is weakness. Why do you think she keeps taking up with these men? She's scared to be on her own, scared to try and do the things that other women do each day. She needs a man there to take care of her, making certain that everything is all right."

"Even if he's not a good man?"

"Even if. I can't explain it, but I know that it's true. I also know something else. Nothing your mama can ever do will break you. You were born so much stronger than she will ever be."

"I don't feel that way, not now."

"You may not feel that way, but it's the truth."

"I mighta believed something like that a few months ago, but now with Brian taking off with some skanky little heifer, I don't know what I feel about anything."

"Maxine, you're not supposed to know everything at your age, you're just supposed to be learning, and you are. Baby, you are learning things that I never knew at your age, how to take care of yourself, even how to be a mother."

"I don't know about that, but I have somehow figured out how to keep Demonee from ending up where I did."

"That takes strength."

"Yeah, but what about my marriage? That takes strength too, and I couldn't pull it off. I couldn't hold on to my husband."

"Maybe, maybe not. I got something to tell you about that. Now go on and eat, baby, and let me tell you what your ex said when he come by here early this morning."

"Brian was here?"

"Yes, he was. He said that he hadn't talked to me for a while and wanted to see me on my special day."

"What did he tell you?"

"You ain't gonna believe what he said to me," she said, laughing. "That's what I love about being old. People think they can tell you anything and you won't repeat it cause you done learned the wisdom of minding your own business, or you so old you gonna forget what they told you anyway. Shoot, I ain't that old. And I say if you fool enough to tell to me, I'm fool enough to tell it to somebody else, unless, of course, you tell me not too. So, girlfriend, let me tell you exactly what Mr. Brian come over here talking about," she said, winking.

"What did he say?" I asked.

"Something about wanting you back."

My eyes widened. "What? You must be mistaken."

"No, I'm not, and you'll know it too, once you hear what I got to say."

"What is it?" I asked.

"Now you just listen up. Brian says he still in love with you," she said.

At first I thought Aunt Freda might be slipping a little, 'cause every once in a while her old age does kick in and she gets things mixed up. Like one time she bought Mama a freezer full of ham hocks for her birthday, when what Mama really said she wanted was a hammock to hang in the front yard. Maybe Great-aunt Freda was wrong again. That's what I thought.

I remember when Brian told me that he loved me for real, not like he usually did in Valentines cards and letters. He told me on one of the worse days of our lives. One evening we were walking home from a basketball game at school. We were taking a shortcut through the alley between Perry's 24 and 7 when two dudes came walking up to us. Before we knew what was happening, one of the dudes pushed Brian down and, when he scrambled to his feet held a knife to Brian's throat.

"Say, dog, you think you slick, trying to get with my lady behind my back. That's my bitch. What you doing pushing up on her?" the guy yelled.

"I don't know what you talking about, dog." Brian said, frightened.

"Yes you do, hell yeah, you do. Don't try to act stupid," the dude with the knife said. He was a little dude, Brian was nearly a foot taller than him. I know Brian would have kicked his butt, if it wasn't for the knife, and the dude's much bigger friend.

"I—I ain't trying," Brian stuttered. "I don't know what you talking about. I don't even know who your lady is. Here my girl, right here," Brian said, pointing to me.

The guy didn't even look at me. "So why you after mine? Why you all over my woman, when you got your own? Why you trying to mess with my stuff? I oughtta do your ass right now," the guy said, pushing the knife harder up against Brian's throat. It looked like the tip was going to go into Brian's skin.

"He ain't lying. He don't know your girl. Please, please don't cut him," I begged.

"I don't, man. I don't. I told you. I ain't trying to get with your girl. Don't cut me man, just don't cut me!" Brian pleaded.

"Cut that bastard," the one without the knife said. "Cut him good. You hear that, dog. He 'bout to put you down. You mama gonna be crying and everything," he said to Brian. "She gonna be saying, 'who stabbed my baby Javon.' Javon, say man, what kind of punk name is that anyway?"

"That ain't even my name, man. Ya'll making a mistake. Ya'll got the wrong man. My name is Brian," Brian said.

"The hell if it is, don't be trying to trick us, punk," the boy with the knife said.

"It ain't no trick, just look at his school ID. He got it in his wallet! Just look in his wallet!" I screamed.

The guy with the knife looked confused. He glanced at his friend, then he moved the knife a little ways from Brian's throat.

"Man, you better not be messing with me. I mean it," he growled. "You got some kind of ID, take it out, take it out right now. Or I'm gonna cut your ass good."

"Okay, okay," Brian said, but he was so scared he couldn't get his wallet out. I reached into his pocket and pulled it out for him. I slipped the ID free and showed it to the guy. He looked at it and cursed.

"Damn, he ain't the dude. He just some school punk," he said to his friend. He poked Brian with the knife a couple of times. "Man, I ought to cut you anyway, for wasting my damn time."

"Come on, dog, we ain't got no time for this punk," he said to his friend. "I got to go find that other dude. He gonna be sorry when I catch him too."

"Yeah, let's roll," his friend said.

The dudes went on out of the alley, and we stood there trembling, until we were certain the thugs weren't coming back. When the coast was completely clear, we went to my house. We stood on the porch because Brian said he didn't want to go inside.

"I'm just gonna go. I don't think I'm gonna be a good person to hang with this evening."

"Okay," I said, understanding how scared and humiliated he was still feeling. I leaned over and kissed him goodbye. I took my key out to open the door to the house.

As I was turning the lock, he whispered into my ear. "You know I love you, Maxine. I ain't never loved and I never will love nobody but you. Ain't nothing better than you in my life, and it never will be," he said, and took off down the steps. I stood there with my hand on the lock, trembling again, but it wasn't like before. I was trembling on the inside, quivering because I knew I had a good man. Most women would say that he told me he loved me because he could have been killed, but I knew he said it because he was going to live. We both were going to live, together forever. Because that's what happens when you have a *real* deep love. I knew he was going to be whispering those words to me for the rest of his life. Or at least I thought that. Now, who knows what I believe? I finished my day out with Great-aunt Freda and left while she was taking a nap in her huge recliner in her tiny living room.

As soon as I walked in the door, I learned that Demonee sure was gonna help me keep my mind off of Brian. She hadn't done a single thing in the living room since I left. The bowl of popcorn was still on the sofa, and popcorn kernels were everywhere. Everything in the room was still covered with a fine layer of white powder. After all the garbage she had put me through, it wasn't too much for me to ask her to clean up some. I flung my handbag on the sofa and headed for her room. I was about to rap on the door and yank it open when I heard muffled voices inside and giggles. I was shocked and mad. She knew she wasn't supposed to have nobody in my house when I wasn't there. A bad feeling hit me, that it might be that little boy she got in trouble with up on the roof. "What in the world is she doing? I know she know better than that," I said to myself. I was a little more open-minded about dating than my mama was, but I still thought boys in the bedroom was a no-no. I pushed the door open.

"Demonee, I know you ain't completely lost your mind up in here," I said, and pushed the door open. I paused, completely stunned. There wasn't a little boy after all. There was Demonee and some little girl with shapely legs sitting on the bed holding hands. They dropped hands and broke apart when they saw me. I got confused and uncomfortable, though I wasn't entirely sure why.

"We weren't doing nothing, Maxine," Demonee burst out.

"Weren't doing what? Demonee, what's going on? You know you ain't supposed to have no company without me being here."

"We weren't doing nothing. We was just about to listen to some CDs," she said.

"I don't care what you doing, Demonee. You ain't supposed to be doing it without my permission!" I said.

"I better go. I'll see you in school," the girl said, getting up and grabbing the CDs off the bed. She glared at me and took off. As she went out the front door, I remembered who the little heifer was. She was that pretty little girl I saw in Ms. Hopkins's room the morning I went to thank her for not kicking Demonee out of school, the one that bumped into me, and then treated me like I should get out of *her* way. I turned back to Demonee.

"Maxine, I swear we wasn't doing nothing," Demonee said frantically.

"I don't know what you was doing, Demonee, but I know what you wasn't doing, cleaning up the living room like I told you."

"I'll get it done," she said.

"I know you will, and let me tell you something, Demonee. I don't want to come home and find nobody else in your room. Do you understand me?" I asked. I was sounding like my mother.

"I do. I promise, I won't," she said, and then completely broke down, water flowing out of her eyes. "I won't. I won't. I swear, Maxine, it won't happen anymore. Please don't throw me out. If you do, I won't have nowhere to go," she cried. "That's what my mama and my grandma did. My mama said she didn't even want me as her daughter no more. She said I did stuff that embarrassed her and my grandma said that too. That's why they sent me to live with my uncle. But he don't know nothing about why they was mad at me. I don't know either, Maxine. I ain't done nothing to hurt nobody. I just feel kind of different sometimes. I don't know why I feel that way. Please, Maxine, just don't tell my uncle!" she said, running over and grabbing me.

She threw herself onto me, crying and sobbing a whole room full of tears. While she was wailing, I honestly couldn't think of what was best to do or say. What was she actually talking about? I didn't know what to do, but I remembered back when Tia and her mama went through a bad situation the day her mama saw Tia and Doo-witty together. Her mama threw a fit, because she thought Doo-witty was too old, and too dumb for Tia. She acted a fool with her daughter, and Tia just up and ran away. She came by my house first that night, and my mama told her she couldn't stay because she didn't want Tia setting her troubles on our back porch. I didn't agree with Mama, but she was my mother, so I stood there without saying nothing and let her turn my best friend out in the streets. I remembered how scared Tia looked when she left my porch that evening. She was terrified, 'cause she didn't know where she would end up. Every time I think about what happened that night, I feel ashamed and angry with myself. I should have made Mama help. Instead, I just watched my Tia walk away. I didn't exactly know what was wrong with Demonee, but I was going to help her. I gently pushed her away from me. When I looked down, I saw my white dress was as wet as her face.

"Look, Demonee, I don't know what went on between you and your family, and what you going on about. But I'm tired," I said, softly pushing her braids away from her frightened eyes. "I been at Aunt Freda's all evening listening to her going on about some craziness my ex done told her. I ain't about to call and tell nobody nothing. And I ain't about to put nobody out on the streets. Now, that living room still looks the same way it looked before I left here. Get out there and do something about it. I'm gonna go take a nap. I'll talk to you when I get up," I said.

"Okay, I'll clean it up right now. I'll clean everything up," she said, flying to the living room.

I waited for a second, to see if Demonee was going to actually do what she was told this time. When I saw her pick up the popcorn bowl and head off to the kitchen, I went to my room. As soon as I got there, I walked over to my bed and fell on top of it. I turned over in the bed and heard the roar of the vacuum cleaner. The sound soon got softer and softer, and I let the quietness carry me away.

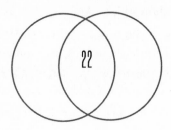

22

ast night I spent two hours talking with Demonee, though I'd rather have been strapped to a rocket and blasted off to Saturn. It was such an awkward thing to do because I really didn't know exactly what to talk to her about. Did I get on her for having company in my house when I had told her not to? Or get on her about the thing that was really bothering me, whatever was going on with her and that little girl? And something was going on, why else would she have freaked out when I got on her about the situation? In an effort to get around talking to her about whatever it was, I first tried stalling her out. I jumped her about not cleaning up when I asked her to. I went on forever about how hardheaded and lazy she was, and told her that I wasn't going to put up with it anymore. I expected her to throw twenty different versions of a fit but she kept her mouth shut. So after that, I started to really ride her about bringing strangers in my house without telling me first.

"Girl, you don't run nothing here but your mouth. You need my permission before anybody can come stepping up in here. Do you understand me?"

"Yes, ma'am," she said obediently—obediently. Can you believe it? I hated it. I wanted her to roll her eyes and tell me off, tell me that she lived here too, and she had every right to have a friend over. If she had said that, I would have gone off on her some more and we would have ended up in a big argument that could have lasted for days, and all the while I would have been happy because I wouldn't of had to go through any of that rough stuff with her.

Before we had the talk, I laid in bed staring up at the ceiling and trying to make my mind accept what I saw, Demonee holding hands with another girl. When I walked into her bedroom, that's exactly what I had seen. Only, what did it mean? She could have been trying to console the girl over something. I remember holding Tia's hand the day she found out she and Doo-witty was going to go to New York. She loved him so much, but she didn't want to go so far away from her family, and me. I told her everything was going to be okay, that she was starting a wonderful new life. Perhaps, that's what Demonee was doing with that little girl. Perhaps she was making her feel better about something frightening or sad in her life. That's what I kept in my mind when I finally got out of the bed and went to speak to her. When Demonee wouldn't take the bait and start an argument with me, I had no choice but to talk to her about what I had seen. I sat down on a folding chair across from her bed and looked at her. Sometime after she finished cleaning up, she had managed to paint her fingers with neon orange polish. The polish was splattered all over her nails and cuticles as if she had put it on with shaky hands.

"You ain't got no fingernail polish remover? Your nails is all raggedy-looking."

She looked down at her small, thin hands. "They don't look too bad, I guess. Besides, I don't think it matters all that much. You gonna kick me out, Maxine?" she asked with a serious face.

"Demonee," I started.

"That ain't my name," she said, shaking her head. "That ain't even what my mama named me."

"What?"

"It ain't my name. My mama and my grandma they just call me that. My grandma said that it suits me 'cause somebody like me just had to be created from some kind of demon. She said that nothing abnormal comes from God. He only makes pure and decent things."

"Pure and decent things?"

"Yeah, not like me. They say I ain't normal because of the things I been doing."

"What you been doing, Demonee? Tell me, 'cause I don't really know."

She looked down at her Hello Kitty bedspread and shrugged. "I don't know, sometimes I'm confused about stuff. You know when I'm with girls. I kinda like 'em, sometimes. You know, like maybe a girl would like a boy. That's why my grandma and mama say that the Devil or somebody created me," she said, sounding like she was about to sob.

"Demonee, don't start no crying, and look me in the eye when you talk," I said.

She looked at me. I saw that she had tears in the corner of her big brown eyes, but she was trying to keep them from falling out. I also saw something else. The face of a little girl that had been beat down by the people who was supposed to be lifting her up. How could a mother and grandma do that? I wasn't gonna knock her down too.

I sighed. "Look, Demonee, I think the Devil got a lot more to do than go around creating little hardheaded girls. There's plenty of major things, like wars and famines for him to create. Plus, you just know he the one making and shipping all them drugs out to folks in this neighborhood. Shoot, even my mama says he's bound to be in them gambling places out in Vegas, where they take money from all kinds of greedy and desperate folks. And just a few blocks down the street there's plenty for him to be doing over at that trashy Obsidian Queens men's club that my uncle Ernie likes to go to. So get over it girlfriend. I guarantee you, with all that going on, the Devil ain't even got time to think about making no little girls."

"You sure?" she asked, with lots of uncertainty in her voice.

"I'm sure. There's a whole bunch of real evil the Lord of Darkness got to do."

"My mama and grandma say it's all dark inside me, and can't no light get in," she said, picking up a stuffed puppy on her bed and hugging it. She looked so young to me when she did that. Like she was maybe seven instead of thirteen. Then it struck me that I had always seen her that way. I didn't want to just help her because I got booted out of my house once. I wanted to help her because from the moment I first saw her all I saw was a scared little kid, not a baby demon. She was just a little girl worried that everyone she met would reject her. I knew how that felt. I was even bigger when I was younger. Brian was the only guy that never teased me about my weight, and Tia was the only girl that never brought it up. However, the other guys and girls at school used to give me crap about it. I often didn't get invited to any of the cool slumber parties that the *IT* girls in our school would throw. I would sit at home while my home girl Tia got to go. Even after I slimmed down some, and got accepted by the kids, I still felt like I didn't belong at any of their gatherings. I was still Fat Maxine, the girl that nobody wanted to hang with. I knew how bad it feels being treated like dirt, simply because you're different.

I got up and sat next to her on the bed. "Demonee, you don't know my cousin Miles. I don't hang out with him much, but he used to come over to my old house sometimes. One time, he came over to borrow a DVD player."

"He ain't got one of his own?"

"Well, it's a long story, but basically it's because his daddy was a hardcore thug, and plain filth."

"That's why he ain't got no DVD player?"

"Yeah, in a roundabout way. You see Miles's daddy was a really bad person. He beat the mess out of Miles's mother while she was carrying him, and on the day Miles was born, instead of being at the hospital, his daddy was out robbing a little restaurant in they hood. The restaurant was owned by an older couple who was raising their only granddaughter. I don't know what all happened the morning Miles's daddy went in there, but I heard that the old man did what little he could to stop him from taking their money. Miles's daddy got mad and shot the man, his wife, and his granddaughter. The granddaughter wasn't but fourteen."

"His daddy did that?" she asked, shocked.

"Yeah. Great-aunt Freda said Miles came into this world covered with the blood of them three innocent people his daddy killed. And that's pretty much what everybody thought. From the time Miles was born, people said that he carried his daddy's evil seed. They was harsh on him when he was kid, but as he grew up people started noticing that Miles was a sweet, gentle soul. He would never harm anybody, and he would give you all the clothes in his closet, if you asked for them. That's what happened to his DVD player. He gave his DVD player to the afternoon day care center at his church. They always short on funding because they give cheap or free day care to poor women at the church."

"So that means he's a good guy?"

"Yeah, that's exactly what it means. See, Demonee, just because somebody say something don't mean it's true. Everybody thought that Miles was bad or was gonna turn out bad because his daddy was trash. They saw darkness in him, even though he really was full of light."

"Oh," she said. "You mean I ain't all black inside just because my mama and grandma said it?"

"Naw, you just black on the outside, like me," I said.

She was deep in thought for a moment, hugging her stuffed animal to her. "I don't know if that's true, Maxine," she said in a bit. "I ain't good like your cousin Miles. I don't do nothing nice for people like he does. Maybe my mama is right. It probably ain't nothing but bad in me."

"It ain't bad to like somebody, Demonee. If it is, everybody in the world is bad, because most people have somebody they care for. Look, at your age you don't even know nothing about nothing. Girls your age got all kinds of weird feelings running through them. It's okay to feel different about things—about girls. Because who knows what you will feel a couple of years from now."

"You mean maybe I won't like to hold hands with them."

"Maybe you won't," I said.

"And maybe I won't go to hell, like my mama say I will."

"Look, Demonee, mamas don't always know how to deal with things. Grandma's don't either. Sometimes they just don't know how to handle stuff. They try, but they end up saying dumb or hurtful things. You're not dark or a demon. You're just a little girl trying to figure out what's what. Right now the only thing you should be worrying about is getting your grades up in school. Just concentrate on that, and while you're doing that, whatever you're feeling or not feeling for girls or *boys* will sort itself out."

"I don't feel nothing but dumb around boys," she said.

"Me too. I felt dumb around every boy I ever met, except Brian. He was different."

"How did you know?"

"He always looked at me like I was covered with diamonds, like I was the most expensive thing he could ever get."

"So how come ya'll broke up?"

"I don't know. Maybe we didn't, at least I didn't. Love is difficult, Demonee, it don't matter who you with. That's why you got to be certain about who you give your heart to—and when you old enough, everything else."

"But will I go to hell if I give it to someone like me?"

"I'm not sure, and I don't exactly know how you get to hell, but I'm pretty certain throwing your own child out on the streets is pretty high on the list."

"You think so?" she asked, all wide-eyed.

"I'll bet you anything," I said.

She looked relieved. "That's good to know."

"Yeah, it is, but that don't mean you get to do whatever you want. I don't want to see any girls or boys in your room. That kind of behavior can't go on."

"I told you, Maxine, we wasn't doing nothing. I mean, I don't even know what we was supposed to do."

"You was supposed to be cleaning the living room up, and she was supposed to not be in my house. So, the next time I catch that little heifer in my house without my permission you and she is gonna be in a whole world of trouble."

"Her name ain't heifer, it's Petal," she said.

"Whatever, you just do what I told you to do and keep that little fast girl out of my house."

"She ain't fast," she snapped.

"She ain't slow either. Otherwise, she wouldn't be teaching you to do things the wrong way."

"How do you know Petal coming here was her idea?" she said defensively.

"I know, because if it was your idea you would have said so a long time ago. You wouldn't let me blame her for something she didn't do. Now I'm through talking. I don't want no foolishness in my house, not if you want to stay here with me. Do you understand me?"

"Yes ma'am," she said, switching back to her obedient tone.

"Good," I said. I got up to leave her room. "Demonee, what's your real name?" I asked.

"It don't matter," she said, and shrugged again.

"It matters to me."

"It's Desmona. I was named after my grandfather Desmond and my grandma Mona."

"Is that what you want me to call you from now on?"

She thought about it for a few seconds. "Naw, I'm used to Demonee. You might as well keep calling me that."

"Are you sure?"

"Yeah," she said.

I left her room and went back to mine. After a long soak in the hot tub I went to sleep that evening tossing an' turning like I was sleeping in a bed filled with pushpins.

When I woke up this morning, I fixed Demonee's breakfast and stayed in the kitchen until she finished and took off. Now ten minutes later, I'm sitting in front of the tube trying to figure out if I handled everything the right way. I hadn't even asked her why she thought she liked girls. Why was she into them? How did they make her feel? Was it the same way I felt when I was with Brian? I mean, could another girl really make you feel like that? A while back when the janitor said he thought she and Destiny were up on the roof with a couple of boys, Demonee kept insisting that she wasn't with a boy. Now I know it was probably true. The janitor said that the boys ran off, so I doubt if he got a good look at them. A girl with a big T-shirt, baggy jeans, and a cap or hat could easily pull off being a boy, especially at Demonee's age, where nobody has much on top. So I'm pretty certain the boy on the roof was actually Petal, Demonee's little friend, or potential girlfriend. Man, I wasn't expecting that. I didn't see no signs at all, if there were signs. I mean, was there any way for you to tell if a girl was thinking about going that way? When I was in junior high, if a girl cut her hair short and played sports, some fool was liable to say that she was different and make her life a living hell.

I didn't like that little girl, Petal. She just seemed like bad news. She was good at doing the wrong thing and leaving Demonee to take the fall for it. She had run off like somebody had told her a bomb was about to go off in Demonee's room. She didn't even try to help Demonee out. She should have tried to explain things to me. That's what somebody who cares about you does. I know, because one time me and Brian were fooling around at Great-aunt Freda's while she was visiting a neighbor. To our surprise, Mama stopped by to bring Great-aunt Freda some fresh peaches she had bought on sale and caught me and Brian messing around on the couch. We weren't actually doing too much, but it was clear that we weren't just studying like we was supposed to be doing.

Mama hit the roof. "Maxine, I know you ain't disrespecting your Great-aunt Freda in this house, cause if you are I'm gonna whip your behind good!" she yelled, barging into the living room.

"Well, you gonna have to whip me also, because whatever disrespecting she was doing I was doing it too," Brian said.

"What? Boy, don't let your mouth start something your behind can't stand. I really will whip anybody's behind in this house that gets on my nerves, and don't think I won't. Now you take your chocolate butt home where you belong!" Mama yelled with her hands on hips.

Brian kissed me goodbye and headed out of the room.

"That boy is out of his mind if he thinks he can talk to me like that!" Mama said, fuming. She ran to the door and let her eyes shoot daggers into Brian's back. Then she came and gave me her standard lecture about being careful with boys.

"Maxine, I know you know better," she started. As usual I tuned the rest out. I couldn't stop thinking about how Brian had told her that he was willing to take a punishment for me. Brian didn't just run off and not say anything like Petal. What was up with that? Naw, I didn't like her at all. If Demonee was gonna have a crush on a girl, I rather she have a crush on someone else. I snapped off the TV and went to look for my backpack in my room. Then out of habit I checked De-monee's room to make sure she had made her bed before she took off. When I came back to the living room, I stopped dead in my tracks.

Brian's daddy had let himself in. He was standing next to the TV, looking over my marketing homework. He had on a jet-black business suit and white shirt and black tie. I knew he was probably on his way to work, but he looked as if he could be going to a funeral. Did he find out she had been kicked out of school for a second time?

"You've answered one of your questions wrong. Instead of sending out flyers, the shop owner should have taken out a quarter-page ad in a local newspaper. It would have brought him three times the amount of customers and pretty soon paid for itself. Most people just toss away flyers that are placed on their cars."

"Oh," I said.

"Yes, that's generally the way it works, and even if they don't toss them, some people make a mental note to not shop at a place, because finding a flyer attached to their windshield made them angry."

"I'll remember that," I said.

He looked around. "Is Demonee here?" he asked.

"Naw, she went to school a little while ago."

"Good, I'm glad to hear that. That's just the way I like it. So, you haven't had any trouble out of her lately. She's been doing everything she supposed to do?"

"Yes, sir. Demonee is doing great. She been doing fine in school. I ain't had to get on her about nothing at all," I lied, my palms starting to sweat.

"Is that right? No more incidents with boys on the roof, and that kind of nonsense? That's wonderful," he said, but there was a hint of suspicion in his voice.

"Yeah, it is wonderful," I said, rubbing my sweaty hands together. "I think she's got a real chance of getting everything straightened out."

"So, has she been making any friends? I mean, besides that little girl Destiny? Does she have any new friends?"

"I guess so, but she don't bring them home, so I really wouldn't know," I said, confused by the question. I hadn't known him to ask about Demonee's friends before.

"Oh, she doesn't bring any friends home?"

"No, she pretty much hangs out with them at school. Why?"

"Oh no reason, I just wondered. I said good morning to your neighbor, Ms. Bartel across the street. She told me she saw a little girl come out of here last night. So I just wondered if Demonee had a new friend?"

"What, oh that little girl? Naw, she was just a kid trying to sell some of them candy bars that the kids be selling this time of year. I told her I would buy a couple, so she came in to wait. As soon as I gave her the money she took off."

"Did she?"

"Yeah, she said her mama and sister was waiting for her down at the other end of the block."

"Oh, Ms. Bartel said that she just ran off."

"Ms. Bartel probably couldn't see them, because she don't see that well no more."

"You're right. She is almost eighty. At her age you are bound to make some mistakes." He said, looking at me intently.

"Me and Demonee done already ate the chocolate. I can't even offer you any," I said, and followed it up with a nervous laugh.

"I don't need any. I'm always trying to watch my figure anyway," he said, and laughed too.

"That's good, I probably should be watching mine as well."

He looked me over. "You're okay, but you could work out some more. Get a little muscle tone. I'll bring you some weights by and an instruction video." He glanced over at Demonee's door. "So you say she's doing all right?" he asked. "She's not getting in any trouble at school and she's acting like a normal girl for a change?"

"Yeah."

"Good. You know, Maxine, that's one reason why I wanted Demonee to live with you. I thought having her stay here would be a good thing. You're her age, and I figured you could teach her how to be a regular girl. My mama couldn't do anything with her, and her mother certainly couldn't. She's completely incompetent. She couldn't teach Demonee how to be a lady, and she has several more daughters that she's probably ruining right now," he said, shaking his head. "Anyway, I have to get to work. I just stopped to see how things were going."

"Yes sir," I said.

"You know the last time I was here there was a lot of drama and shouting. I don't want to have to come in here like that again. And I won't have to, not as long as Demonee does what she's supposed to do and handles herself like any average normal girl would do. You can make sure of that, can't you, Maxine?" he asked.

"Yes sir. I can make sure Demonee stays out of trouble," I said.

He nodded. "All right, because you're her last chance. I'm trying to do right by the child, but I'm not fooling with her anymore if you can't straighten her out."

"I know. It's all cool, sir. Thanks for everything," I said.

I followed him to the front door and latched it after he was gone. I breathed a sigh of relief. Damn, why did he suddenly pop over to see how Miss Thing was doing? Man, if only I had left the house a little earlier. Staying at home later just gives everybody the opportunity to come running at me with something. Speaking of running, what the heck was Ms. Bartel doing telling Demonee's uncle who was running out of my house? She was one nosy old cow, if ever there was one. She lived right across the street from me and all she did was sit on her front porch minding other people's business. I

walked over to the sofa and picked up my marketing homework. He was right, the merchant wouldn't have earned a
large profit by using the flyers.

I took my black ballpoint out of my hair and scratched
out the old answer. He knows, I thought, as I wrote in the new
answer. He's always known. All that junk about me making
certain that Demonee was like other little girls didn't have
anything to do with her school behavior, it had to do with her
crushing on girls.

Demonee told me last night that her uncle didn't know
why her mama and grandma was angry with her. Bless her
heart, she doesn't have a clue. Her uncle knew a long time ago.
There's no way her grandma would have kept that a secret.
Her grandma had to let Demonee's uncle know why she didn't
want Demonee in her house. She also had to let him know
why Demonee's mother was trippin' over her too. I knew
enough about Brian's family to know exactly how the conversation went.

"Me and her mama done talked, and we can't have that
kind of weird stuff in our houses. It's a shame before God. I'm
a Christian woman. I don't know nothing about that kind of
mess. She can't do that stuff here," Demonee's grandmother
probably told Demonee's uncle, while Demonee was packing
her bags.

Demonee's uncle had passed her on to me like her mother
had passed her to her grandmother, like her grandmother had
passed her to him. To her family she was like a virus, and they
kept passing her from family member to family member hoping that someone would cure her. I didn't know if I should be
flattered that they still considered me a part of their family or

pissed, but what difference did it make? Could I really change what was going on inside of Demonee? Did I or anybody else have that power over her?

I switched my answer on my homework and stuck the folder into my backpack. Then I clicked off the TV and went out the door. As soon as I got outside, I saw Ms. Bartel sitting on her front porch swing, staring at my house. I waved to her and realized that from the beginning she had probably been keeping an eye on me and Demonee, just waiting for a chance to tell Demonee's uncle about any unnatural behavior she had seen. That bothered me, but not as much as realizing my true purpose. I was not only supposed to make certain Demonee didn't screw up in school, I was supposed to make her into what her family thought was a real girl. What was that? I thought that dressing pretty, keeping a clean house, making nice lunches and dinners is what a real girl did, a girl that any guy would want to be with, and then my man took off with a girl that obviously didn't care about any of those things. So, I wasn't even sure anymore what a real girl was. How could I teach Demonee to be something that I didn't know how to be myself?

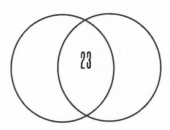

23

During lunch today I suddenly got the urge to go to the library and check out some books that would give me a little information on what Demonee might be going through. I wanted a little more help dealing with her situation, so after I finished eating my slice of cheese pizza, I headed to the library. There were only four students studying when I went in. However, there might as well have been four hundred. When I walked up to the counter and whispered to Sean Ralston, the library assistant, that I wanted a book about gay feelings, it felt like every last one of those kids and all their classmates were standing right behind me, staring at my back. I was grateful when Sean beckoned for me to follow him to the other side of the library. "This is all we got. You want something for a boy or a girl," he said, stopping in front of a small rolling cart. I looked and saw seven or eight books and DVDs.

"A girl, I guess," I said.

He smiled. "Girl, don't act so nervous. It's going to be okay. There's nothing wrong with being different," he whispered.

"I'm not, and I don't even know if anybody is. I mean, not for real. I—I just don't know what I'm looking for, what I need," I said.

"Don't worry girl. I can hook you up. I read or watch everything that comes in here." He pulled out a DVD. "This one is really good," he said.

He pointed to our tiny media room. "You can watch it back there, if you want to," he said.

"Okay," I told him.

I took the DVD and went over to an empty DVD player in the back of the room. As soon as I sat down in front of the TV, I couldn't make up my mind about playing the DVD or taking it home. I didn't really want to take it home. I wanted to watch it in the media room, only I was scared that some big mouth would come in while I was viewing it. Everybody in school knew that I used to live with my husband, and it wouldn't take long for a rumor to spread about me. "Maxine's husband dumped her because she likes the honeys," they would all say. No, it was better for me to check the DVD out and take it home. I placed it underneath my backpack on the table and pulled out a novel I was supposed to be reading for my English class. It was really boring, about a group of boys who get stranded on an island. I tried reading it for a while, but my eyes slowly got heavy and I went to sleep. I'm sure I was snoring away when I felt someone shake my shoulder.

"Maxine, dang, you sleep or what?" Madona asked.

I sat up straight in my chair and rubbed my eyes. "Naw, I'm not asleep. What do you want?"

"I seen you in here. It's been a while since we hung out. I just wanted to catch up."

"Yeah, I'm sorry that I haven't been hanging with you. I'm just stressed out from dealing with Brian and Demonee."

"I hear you. What's up now?"

"The same junk. I found out Brian has been messing with that Shell girl for a long time."

"He admitted it?"

"Naw, I haven't even said anything to him yet."

"Why?"

"I don't know. I guess I don't want to hear him say it to my face. Shell's not the first girl that was pushing up on him. She just the first that he actually took off with. I should have known there was a big connection there. I should have been able to see it with my own eyes, without anybody's help."

"You didn't want to see it."

"Naw, and I still don't. Anyway, that's enough about my man."

"Do you still call him *your* man?"

"Yeah, I guess I always will, until I feel like he's gone for good."

She rolled her eyes. "I wish Bonita's boyfriend was gone for good," she said.

"Trying a spell didn't work, huh?"

"Naw, it's worse than ever. She's still sneaking around with that fool, and the other night she didn't even come home. If Mama would have known that, she woulda blew the roof off of the house."

"Shoot, I'll bet she would have. What is Bonita thinking?"

"She ain't. That fool she dating got her head all turned around, and every time I say something to her she gets pissed at me. Maxine, I'm really worried. I ain't never seen her act this crazy."

"Well people do crazy things for love. I know I sure did."

"You mean marrying Brian or lying about being pregnant?"

"I don't know. Sometimes I think I mean letting Brian go."

Madona hunched her shoulders, grabbed the tail of her oversized T-shirt. "Maxine, I'm just a big ole tomboy who likes to wear huge shirts and jeans. I don't do nothing with my hair, and the popular boys ain't never been into me. If Brian would have been my man, I would have been a fool for him too. He certainly would have been my whole world. But you know what? I would have kicked his behind out too. I would have thrown him right out, if I found out he was trying to be a player with another chick."

"For real?"

"Yeah, I ain't telling you nothing but the truth."

"Thanks. I wish Bonita would listen to you sometimes."

"Me too. I'm really scared Bonita is the one gonna end up pregnant like Shell, or in some other kind of trouble. This dude she hanging with, he used to be into some bad stuff and I think he still might be."

"You know that for sure?"

"Naw, but I been hearing things around the hood, stuff about gangs and drugs. You know, what some of the thugs in our neighborhood be into."

"Aw, no, for real?"

She looked really upset. "I don't know. I don't even want

to talk or stress about it anymore," she said, waving the topic away with her hand. "I'm just gonna hope she dumps this loser soon. I'm going to class. Can we hang out this evening? I promise I won't ask you to do any spells."

"That would be nice. I'll drop by after I fix Demonee some dinner."

"Okay, I'll see ya later," she said, walking away.

When she was gone, I decided to watch the DVD. It was pretty good. It gave statistics on how many girls under the age of eighteen were sure of their different feelings, but I don't remember how many. What I did remember was how the friends of the girl in the DVD treated her when they found out she was gay. She was living in a small town. She was very pretty and popular, like Demonee's annoying little friend Petal seems to be. When some of her friends found out she was different, they started treating her like she was a smelly dead skunk on the side of the road. When they saw her coming down the halls, they would go to the other side as if being near her would cause them some distress, or they wouldn't even speak to her at all. Then there were the friends who went out of their way to hurt her.

I don't know how the girl in the DVD put up with it. She was obviously really strong. A part of me was worried that when the time came, Demonee wouldn't be as strong. She had already been beat down by her own family. How would she pull herself up if she started getting beat down at school too? I hoped it never came to that. I don't think either one of us were ready for Demonee's feelings to be exposed to the entire school.

* * *

After the DVD, I sat bored through my last two classes and headed home. When I walked by Bonita's and Madona's place, I considered checking to see if Bonita was there yet and soon changed my mind. Running into Bonita would not be a good thing right now. I didn't have anything to say to her except get on her butt about how she was ditching her classes and treating her sister. The day that I spoke to her in the hall I was really hoping that she would shape up, but she was screwing up now more than ever. I hardly ever saw her in class anymore, but what could I do about it? Her sister and I were both trying to get her to see reason, but only she could control what she wanted to do with her life. I made a note in my head to try and talk to her again about it, then I passed her house and went straight home. When I got there, Demonee wasn't at home yet, and the phone was ringing off the hook. I threw my book bag down and ran to get it. My mood brightened some. It was my girlfriend Tia.

"Hey, girl," I said. We got started on a friendly conversation when the doorbell rang. "I'm coming!" I hollered out.

"I gotta go girl. Demonee is home, and I need to talk to her about something important before she stomps off to her room and slams the door shut like she usually does. After that, it's a whole lot of drama to get her to act like she got some sense and talk to me," I said to Tia.

"That's because she ain't got none," Tia said playfully.

"True that," I said. The bell sounded again. "I gotta go," I repeated.

"Wait, when you coming out to visit me and Doo-witty? We'll pay for it. You can get some real cheap tickets off the Internet now."

"I know you can, but what am I gonna do with Demonee

while I go away? I got a kid to think about. I love you and I'll call later," I said, and hung up.

I dashed to the door, expecting to see Demonee without her key again. To my surprise it was Uncle Ernie standing at the door in a pair of baggy black jeans and an NBA shirt. I sighed. He was the last person I wanted to deal with right now, but I still owed him big for Demonee, so I opened the door with a smile.

"Dang, girl. Why it take you so long to get to the door? You move slower than a three-legged blind dog."

"How do you know? You ain't never seen no three-legged blind dog."

"Yes I have. My girlfriend Quanda's grandfather got one. It's one of them little hairy dogs. He lost his leg being fool enough to start a fight with a pit bull and he lost his eyesight when one of them mares her grandfather keeps on the farm kicked him in the head."

"Ouch, for real?"

"Yeah, for real, and he slow, cause it takes him forever to get anywhere, limping and running into stuff at the same time."

"Quit lying, that ain't even funny," I said.

"Yeah it is, and you know it," he said laughing.

I opened the door wider for him to come in. He stepped inside and started looking around.

"What's up with you?" I asked.

"I was just looking for that little daughter of evil you live with. I don't want her coming out of her room and putting some kind of hex on me."

"Shut up," I said. "Besides, if you worried about getting a spell put on you, you'd be better off staying away from my friend Madona. She the one been running round lately trying to put hexes on people."

"Really, that twin girl you always hanging with? She into them black arts?" he asked, with a shocked face.

"Naw, not really. It's just some stuff going on between her and her sister, and a new boyfriend."

"Oh, that's a shame, but I can't be putting her troubles in my basket today," he said. He walked over to the table and sat down on it.

"Don't be putting your behind on the coffee table," I said.

"Why not? Girl, quit trippin'. I know you ain't trying to act like this warehouse liquidation furniture come out of an antique shop or something."

"Just get off my table, please, Uncle Ernie," I said, and laughed.

He hopped off and settled on the sofa. "You know, you need to be talking better to me. I'm your elder. I used to help change your diapers," he said.

"Yeah, right. It'll be a blizzard in Houston if you ever change a diaper."

"All right, all right, but speaking of diaper changes, that's what I'm here for. My ex, Rayena, said she gonna drop Bethany and Netta off at my house on Saturday. She been bitchin' at me all over the place, saying I need to spend some time with my children and be a real daddy, or something like that."

"Something like that," I said.

"Don't start nothing with me, Maxine," he said.

I giggled.

"Anyway, I just wanted to get Rayena off the phone, so I

told her I would keep them all Saturday and bring them back home on Sunday morning."

"That's nice."

"Oh no, it ain't. Shoot girl, you know I ain't about to do that. That's why I'm coming to you. I need somebody to keep Bethany and Netta while I go to the clubs Saturday night. It's a lot of fine women in them clubs on the weekend, and I don't intend to disappoint none of them. What I'm saying is, I can't be held back by kids."

"But I can."

"Yeah, well, what else you got to do? You ain't old enough to get in nowhere good, and I know you sho' ain't fool enough to be going nowhere on Saturday night and leave Hell Girl in the house all alone."

"No, I probably won't, and stop calling her names like that," I snapped. "Her name is Desmona."

"Desmona, since when?"

"Since the day she came out of her mama's belly. It's her real name."

"So why everybody call her Demonee?"

"I don't know. The name just popped up somehow. She just got stuck with it."

"Oh, that's too bad, but what about my girls? You gonna keep them or what?"

"I'll keep them until twelve o'clock, that's just about when I go to bed."

"Until twelve? Girl, most of the clubs don't even catch on fire until then!"

"Well, you better find one that strikes a match a little earlier, cause I'm dropping them off on your doorstep between

12:00 a.m. and 12:30. And if you ain't there, I'll be taking them over to they mama's house, and I know you don't want that."

"Naw, I sho' don't. But damn, that's cold."

"Ice cold," I said.

"Well, I guess it's better than nothing. At least I'll get a little break from all that hollering and screaming for a little while. I mean, I can only take so much, and man won't I be glad when Netta finally gets potty trained."

"Me too," I said, remembering the last time I kept Bethany and Netta. I had to change Netta every hour. I never seen a baby fill a diaper so much.

"Well, I best be going before hurricane Desmona comes ashore," he said, getting up and going to the door. I couldn't help it, I had to chuckle at what he said. I opened the door and we both went out. On the porch we spotted Demonee coming up the sidewalk with Petal.

"Oh no. Here comes dangerous high winds," Uncle Ernie said, and I couldn't even tell him to hush because it was true.

Damn, why was Demonee bringing that little Petal girl back to my house so soon? I glanced across the street. Thank God Ms. Bartel wasn't there. She was probably in the house looking at her afternoon court shows. It was the only other thing I knew she was interested in more than other folks affairs. "Thank God for *Divorce Court* and Judge Alex," I mumbled under my breath.

"What did you say?" Uncle Ernie asked.

"Nothing. Bye," I told him. He left the porch and took off down the street. When he came upon Demonee and Petal, he held up two crossed fingers like he was trying to keep a couple of vampires away.

"That's so funny I forgot to laugh," I heard Demonee say. Uncle Ernie just laughed at himself and hurried past her.

I closed the front door and went back inside. My plan was ruined. I wanted to talk to Demonee again about the whole liking girls thing, and about what I saw on the DVD. Now I would have to put all that aside because of Petal. I sighed and went into the kitchen to get a drink of anything I could find and something to snack on, even though I wasn't very hungry. I took my time mixing some chocolate syrup and cold milk, and making a peanut butter and sliced strawberry sandwich. When I came back to the living room, I didn't see either one of them. I went straight away to her room, hoping that I wouldn't find them in a repeat of what I had seen before. I knocked on the door, heard the bed creek, and I groaned.

"What is it?" Demonee asked.

"Open up the door and come see," I said. A few second later the door opened. I was relieved to see nobody holding hands and Petal was sitting in the chair next to Demonee's bed. She was wearing a pink tank top and miniskirt set that said Queen Bee on the tank in gold letters. I had seen a ton of tanks like it on girls before, but this one definitely suited the wearer. When she saw me, she batted her thick black lashes. I guess she was trying to charm me or something. It was a good move. She couldn't run because I was blocking the door. When you can't run, seduce. Petal already knew that at thirteen.

"What you want, Maxine?" Demonee asked.

"I just came to say hey, and see what ya'll was up to," I said.

"We was just talking, that's all," Demonee said, defensively.

"Fine, just leave the door open while you do that," I said.

"Why?"

"Because, if all you doing is talking, it ain't gonna matter if you doing it with the door open or closed," I said.

She gave me a mean look, like she wanted to fight about it, but thought better. "Okay, whatever," she said.

Petal just smiled or smirked. I couldn't tell the difference.

Demonee walked back over to the bed and sat down. As she did, I noticed a new gold bracelet dangling from her left arm. I walked into the room and caught her wrist. "What's this?" I asked.

"Nothing, just a bracelet," she said. She moved her arm away, and I got it again.

"Demonee, is this real?" I asked.

"No," she said.

I twisted it around on her arm and studied it more. She was lying. I didn't have much, but I knew real gold when I saw it. It wasn't the cheap 10k junk either. It was good gold, and when I looked closer, I saw a small diamond in it. "Girl, you lying. This thing is real. Where did you get it?" I asked.

"Petal bought it for me," she said.

"Not this she didn't. Ain't no kid got money to buy nothing like this," I said.

"Petal does, and she did buy it."

"No, she didn't. This ain't none of that cheap crap that they sell at the flea market. Demonee, where you get this from? Don't lie to me. That would not be a good idea," I said.

"I ain't lying."

"Yes you are, and I'm gonna ask you one more time where you got it."

"Okay, okay, Ms. Hopkins gave it to me," she said.

"Ms. Hopkins, what for? Demonee, I know that lady ain't gave you nothing like this. Ain't no teacher gonna give a student something like this, so you still lying."

"I ain't lying. She did give it to me. She said it was because I was trying harder in her class, doing better."

"So she just hauled off and gave you something like this cause you been doing your math homework."

"Yeah, she did!" Demonee shouted.

"Don't be hollering at me, little girl!" I yelled back.

"Well, stop calling me a liar. Cause Ms. Hopkins gave it to me. You can ask Petal. She was there."

"Yes ma'am, she did. She does stuff like that sometimes. It don't cost her nothing. She says her daddy owns a jewelry shop," Petal spoke up.

"Is that right? Her father owns some kind of jewelry shop, so she can just give her students bling," I said.

"That's right," Petal said.

"You cracked if you think I believe that, little girl," I told her. "It don't make no sense at all. Ain't no teacher gonna give nothing like this to a student. I don't care who her daddy is or what he do. Take that thing off and give it to me, right now," I said to Demonee.

"No, it's mine—she gave it to me," Demonee said, jerking her hand away. I snatched her wrist.

"Take it off now and give to me!" I yelled.

She yanked it off and threw it at me. "You make me sick," she said.

"If you sick, take some Pepto-Bismol and get better, cause I'm gonna take this back to Ms. Hopkins and find out what's going on. And if I find out you done stole this from her or any-body else you gonna be in big trouble. And you can believe that," I said angrily.

"I ain't gonna be in nothing, 'cause I didn't steal from no-body," Demonee said, glaring at me.

"Well, then it sho' won't be no problem with me finding that out for myself," I said.

I picked the bracelet up off the bed and placed it in my pocket.

"That's not fair. It's mine," Demonee said, starting to cry.

"Yeah right," I said, turning to leave the room.

"Don't worry about her. You my girlfriend, I'll hook you up with something better than that, Demonee," Petal said. Then she glared at me. "It ain't your bracelet to take; it's hers. You ain't her mama. You don't have the right to take nothing from her," she said. It caught me off guard for a second. I know the little mare didn't think I was gonna let her talk some smack to me in my own place.

"I got a right to do anything I want to do in my house, and Demonee knows that. She also know I don't put up with no trash-talking from some want-to-be-grown little girls," I said.

"I'm not a little girl," she told me. "And you ain't that much older than me."

"But I am older, and this is my place, so you get out my of house, before I smack them pretty eyes you got clean out of your head," I said.

"I wish you would," she told me, and got up in my face as if *she* could hit me.

"Petal, don't start no fight," Demonee pleaded.

"She better not start nothing, 'cause I'll lay her little behind flat!" I said. Then I came back to myself. "Just go. I don't want you in my house anymore," I said, pointing to the door.

"Whatever, I don't want to be here anyway," she said, and left the room. She went out the front door and slammed it hard. I had a good mind to go after her and give her the slap she deserved. Instead, I looked up at the living room clock. Demonee's school had only been out about forty minutes. If I went fast, I could probably catch Ms. Hopkins before she left her class.

"You didn't have to talk to her like that," Demonee cried.

"If I had my way, I wouldn't have ever talked to her at all. Demonee, I don't know what's wrong with that little girl, but I don't want her in my house. She got some serious issues."

"No, you just don't like her 'cause she likes me," she sobbed.

"I don't like her because every time she walks in a place, trouble comes with her, and that ain't got nothing to do with who she likes or don't like. That's just a fact. Now, dry them tears up and get your homework done. I'll be back in a little while," I said, and took off straight to Ms. Hopkins.

Ms. Hopkins just confirmed what I already suspected about the bracelet, and it really upset me.

"I'm not certain where this came from, but I sure didn't give it to Demonee. I'm happier with her these days. She's been studying a little harder, and her grades have been coming up. I'm pleased, but not so pleased that I would give her such a nice gift. I sometimes give my students ten-dollar gift certificates, but that's about it. Where do you think it came from?" she asked.

"I don't know. She said you gave it to her. I figured it was a lie, but I still had to ask," I said.

"I would have too," she said, placing a stack of notebook papers in the chair next to her neatly organized desk. "Maxine, I can't tell you where that bracelet came from, but I agree. It probably is stolen. If I were you, I would let her uncle know immediately. If she gets caught taking something like this, she could end up in a lot of trouble. This is the type of thing that usually gets a child put in the criminal justice system."

"I know, and I can't even figure out how she got her hands on it. I mean, it's real gold—good gold. I looked inside. Its says 18K."

"I saw that too. And I don't know where it came from, but my father owns a couple of pawn shops. Kids are always trying to buy or pawn jewelry there. You'd be surprised how easily kids can get their hands on things they want."

"I guess. Thanks. I just needed to know," I said.

"You're welcome. Maxine, you've been here twice to speak with me. It's almost as if you're Demonee's guardian and her uncle isn't," she said.

It caught me off guard. "No, her uncle is the one who takes care of her. He's just busy. So Demonee stays with me sometimes. I promised to look after her while he's away. I'm here because I don't want him to come back and find out that she's in trouble again," I said.

"It's good that you're looking out for her. Do you mind if I ask you how old you are? You seem pretty young."

"I just turned twenty. Well, I better go," I said, trying to get out before she quizzed me further and found out the truth.

I was out the door, when something struck me. I turned back. "That little girl that Demonee is hanging with now—Petal. Is she as bad as I think she is? I mean, something don't set right with me about her."

She looked stunned by the question. "I can't really discuss too much about another student with you, but Petal can be difficult when she wants to be. You've seen that for yourself. She has issues. I think I mentioned that before. However, she is popular. She has a lot of friends. Sometimes that's good for a girl like Demonee, it gets her more acceptance, allows her to expand her social group."

"I guess, but I don't think it's like that between them. It's different. I don't think Petal is interested in Demonee meeting her friends. To be honest with you, I think she's interested in getting her in trouble. Anyway, thanks for your help," I said.

I took the bracelet and walked outside. In the hallway, I wanted so much to drop it in one of the aluminum trash cans, because I didn't want Demonee with it. If her uncle saw it, he would be asking all sorts of questions, and I didn't need that. Plus, there was something up with that bracelet. I wasn't gonna do anything with it until I figured everything out. I went straight home. When I got there, Demonee was sitting on the sofa waiting for me in her terry bathrobe and slippers.

"Demonee, what you got on your night clothes for already? You going to bed early?" I asked.

"I ain't going nowhere until you give me my bracelet back," she said.

"I ain't giving you nothing, and don't start that, Demonee," I said.

"It's my bracelet. You ain't had no right to take it."

"I had every right, and I did, so you might as well quit trippin' over it."

"I ain't trippin'. You trippin', Maxine, and you too much into my business," she said, wagging her finger at me.

"You ain't got no business, Demonee. Ain't nobody thirteen got business. What you got is a whole lot of trouble, if you keep pointing that skinny finger at me."

I walked over to the recliner across from her and sat down. She glared at me as if she wanted to pick up the chair and dump me out of it.

"Demonee, don't be staring at me as if you can put an evil eye on me," I said.

"Give me my bracelet back."

"No can do, sweetie. I'm not giving you jack."

"Why not, Ms. Hopkins gave it to me!"

"No she didn't, and you know it!" I said.

"Yes she did. She gave it to me 'cause I been doing good work."

"Not that good. Not good enough for this," I said, taking the bracelet out of my purse. "Besides, I spoke to her and she busted you out. She said she didn't give you a darn thing," I said, holding the bracelet up. She ran over to me like she was gonna snatch it. I threw it back in my purse.

"Give it to me! It's mine!"

"I'm not giving you nothing. I don't know what's up with this bracelet, but I do know that your uncle will be asking all kinds of questions if he sees it. He'll know that I ain't bought it, and you sure didn't. So get over it, sister, and go find something else to do," I said.

"I hate you, Maxine. You think you run everything!" she hollered.

"Not everything, just you," I said. "And by the way, since you got your night clothes on, why don't you take your behind to bed."

"Fine, at least I won't have to talk to you," she said, and stomped off toward her room. She slammed the door, and I sat there feeling happy the conversation was over. I took the bracelet out and looked at it again. It was wrong, and I felt it. It wasn't the feeling I got at all when Brian slipped a promise ring on my finger years ago. There's was love behind that ring, and a hope of something special to come. I didn't feel anything special was coming my way from Demonee's bracelet. It was trouble. I knew it the moment I saw it on her wrist, and nothing was gonna make me change my mind about that.

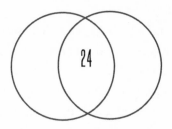

24

ditched school today. All I ever do is get on Demonee about going to class and making sure she does her work, but this morning I said to hell with it all and skipped my own classes. I needed to think about some things, and I couldn't do it while my Marketing teacher was going on and on about the importance of knowing your customers, so you could take care of their needs. Shoot, I needed my needs taken care of too. And right now what I needed was to be by myself, so I could pull my thoughts together. If I had a car, I would have driven down to the beach at Texas City or Galveston and sat by the ocean. That's what people did in the movies and on TV. When they needed to think, they went down to the ocean or seaside and spent hours just walking the warm beaches, staring into the cool blue waters. There was no way I could do that. I went to the backyard instead and pulled out the big inflatable pool that Uncle Ernie bought for when he brings one or two of his kids over. I hooked the water hose up to the kitchen sink and filled it with warm water. When the tub was full, I put on my Hawaiian print two-piece and sat down in it. The water was soothing. I let the comfort of it wash everything away. I was thinking of absolutely nothing at all when the back gate creaked. I looked up and saw Brian at the fence.

"Can I come in?" he asked. My whole soul jumped. I guess it's true. You never get over your first love.

"You already in," I said.

"Yeah, I guess you're right," he said, closing the gate behind him. He was looking good, in a short-sleeved, baby blue shirt, with a pair of navy slacks and a matching tie.

"Where you going all dressed up?" I asked. He shrugged his shoulders.

"Nowhere, just here," he said.

"You got all dressed up for me?"

"Something like that," he said. I didn't know what to make of his answer, so I just left it alone.

"How did you know I was here?" I asked. He walked over to the pool.

"I waited for you in front of the school all morning and you never showed up. I just figured if you wasn't in school, this was the only place you could be. What are you doing here? Don't get me wrong. I can stand here watching you lounging around in that swimsuit all day, but ain't you supposed to be in school?"

"Ain't you supposed to be somewhere else too?" I asked.

He grinned. "Yeah, probably, but you a trip, Maxine. You always trying to turn things around on folks. You always a step ahead of other people."

"Not lately," I said. He grabbed a plastic lawn chair next to the pool and pulled it up.

"What do you mean by that?" he asked. I hesitated for a moment, wondering if I should keep my thoughts to myself, but I decided against it. Brian had already kept one secret about Demonee. I figured he could keep two, and I really needed someone to talk things over with.

"Did you know that your cousin is into girls?" I asked.

"What cousin?"

"Demonee, did you know that she's been crushing on girls?" I asked.

His mouth flew open.

"She's into girls? I didn't know that. Ain't nobody told me nothing about it."

"Me either. I just came home the other day and caught her with some little girl in the house. They were in her bedroom."

"Doing what? Are you for real?" he asked.

"Did I ever lie to *you* about anything? And I don't know what they was doing. It looked kind of innocent, though. I think they were just holding hands. I didn't even think too much about it, until Demonee freaked out."

"Really? Damn. I wasn't expecting that at all," he said.

"Me either—I mean—I don't know what to think. I mean, she's too young to even know what she feels about anybody. Plus, you know how kids can be. Remember that girl Cassandra in junior high?"

"The girl who dressed like a boy and liked to play basketball?"

"Yeah, her. Remember what I said happened in the locker

room one day before gym class? A bunch of girls refused to change because she was there."

"'That freak is gonna be staring at us in our underwear,' one dumb girl said. Fortunately another girl busted her out. 'With your tiny boobs and flat behind, she won't be looking at much. Besides, who wants to see you in them raggedy drawers you always got on,' she said. The rest of us laughed and we *all* went into the dressing room. I was glad everything went down that way, but you know how it is. Kids who look or act different can get treated like a dog, or even get jacked up. You know how many kids get beat down for hardly anything at all?"

"Yeah, you right about that. There's always a girl or boy getting their butt kicked just because somebody decides that they don't like them. Anyway, man, I can't believe that my little cousin is leaning that way, and nobody didn't know it," he said, looking amazed.

"They knew, her mama and your grandma. That's the real reason why she here with me. They think she some kind of baby demon or something because she got different feelings."

"Lord, that don't surprise me none," he said. "My family is as backwater as they can get about stuff like that. One of my daddy's cousin's sons is gay. His father is one of those military guys that spent most of his life in the army, and when he found out he completely cut his son off, and so did the rest of the family. They stopped inviting him to any family gatherings and my uncle gets pissed at anybody who brings him up."

"You never told me that, but it don't surprise me either," I said.

"'Cause you know my family. So anyway, my aunt and

my grandma kicked Demonee out, and that's how she ended up with my daddy?"

"Naw, that's how she ended up with me. Your daddy ain't said nothing, but he knows too. That's why he put her off on me. I think he was hoping that I could turn her into what he thinks she's supposed to be. And, if I can't, it will be just one more excuse for him to let her go off into the system. Then nobody will have to worry about her shaming them."

He frowned. "That sounds like my dad too. He's a control freak, and when he can't control a situation, he just walks away."

"I guess that runs in the family, walking away."

"That was cold," he said.

"Yeah, it was. I'm sorry. I wasn't trying to go there."

"I know."

"Yeah, it's just because of Demonee."

"Maxine, you know that you're not really her mother. You're not supposed to be the one that saves her."

"Deep down I know that, but I'm just trying to do what I can. She ain't the kind of child that people want to take care of."

"I know," he said.

"Then you know that if she ends up in a home there won't be anyone there that cares what she has been through."

"Maybe her mama will. Maybe she'll wise up and be there for her."

"My mama didn't. Do I have to remind you that she wasn't there when I missed meals because my foster mom was too lazy to cook? She wasn't there when I didn't have clean clothes to go to school in, when I needed help with my math or reading, or when I got sick with chicken pox or the flu. She wasn't there for any of that stuff."

"I know," he said.

"Yeah, you know, and you know that there wasn't anything even wrong with me. Nothing that should have made my mama not give a damn about me. Now look at Demonee, with all her problems—do you really think that her mama will show up for her?"

"Naw, I guess she won't."

"That's for sure. It's why I'm just trying to make certain that she don't end up in a foster home, with nobody caring what she's doing, or how she's being treated."

"I'll care about Demonee, if you really want me to," he said.

"Desmona, that's her real name. Let's call her that for this conversation. You did know that was her name right?"

"Yeah, I knew. So what's been going on with her?"

"I don't know," I said, running my hand through the warm water. "This girl that she's into is getting her into trouble. They were up on the roof together with some more kids, and there may have been drugs."

"Drugs? Dang."

"Yeah, maybe, and something else weird."

"How weird?"

"I don't know. They came home the other day with some expensive bracelet. I immediately thought that Desmona stole it, so I jumped all over her. Then she said her teacher gave it to her."

"Did she steal it?"

"If you shut up, I'll tell you," I said.

"Well go ahead. You ain't got to be all funky about it."

What I told Brian he probably didn't *really* want to hear,

because it meant that I was pulling him further into his cousin's drama. But like Tia's grandma Augustine would say, I needed a post to lean on, and he was the post.

"So where is the bracelet, now?" Brian asked me after I finished telling him the whole story.

"It's in your old underwear drawer."

"You're not gonna give it to her?"

"Would you? Look, Brian, I don't know what's going on with that thing. It's expensive, and I don't know where it came from. I'm not going to have her walking around in it. What if the person she ripped it off from sees it? What if they press charges or something? That's something that none of us needs."

"For real," he said.

"Anyway, I just get a bad feeling from the whole situation. Plus, I'm already dealing with all the other secrets and lies. I don't want to deal with stealing too.

"Then there's this girl, Petal, she's hanging with. She is working my last nerve, getting Desmona into trouble, and getting in my face. The first time I met her she bumped into me and had a funky attitude about it, then she run off and left Desmona alone in the house when I caught her in Desmona's room. I thought, okay, she's that kind of girl. She acts a fool sometimes, but deep down she knows when to cool it. She got caught somewhere she wasn't supposed to be. She bolted, and had better sense than to say too much to me. But when I took that bracelet from Desmona, she got all on me again. She acted like she was gonna do something. I didn't even see it coming. Man, I wished she would have tried something. I would have beat all the black off of her little pretty behind, because I'm tired of the nonsense she's been putting down."

"You sound like it."

"I am."

"And you say she pretty?"

"Yeah, and popular. That's why I can't figure her out. Girls like that don't usually like to mess up what they got going on. She seems like a kid that's looking for some kind of drama, but I don't know why."

"Well, some kids like to go for bad during that age. They act tough, hoping that nobody don't mess with them and find out what they really like."

"Hey, I'm not messing with that heifer, she messing with me. I sympathize with whatever issues she might have, but I don't want her problems becoming Desmona's problems."

"I hear you."

"Yeah, I hear me too. I just don't know what I'm going to do about all of it. I don't know how I'm gonna keep things damned up. If the floodgates open, everything is gonna come pouring out. Everybody gonna find out that Desmona been staying with me. If that happens, your daddy is gonna freak and kick us both out. I don't want to be back in the house with Mama and her boyfriend, and I sure don't want to see Desmona end up in a home."

"Me either," he said.

I looked surprised. "I thought you didn't even care all that much about your cousin?"

"I don't, but I care about you, and I don't like to see you upset," he said.

"Since when? You didn't mind me being upset when you took off with Shell. You didn't care if I was upset then."

"Well, I do now. I care a lot."

I searched his face to see if he was actually telling the truth.

Honesty was written all over his ordinary-boy looks. But I didn't care. His honesty wasn't enough to take away my pain.

"Is that why you came over here all dressed up. You trying to hook up with me again?"

"Probably, maybe," he said.

"Maybe," I repeated. "Great-aunt Freda said that. I thought she was getting things mixed up again. Dang, I guess it is true."

"She shouldn't have told you."

"No, *you* should have." I shook my head. "Anyway, Brian, I don't think so. I got too much stuff going on right now to be fooling with you. I got school, I got Desmona or Demonee, whichever one you want to call her. That's enough drama in my life for now."

"I know what you saying, but I still want you back. I made a mistake when I left you. I'm through with other girls. I wanna get back in the house with you."

I rolled my eyes. "Are you kidding? Brian it don't work like that. I'll bet you do want to get with me, but you got Shell and a baby to think about."

"Yeah, maybe," he said, in a really blue tone.

"What's up with you? Did Shell leave you? I'll bet she done took off with some other dude and left you sitting in that raggedy house with that tragic family of hers," I said sarcastically.

"What's that got to do with it?"

"You tell me," I said, realizing I had touched a nerve.

"I ain't got nothing to say about that. I'm just concentrating on the present, trying to hook up with you again."

"I see," I said.

I stood up and dripped for a moment, before I got out of the pool. Then I walked to the back porch and picked up my beach towel off the steps. I wrapped it around me. "I may not have this house much longer, Brian. But if I do, I'll have to think long and hard about sharing it again with you. Been there, done that, and I'm not so sure I ever want to do it again. You broke my heart, and all the pieces still ain't back together," I said.

He looked guilty. "I know. I'm sorry I did that. I know that I didn't do you right, but I'm just trying to let you know how I feel about being with you right now. I'm trying to be honest."

"Me too, and telling you that I don't need you all over me at this moment is as honest as *I* can get," I said.

"All right, but you gonna miss me when I'm not here," he said.

"Brian, you haven't been here in a very long time, in case you haven't noticed," I said and went back in the house.

Brian hung around the yard a little while looking depressed, and waiting for me to come back out to the pool. When I didn't, he left through the back gate.

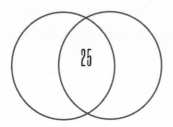

25

My friend Bonita's skipping has gotten to be routine and, to make matters worse, when she does come to class she comes covered in hickies. Last week our English teacher sent her to the office for showing up with the red love bruises all over her neck and, of course, missing way too much class. She was there for three periods until her mother came and picked her up. Madona said that her mother was really pissed and did a lot of yelling.

"Bonita called me and told me to come down to the office because she thought my mama was going to knock her head off or something. When I got there, Mama was yelling so loud the whole office was shaking. I couldn't believe what was going on. Mama is strict, but she never goes off like that. She told Bonita that if she got called off her job again she was gonna kick her butt. I didn't know what to do, so I went back to class before I got into trouble for skipping myself. It's been bad ever since then. Bonita is hardly speaking to either one of us. I hate the way things are right now," Madona told me in Science class.

"Man, I can't believe how much your sister is screwing up," I said.

To make Madona feel better I decided to run over to Diamonds after work and buy a doll outfit for one of the dolls that she collects. I found a red velvet dress with a matching beret. It was cute and classy. I immediately thought that it would be a lot nicer gift for a sister to give a sister, and I wished Bonita was the one purchasing it. However, when I left the store I felt good that at least I was going to do something for Madona that would hopefully put her in a better mood. With that in mind, I also started to feel better myself, but the better turned bitter when I spotted Brian coming toward me in his black work slacks and a clean white shirt that I used to press once a week. My heart jumped a little again. I wondered how long it would keep doing that? When would Brian just be Brian to me? I think I wanted that. I hated feeling like I should be kissing him, when I should be trying to get far away.

"Hey, Maxine, wait up," he said. I stopped in the parking lot and waited for him to make his way through the rows of parked cars.

"Hey, pretty brown sugar. Where you off to?" he asked, walking up.

"That's my business. Brian, what are you doing here? And don't call me your sugar. I'm not that anymore."

"You'll always be that, Maxine," he said. Then he leaned over and kissed me on the mouth. He lips felt warm and sweet, and I returned the kiss before I even knew what I was doing. It was just instinctive. Brian and I had been kissing forever. My body gave in, but my mind didn't. I came to myself and pushed him away.

"Brian, what are you starting this for? I'm not even going there," I said.

"You already did. Girl, you know you enjoyed that kiss, just as much as me. Don't even trip," he said, and grinned.

"Brian, what do you want?" I snapped, irritated at the truth.

"You know what I want. I already told you. I want you back. I want us to be together."

"Yeah, I saw that DVD. You don't have to play it for me again. I already told you, I'm not ready for you to move back."

"Well, when you gonna be ready, Maxine? What do you need to get ready?" He took me into his arms, and I didn't pull away. "Look, Maxine, this is me. You been knowing me most of my life. There ain't never been nobody but you and me. You know how I feel about you," he said.

I wriggled free. "Yeah, I know how you feel about me, but it didn't stop you from screwing around with somebody else. Brian, how long was you really screwing around with Shell? And why her, Brian? It was always just you and me. You never ever let a girl come in between us, and then here she comes. Why her? Why did you let her tear us apart?"

"What—what difference does that make? Does it really matter?"

"It does to me. You were always supposed to be just mine, and then I found out about you and her. Why her, Brian?"

"I already told you. I just liked being with her."

"And you liked all the drama that came with her too?"

"It wasn't that way, at least not at first. We was just chillin' and then she said that she was gonna have a kid."

"How long, Brian? How long was you just chillin'? Was her mama the one who cleaned your mama's house when you were little. Is that where you met her? Were you hooking up with her the whole time you was with me?"

"Maxine, why do you want to go there?" he asked.

"Because I can, because I have to. How long were you with her? Did you go on those trips with your dad to Dallas, so you could spend time with her?"

"Maxine, I'm not going to tell you something that's gonna make you even more upset. I told you, it's over. It's just you and me, Maxine. Nothing else matters."

"To me it does, and it always will. It's going to always matter, so you tell me, why her?"

"It don't matter, Maxine!" he shouted. "If it wasn't her, it probably would have been somebody else. Girl, I just wanted out. I was feeling all squeezed with the marriage and all. I tried to tell you how I was feeling, but you wouldn't listen. I asked you more than once if marriage was really something that we should do."

"No, you asked me if was I sure, and I always was. Even on the day that I kicked you out I was, but not anymore," I said.

"Maxine, don't be like that. Girl, Shell didn't mean nothing to me. I liked her, but she wasn't who I really wanted to be with. It's just you, girl. Shoot, we can go back to the beginning, baby, all you got to do is let it happen," he said, reaching for me again.

I slapped him as hard as I could. I didn't mean to, but my hand had drawn back and whacked his cheek before I even knew it wasn't at my side anymore.

"What the hell?" he said, grabbing his face.

"Yeah, what the hell?" I angrily asked. "What the hell was wrong with you for taking off with Shell? What the hell was wrong with you pretending you didn't even know her the moment she stepped in our house? You knew who she was and why she was there. You knew that she was there to get you. Dang, you made such a fool of me. I'm not letting nothing happen right now, Brian, and I got somewhere important I need to be," I said, storming off. He caught my arm.

"Maxine, I know you mad. Baby, you got a right to be, but this is important. You and me, right here. It's real important, because I got things I'm having to deal with too. I'm going through changes too."

"Yeah, and I went through a lot when you took up with Shell. You betrayed me, Brian. You made it seem like all the years we were together didn't mean nothing."

"I never said that," he said.

I slapped him again, and this time on purpose. "You didn't have to. You took off with that skank. I would have never done that to you. I never even looked at nobody else. It didn't matter if some boy tried to push up on me, I would always tell him to back off. I got a man, I would tell them."

"And you still do. Maxine, I'm right here, and I'm trying to make things right between us again. All you have to do is let me do it."

"Let you do what, Brian? I'm supposed to let you break my heart again? Naw, that ain't happening," I said, shaking my head. "I'm leaving. I love you, but being with you ain't on my to-do list right now," I said, and marched off.

I dropped the present off at Madona's house, and she gave me a big hug when she got it.

"Maxine, you so sweet," she said.

"I just thought you would like it, but I gotta run. There's some stuff I have to take care of at the house. Let's catch the bus to the mall and go try some clothes on at Lane Bryant's this Saturday," I said.

"Okay, maybe we can get Bonita to go with us. You know, like she used to."

"Maybe," I said. I gave her a kiss and took off.

As soon as I got to my home, I noticed that Demonee wasn't home yet. It pissed me off, until I remembered that she was supposed to be working on a book report in the library that afternoon. I put my book bag down and started dinner. I was cutting up some fresh catfish when the doorbell rang. "Please don't let it be Brian again," I muttered. I yanked the door open.

"You think you slick, Maxine!" Shell spat, before my eyes even registered that it was her on my doorstep. "You gonna let me in or what?" she asked, with one hand on her watermelon belly. I didn't know what to say. She was the last person I expected to see on my doorstep.

"Whatever you got to say you can say it out here," I said, folding my arms across my chest.

"You not getting my man, you not getting Brian back. That's what I have to say," she said.

"Excuse me."

"You heard me, heifer. I said you can't have Brian back. I know you been calling him, trying to pretend that you need help with that bad-ass cousin of his."

"I do need help, and I can call Brian anytime I please. You ain't got nothing to say about it, *fat cow*!" I said.

Her face went sour as if she had something nasty in her mouth.

"I got everything to say about it. Brian is my man. I'm the one he wants to be with."

"Well, why does he keep coming around to see me?" I asked.

"He don't, you keep luring him back here," she said.

"Look, Shell, I'm not luring Brian anywhere. We been together since we were little kids. You can have as many babies as you like, but you can't get in between that."

"Are you for real? Do you think you the only one who knows Brian? I'm not trying to get in between nothing. I'm already between it, me and this baby I'm gonna have," she said rubbing her belly.

"Shoot, that thing probably ain't even Brian's," I said.

"It is, and you need to stay away from him. Why can't you see that? Why can't you stay out of my life?"

"Why can't you stay outta mine?" I screamed. Was she kidding? She had already taken my man, and now she was on my porch telling me that I should stay away from him. "Shell, you are out of your mind. You are like some crazy-ass broken record. How you gonna come here in my face again about my husband!"

"Your ex-husband!"

"No, my husband. Me and Brian ain't got no divorce. He

still mine. And you know what? He came by my house and told me that he wanted me back."

"You a liar!" she hollered.

"No, I'm not, and you know it. That's why you here. You all up in my grill, because you know Brian is about to walk away from that thing you carrying."

"No he not!"

"He is, if I ask him to. Now get off my porch, and take your raggedy behind back to your raggedy life!"

"I hate you, Maxine!" she hollered.

"Fine, just hate me somewhere else," I said. I went to slam the door and she pushed it back on me. I pushed it again, and shoved her big belly out of the house.

"You make me sick!" she hollered, banging on the door.

"Then die!" I yelled. "And stop hitting my door before you break it." I walked back through the living room muttering to myself when I heard a loud groan. "Maxine, Maxine, help Maxine. I don't feel so good," she cried out. I hurried back to the door and flung it open. She was standing there with a pained look on her face holding her left arm.

"What's wrong with you?" I asked.

"My arm hurts real bad, Maxine. It's aching a lot."

"Because you were banging on my door," I said.

"Naw, something is real wrong, Maxine. It hurts real bad, and so does my head. It's been hurting me all morning. I think I might be having a heart attack or something. My grandma was feeling like this before she had one."

"What? Girl come in and sit down," I said, helping her in the house. With her expanding tummy, she was heavier than I thought. I could barely get her to the sofa. As soon as her butt hit the sofa, I ran to the phone. "I better call an ambulance," I said.

She vigorously shook her head. "Naw, don't, we can't afford nothing like that. Run to the house and get my uncle. He up here from Dallas, working on the pipes underneath our house. He'll run me over."

"Okay," I said. I wasn't a runner, so I took off walking as fast as I could to her place. I didn't really know what was wrong with her, but I figured she had to be in great pain to ask me to help. There was no way she would put her life in my hands if it wasn't an emergency. God, why did she have to get sick at my home? Now she was laid up in my living room, in the house that was supposed to be for me and my man. "How in the hell did this happen?" I cried aloud.

As I headed up the block to Shell's place, I realized for the first time that I wanted to be out of it. I didn't want to deal with Brian or Shell anymore. She could have him. I wasn't going to ask him for anything ever again. I was going to let him live his own life, which is what I should have done months ago. The marriage was a mistake, and the only way to correct it was to get Brian out of my life for good. Before I reached the next block, I realized that both Shell and I were so panicked we weren't using our common sense. If I could call an ambulance, I could call her house. I had my phone in my shorts' pocket. I stopped and pulled it out. I rang Shell's place, and wouldn't you know Brian answered the phone.

"Shell's at our place. She's feeling pretty bad. She needs her uncle to run her over to the hospital," I told him, out of breath.

"What? I'll get him right now. We're on our way over," he said, and hung up.

I walked to a boarded up house a few feet from the sidewalk and sat on the dusty porch. I wasn't going home. I didn't want to see Brian helping the mother of his child. In fact, I didn't want to see him at all. I looked at the boarded up house and wished I could take the boards down and move into it right away. I could start a new life here away from Brian. I deserved that. What I didn't deserve was a pregnant girl and an unfaithful husband in my living room. What a strange and ugly mess Brian had pulled me into. I was going to do everything I could to get out.

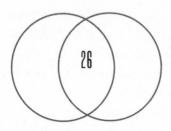

26

S hell is fine. She didn't have a heart attack or anything. Her blood pressure was sky high, and that's what was causing the wooziness and pain. The doctor kept her overnight and sent her home with some medicine. She's supposed to be on bed rest for a while. Brian called me on the phone this morning and told me the information.

"Good for her," I said, and abruptly hung up the phone. I thought our conversation was over but then he showed up on our doorstep a few minutes later. Demonee saw him through the peep hole and refused to answer the door.

"It's Brian, you wanna talk to that fool?" she asked.

"Not even," I said.

"Go away, Cousin Brian. Don't nobody want to talk to you," she hollered out.

"Girl, you better open up this door!" he hollered back.

"Make me!" she said.

"Demonee, I'm not playing with you," Brian said, and

started banging on the door. I didn't want his blood pressure to somehow go up and end up at the hospital like that trashy Shell, so I went to the door.

"Brian, what do you want?" I asked.

"Open the door," he said.

"Naw, I'm not going there. You got something to say, say it through the door."

"It's personal," he said.

"I don't care, Brian, just say it. I'm not in the mood."

"Why you so mad?"

"I'm not mad. I just don't want to talk about you or Shell. You got something to say. Spit it out."

He hesitated.

"Spit it out, Brian," I said.

"The baby ain't mine," he said through the door.

"What did he say?" Demonee asked. I was so stunned I couldn't answer.

"The baby ain't mine. Shell told me at the hospital. She was really sick with her blood pressure, so she told me the truth. It ain't mine, Maxine. It's some boy she was messing around with in Dallas. Did you hear me?" Brian asked a little louder.

I still didn't know what to say.

"She heard you. Now go away," Demonee told him.

"Girl, this ain't none of your business," Brian said.

"No, it's mine. Go home, Brian," I spoke up.

"Oh come on Maxine, don't do me like that!" Brian begged.

"You heard her. See ya!" Demonee said.

"Girl, you better not let me get my hands on you," Brian told her.

Demonee laughed.

"All right fine, but we gotta talk," Brian said to me.

"Talk to yourself!" Demonee hollered out.

"Go away, Brian," I said.

"Yeah, go away!" Demonee hollered.

"Maxine, let me in. Don't do this! I really need to talk to you."

"No, you don't, just go get out of here," I said.

I walked away from the door and sat down in front of the TV. I didn't know what to think.

"Dang, you think he telling the truth?" Demonee asked.

"Yeah, I do," I mumbled.

"Does it matter?" she asked.

"I don't know. Why don't you go get ready for school," I said.

"Okay, but I wouldn't. I wouldn't take him back. He just gonna hurt you again. Why you gonna let him do that?" she asked earnestly.

"I'm not, Demonee, it's complicated. Me and Brian got a lot of history."

"So, it don't mean you should let him treat you like that. Anyway, my mama say that you can't trust no kind of man."

"That's not true, Demonee. Not every guy does what Brian did. At least I hope they don't. Go finish getting dressed."

She went to her room. I turned on the TV and stared at the screen. I wasn't watching nothing. I just wanted the noise to drown out the shocking thoughts in my head, thoughts about my husband and a baby that had turned out not to be his. I couldn't believe it. My marriage had begun and ended with a lie. How was I going to handle that revelation? I turned off the TV and went to get dressed.

I let my feelings lie. I didn't want to think about Brian or Shell while I was getting dressed or even on my way to school. I was saving my feelings to talk over with my friends. Girl talk always made things better. I got to school and zombied my way through my first two classes. I didn't volunteer to answer any questions the teacher asked, and I pretty much ignored anybody who tried to strike up a conversation with me. When the lunch bell rang for Study Hall, I waited outside of my locker to see if either one of my friends would show up. I was happy when I saw Madona coming, until I saw the distressed look on her face.

"Bonita is gone," she said.

"What, gone where?" I asked.

"She didn't have no choice," Madona said, with tears streaming down her face. "You know how mad Mama was with her. I told you that things been bad at the house. Well, yesterday Mama found some crack that Bonita was holding for that boy, Billy. It was in a suitcase underneath her bed. Bonita tried to defend Billy by saying that he was just selling rocks, so he could buy a new car for his family."

"Yeah, right!" I said.

"Mama didn't buy it either, plus she had already told Bonita that she didn't want her sneaking around with him. She told Bonita that she wasn't going to sit around and watch Bonita mess her life up with some street trash. She told her that she was gonna send her to stay with our relatives in another state."

"What, for real?"

"Yeah, then Bonita said that she was just gonna run away. She told me that. She didn't say it to Mama, but I guess Mama must have figured it out. She called some cousins she got down in South Texas. They drove all night. As soon as Bonita woke up this morning, they pounced on her and took her away."

"Pounced on her?"

"Yeah, that's the way it was. Bonita was crying and throwing a fit, but Mama got some big cousins. They both females, but they both work construction all day putting up buildings. They hauled Bonita off kicking and screaming. They gonna drive her out of state to stay with our relatives. Mama is at home packing her stuff up right now."

"Oh Lord!"

"I miss her so much already!" Madona cried. "I knew if Mama found out she was gonna be pissed, but I wasn't expecting her to take my twin sister away. Now it's just me in the house. I hate it. I wish Mama would have made me go too."

"I know you do, but it will be all right. We can catch a Greyhound and go see Bonita when she gets settled in," I said, hugging her.

"I know, but it won't be the same. Nothing will ever be the same," she said, pulling free.

I pulled her to me and kissed her on the forehead before she walked off, but I know it didn't do much good. Bonita had been putting little cuts in their relationship for months. Now her mother had finally sliced the cord and separated them for good.

I leaned against the locker dazed. Bonita was gone. It was the second most shocking thing that had happened to me in the week. I wasn't going to be able to talk over my issues about Brian with her and Madona anymore, because she wasn't going to be there to listen. I felt like bawling in the halls like Madona, not just over Bonita, but mostly over my marriage and all the weird, unfair things that kept coming my way. I left the lockers and headed to the girls bathroom. As soon as I got there, I sat down in a stall and rang Tia. She didn't answer, so I left a message anyway. "Brian say that the baby ain't even his, and now Bonita is gone. Her mama done sent her off. Girl, everything is so crazy and screwed up. Give me a call, please," I said, and hung up the phone.

I sat in the stall for a while and collected my thoughts. When I was halfway pulled together, I headed to my class. I was there for a little while when one of the student office helpers came and gave me a note from Great-aunt Freda. "I need you to come by my house as soon as possible. Stop by on the way home. It's important," the note said. I sighed. I really wanted to just go home and curl up in the bed, but I checked to see if I had enough for bus fare to her place. I had a few coins in my pocket, so when I got out of school I used them to get to her apartment as quickly as I could. She was standing out in the yard in a beautiful ankle-length white lace dress and a big white hat with a blue bow. I took her style of dress as a sign that nothing bad was up and calmed down.

"Aunt Freda, what's up?" I asked as I entered the court-yard. She sat down at the wooden picnic table in front of her place, and I sat across from her.

"So what's the deal? You don't look bad or nothing."

"Little girl, do you really think I'm sick?" she asked. I looked over her wrinkled face. Her eyes were shiny and full of life.

"Not really. So what's up then?"

"Brian, that's what's up."

I shook my head. "Not that again. Look Aunt Freda, I don't know what Brian been saying to you this time, but I already told him I don't know about us getting together again. I really don't need no extra drama in my life."

"Is that what Brian is? Is that really how you see him?"

"Right now it's how I see him. If you want to know the truth, I feel like I'm one of them pole hangers."

"Pole hangers?" she said, looking confused. Her creased forehead seemed to gather a few more wrinkles.

"Yeah, a pole hanger. You know one of them people that's holding on to a pole for dear life in the middle of some kind of . . ."

"Storm, is that what you gonna say, baby? Cause let me tell you, Maxine, you ain't got no real storms in your life. You're young and healthy, and everything that's laying heavy on you will soon disappear, like fallen ice cubes on hot pavement."

"How do you know?"

"I just do. Now about Brian. You know he talks to me, just like you do, and you know that I love both of ya'll."

"I know, but do me a favor, don't go there today. I don't know what Brian is putting you up to, but I'm not interested. I know he probably told you that Shell's baby ain't his. I'm glad about that, but I'm not ready to deal with it right now."

"Well, you better get ready, because it's about to be too late. Brian's about to leave," she said sternly.

"What, leave where?"

"Brian is joining the Marines. He been talking to a recruiter over at that Redesign Center for months. You know they help them boys get into the military if they want to."

"I know that, but what are you talking about?"

"Baby, I wanted to tell you before, but I promised that I wouldn't. Plus, I didn't know if it was really gonna happen, and I didn't want you to get upset over nothing. He started talking to me about it before you even got married. He said that his father was pressuring him to come work with him when he graduated school, and he didn't want to do it, so he was thinking about joining the military. Of course, now he's not just thinking, he's planning to go."

"You're kidding."

"No, I'm not baby. He told me himself. You know I wouldn't lie to you about something like this."

"No, of course not, but you probably heard wrong. Brian ain't even like that. His daddy couldn't even get him interested in contact sports. I know he ain't about to go through no boot camp."

"He is, if you don't give him a reason to stay."

"A reason to stay where? Aunt Freda this don't even make sense. Brian ain't said nothing about no Marines. All he been talking about is getting back with me."

"Is that all?"

I thought for a second. "Wait, when he came to my house he said I was gonna miss him when he wasn't around no more, and when I saw him in the street, he was talking about going through some changes. Is that what he meant? Why didn't he just tell me?"

"He didn't have to. I'm telling you. He been thinking about it for a while, and now that he knows Shell's baby ain't even his, he ain't got much reason to stay with her. Plus, going into the Marines will give him something to be proud of."

"I'm sure it will, if that's what he wants," I said.

"What he wants is you. That's what he wants."

"Aunt Freda."

"Don't Aunt Freda me," she said, shaking her finger at me. "Maxine, you love Brian, and God knows he still loves you."

"I know, but I'm not sure it matters. To be honest with you, Aunt Freda, I kinda like being on my own again. I like being just a girl in school, and not a wife. I mean, when I see my future, I don't see me being all tied up again."

"Is that the way you looked at your marriage?"

"Naw, not really, but Brian did. That's why he left me. He felt like I was holding him down."

"Well, he don't feel that way now."

"I don't know how he feels, not really. And right now I'm not sure I even want to know. Aunt Freda, he thought Shell was having his baby, so he went off with her. That is so messed up."

"Yes it is, but are you sure you don't want to give him another chance? I mean, honey, I don't want you to end up like me, old and broken down with nobody, or like your mama, with no real love in her life. She goes from man to man thinking that something great is gonna happen, but nothing ever does, except she pushes you further and further away. I don't want that for you. I want you to find that kind of passionate wonderful love that me and your mama have never had."

"I understand, Aunt Freda. I really want to give Brian

another chance, but to do what, run away again? Fool around on me? I mean, what kind of chance am I supposed to give him?" I angrily asked.

"Whatever chance that keeps him from ending up someplace in the Middle East."

"So that's on me. If he ends up somewhere in a major war, it's my fault? I'm sorry, Aunt Freda, I don't see it that way. If you think I'm just gonna up and get screwed over by Brian again, you got something loose in your head," I said.

"No I don't, little girl," she said, reminding me not to talk to her that way. "And I don't think it will be your fault if Brian goes off to the military. He's a strong boy, and it is an honorable thing to do. I'm just letting you know if you still want him around you better speak up now, because in a little while he might be miles away. And with the way things been going, it's possible that he won't be coming back."

"Okay, you told me. I hear what you saying. And I love Brian, so I don't want him to make a bad decision just because I won't take him back. But I also don't want to be pressured right now, and I'm not going to have what Brian does or doesn't do on my conscience." I got up from the table and walked around to her. She got up from the table too, and I was about to kiss her goodbye when my cell rang again. I took it out of my purse and opened it.

"Dang, this better not be Brian," I said.

"Hello, Maxine. This is Ms. Hopkins, down at Demonee's school. Demonee put you down on her emergency contact list," she said. My heart dropped in my feet. What now? More drama?

"Yes ma'am, what can I do for you?"

"I need you to come by the school as soon as you can."

"What for? Is something up with Demonee?"

"I'll tell you when you get here. I just need you to come up to school. I teach an after-school Math Workshop in one of the portables out back. I'll meet you out in front of it. The number is 147."

"Yes ma'am, I'm on my way," I said.

"Something wrong?" Great-aunt Freda asked.

"Lord, I hope not. I surely do hope not, but I got to go to Demonee's school," I said.

"Again?" she asked.

"Yeah, again. I gotta run."

"Well, if you gotta, you gotta." She pulled me to her and kissed me goodbye on the cheek. "Maxine, you're a better mother to that little girl than her own mother was," she whispered to me.

"You don't know how true that is," I said.

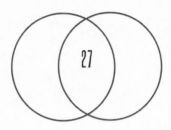

27

"Y ou see that chemical plant?" Ms. Hopkins asked me as we stood in the alley next to the portable that she worked in. I looked where she was pointing and noticed thick yellow gasses streaming out of the smoke-stacks of the company just a couple of miles from our school.

"Why are you asking me about that?"

"Because I'm standing here angrier than I've ever been, and I needed something to calm me down," she said, shaking.

"So do you see it?"

"I see it," I said.

"Yes, those gasses come pouring out, polluting the air, the water, the soil, and the people. It's a crime, really, but crimes like that don't ever get punished. However, Demonee's crime will."

"Oh no! What did she do?" I asked.

"Maxine, have you ever done anything really incredibly dumb, besides taking on the responsibility for a thirteen-year-old girl that you're not even related to? And don't take that the wrong way. I know you only mean to help Demonee, but I've known for a long time that you're not really her cousin," she said.

"That's not exactly true. She's my husband's cousin—that makes her my cousin through marriage," I said.

"I see, I didn't know you were married. You look so young."

"I am, kind of."

"Anyway, Maxine. I called you about Demonee, but first I have to let you know something. The little girl that she spends time with, Petal, is actually the daughter of a very good friend."

"Okay," I said.

"I'm just telling you this because I want to be completely honest with you. I need to be, because I've probably been a lot more lenient with Petal than I should have been, and that has caused some problems, for all of us, especially Demonee."

"How is that?"

"Petal's not a nice girl. I don't usually say that about my students, but it's the truth. She's a bad influence, and real trouble when she can't get her way. There's been one negative incident after another, way too many for me to tell you about."

"You don't have to. I get the picture."

"Anyway, I was hoping that things would turn around, but they haven't. They've gotten worse, and then there's Demonee. Believe it or not, I never had a problem with Demonee until she started hanging with Petal. Petal's been able to get Demonee into all kinds of things that I don't think Demonee would normally be into."

"Are you saying that's the reason Demonee threw that book at you?"

"Yes, I believe Petal was behind that. She was angry because I wouldn't change a quiz grade. She passed that anger onto Demonee, and—trust me—I've been experiencing it ever since. There have been days when those two girls have turned my class upside down."

"Why didn't you turn them in?"

"I don't know. I was just hoping that one day I could get through to at least one of them, but that was before the bracelet."

"They stole it didn't they? Where did they get it from? Did they take it from a teacher?"

"No, it's worse, much worse. They stole the money to buy it."

"Stole the money. From where? Where did they get that kind of cash?"

"That's the much worse," she said, shaking her head. "They got it from the project we've been doing to help out some needy families. You may remember that I was talking about it the first day that we met."

"I think I do. I overheard you talking about selling merchandise from a catalog."

"Right, well it seems that Petal was selling her merchandise after all. She told me that she couldn't get anyone to buy the products, but in reality she was selling them and pocketing the money. And if you think that's bad, when she ran out of goods, she told some of the other students that she would sell theirs too. She's cute, and can be very charming. She went through eight order forms. She and Demonee sold things and then kept all of the money. They've been using it to buy gifts for themselves."

"Gifts? You mean she got more stuff?" I asked.

"Yes, I'm sorry. I think if you check her room you'll find that she has merchandise stashed all over the place."

"Oh damn. How am I going to get her out of this? Her uncle is going to freak."

She shook her head. "I don't know how to help you Maxine, but as I've said before, I get the feeling that you are more responsible for Demonee than you've let on. I think her uncle leaves her in your care most of the time. I'm not here to question that, I'm just here to give you the heads-up. I'm about to go into the office and tell the principal. I have no choice. The other teachers have already turned their money into the office. How can I explain that my class is over a thousand dollars short?"

"Over a thousand!"

"Yes, nearly sixteen hundred dollars. Maxine, the merchandise we were selling was all twenty dollars or more. The fund-raiser was designed to bring in a lot of cash, to give to victims of the recent hurricanes, people who have lost everything and don't even have a place to stay. So, I have to make an account of it. The amount of money that they stole is a felony. When I report it, there is no doubt in my mind that they will be arrested."

"Arrested?"

"Yes, for the money, and the threat, and my car."

"Threat? What car?"

"The threat was against me, and apparently my vehicle. After I told Petal that I was going to report everything, the girls threatened to beat me up if I said anything. I should have called security and had them both taken to the office right then and there, but I had a table full of students waiting to be tutored in the library. Plus, I really did believe that they were just blowing off steam, until I saw my car. The girls smashed it up pretty bad. With what, I don't know, but there are dents everywhere. Also, they slashed my tires, cut up my seats, and if I didn't know how to spell the word *bitch*, I do now. It's spray-painted on every inch of what's left of my car in silver paint."

"Petal really did that?" I asked, in disbelief.

"Yes, and Demonee. Look, I have to go, Maxine. I just thought I would tell you first. I'm angry over my car and the money, but I know that Demonee is probably a victim in this too. I know she's just a child who wants to be loved. I've sensed it. I was her when I was younger. I was a stepchild, with two new siblings, and my mother never seemed to have much time for me. Eventually she sent me to live with my father. He was a very good man, but he had no idea how to raise a mixed-up little girl. Maxine, I know that Demonee is different. I picked up on it the first days of my class. I see how she responds to and looks at the other little girls. It's something that I understand from my own childhood. I was hoping that I could help her through some of the awkward feelings that she's been dealing with, and I think I could have, before Petal. But now all I can do is try to help her out of this mess. She will fare better in this if she's honest and tells the principal that none of this was her idea. I believe that with my whole heart. For instance, it was Petal who started the threat, and Demonee who was silly enough to chime in. I think she's been chiming in one way or another for months, until it's led to the kind of behavior we've witnessed today. I'll tell the principal as much, but it won't do much good if she doesn't speak up for herself. Tell her that when she gets home. Tell her that she has to look out for number one. I'm sorry that you are having to deal with this, Maxine," she said, walking away.

I followed her away from the portables and turned off to go to the back parking lot. I saw what had to be her car. She had a nice ride, a Toyota Camry, and it was definitely totaled. It looked like somebody had taken a baseball bat or a sledge hammer to it. Everything was caved in and glass was all over the place. I couldn't believe two teen girls could make so much damage. I felt deeply ashamed. How could I be looking after a kid that could be so mean, and so stupid?

I got home and sat down on the porch to wait for Demonee. My pulse was racing, and I was seriously freaking. The phone in my pocket rang. I picked it up, hoping it was her. It was Uncle Ernie, and before he could ask me to babysit for one of his kids, I spilled everything to him. I told him how much trouble Demonee was in and that she might be okay if she would put it all on her girlfriend. I told him that I was scared and confused about the whole thing. I didn't expect him to give me good advice, but he was surprisingly helpful.

"Maxine, I don't know why you telling me this? You should be going to Demonee's uncle with something this big. You done tried to do all you could for that little girl, and all she been doing is screwing up. This shouldn't be your job. You ain't nothing but a kid yourself."

"I'm not a kid," I said.

"Let me finish. You know why I went and helped you

that first time with Demonee? It wasn't because I need you to keep my kids sometimes. I'm not crazy. I love your mother, but I know there are times that she don't do right by you. I know it's a big reason why you wanted to get married and move out of her house. I know that sometimes she gets all up under her men and forgets you are her daughter. I don't like that, 'cause I ain't never ever seen a mama do it. I mean, when I'm fool enough to hang out in the club, instead of being with my kids, my babies' mamas get after me. And they do it because they don't like me hurting their kids. They stand up to me, get in my face, and yell. Lord, how they yell! They scream so loud sometimes I wish I was born without ears. They right to get on me though, 'cause that's what good mamas do. So, when I see my sister not doing you right it just breaks my heart. That's why I agreed to go up to that school and make a fool out of myself," he said with a bucket of emotion.

It caught me off guard. Uncle Ernie rarely gets serious about anything. "I don't know what to say to that," I said.

"Ain't nothing to say, Maxine. This ain't even about that. I'm getting away from the point, 'cause I don't really know the right thing to say. Look, life ain't nothing but one big crap shoot. All you can do is put something down and throw the dice, hoping that when the game is over you come out ahead."

"What does that mean?"

"You know what it means, Maxine. It means you gonna have to tell that girl to give up her friend, if she wanna keep out of the juvenile system for a long time, because, Maxine, I've seen kids locked up for a long time for a lot less, and look what she's done. Honey, you gonna have to tell her to stop being a fool and look out for herself. You got to give something to get something. That's the way it generally works."

"She's already given up so much," I said.

"No, everybody done gave up on her, except you, Maxine. You ain't been doing nothing but helping that child. Now you just asking her to help herself."

I spotted Demonee coming up the walk. "I gotta go, Uncle Ernie. I love you," I said.

I put my phone away and waited. Demonee came walking up with a stupid grin on her face, like she hadn't done anything wrong.

"What you doing sitting out here? You need to be in the kitchen cooking. What we gonna eat for dinner?"

I rolled my eyes. "Demonee, don't start nothing. You in enough trouble already."

"For what?" she asked.

I looked around to see if my nosy neighbor was sitting on the porch or camped out at the window. She wasn't, so I answered the question.

"Guess, Demonee, guess why you could be in trouble."

"Maxine, I don't even know what you talking about," she said, placing her hands on her hips and shaking her head.

I noticed that she had on a new slammin' pair of gold hoops that I hadn't seen before. I was certain she had bought them with some of that stolen cash. It further pissed me off.

"Demonee, don't play no fool with me. You know darn well what I'm talking about. You a thief and a thug."

"No, I ain't!"

"Oh yes, ma'am, you are," I shot back. "You and that little friend of yours been ripping off folks in need, you been ripping off a school project. You took the money and bought that gold bracelet and God knows what else. Ms. Hopkins told me to look in your room, but I can't bear to do it. I know you got more stuff in there and I know that you and your friend Petal got mad and smashed up Ms. Hopkins's car."

"No, we didn't. I don't know what you talking about," she said, looking shocked.

"I ain't gonna argue with you. I know you lying, little girl," I said, pointing my finger at her. "I know you lying and I know what you been up to."

"I ain't been up to nothing, and Ms. Hopkins is the one lying. None of that junk is true."

"The hell it ain't! Demonee, you threatened her. You destroyed her car."

"Well, so what? She deserves it anyway. I don't even like her!" she snapped back.

"I can't believe you said that. You gonna act like a thug, and then say it's somebody else's fault. Do you really think Ms. Hopkins deserves to be mistreated by you?"

"Why not?" she asked.

"Because she's your teacher, and she ain't done nothing to you but ask you to come to class."

"So."

"What do you mean so?"

"So what? I don't care."

"What, little girl are you crazy?" I snatched her by the arm, and pushed her down on the steps. Then I got in her face.

"You better care, little girl, because you're in big trouble. You can't threaten a teacher. You can't tear up her ride. Ms. Hopkins is in the office right now. She's gonna tell the principal about everything, and you know he's gonna tell the campus police."

"No, he ain't. You making all this up. Ms. Hopkins likes Petal. She ain't gonna do nothing mean to her," she said with an unsure tone.

"Mean to her? What about what you idiots did to her car, and her trust! I can't believe you stole that money. No, Demonee, I ain't making nothing up. You done really done it this time, little girl, and I can't help you out. Ms. Hopkins says that what you did is a felony. What were you thinking? You didn't have a right to hurt her, and you certainly didn't have a right to hurt those people, people who probably ain't got nothing left after the storm. That's what bothers me, here you and me struggling, we wouldn't have nothing if it wasn't for your uncle. Plus, you know whats it's like to be in need," I said, pointing to the small crumbling rent shacks that made up every other house on our street. "Look around you, girl, this is a neighborhood where ain't nobody got nothing, but even these people understood that you help someone when they down. You don't kick 'em in the teeth. That money that you stole, they donated it, out of whatever little cash they make once a week. You didn't just rip the school off, you ripped off everybody in this neighborhood. And for what? Those stupid hoops you got sticking out of your ears, or that bracelet I wouldn't let you have. Is that why you took something that didn't belong to you? Demonee, that's all junk, just material things. You don't hurt people for that."

"I ain't hurt nobody," she said, scrunching up her face.

"Yes you did, Demonee. You hurt all those people, and you especially hurt Ms. Hopkins. She did nothing but try to look out for Petal—and you, and ya'll used it against her. Maybe your uncle is right not wanting to have anything to do with you. Who would want to care about you, if you gonna do stuff like this? I'm for real, Demonee. I'm sick and tired of fooling with you. I don't like thieves, and especially don't like people who steal from folks that already ain't got nothing," I said.

I sat back down on the steps, exasperated. I really was finished with her and wanted her to know it. If she couldn't find it in her somewhere to care about what she had done, I certainly wasn't gonna care about how she ended up. "Demonee, do you hear me? I'm through talking to you. I'm going in the house," I said. I stood and started up the steps.

"Wait, Maxine, don't be mad at me," she said, in a little girl voice. "I didn't wanna do none of that stuff. I just did it because Petal wanted me to do it."

"Look, Demonee, I don't know much about Petal. Somewhere in her might be a nice kid, but I ain't seen it. What I do know is you in a world of trouble, and the only way to get out of it is to tell the truth. You gonna have to say that it was all Petal's fault. It should be easy. After all, she was responsible for most of it. She was supposed to turn in the money."

She started shaking her head vigorously. "I can't do that, Maxine. I can't do something like that to Petal. She cares for me, and I don't want her to go to jail or nothing. Please don't make me do something like that," she said frantically.

"I'm not, Ms. Hopkins is," I said.

The tears started to show up in the corner of her eyes. "Maxine, don't make me say it was all Petal's fault. She's nice to me. Don't make me turn on her. I know she don't always do right, but she my girl. We just alike, and I always feel good when I'm with her."

"Always?" I asked.

She hung her head.

"Always?" I asked again.

"Well, I don't like it when she acts like she don't know me around her cool friends, and I don't like it when she comes up with a bad idea."

"And she has a lot of them, don't she? I'll bet she got some I don't even know about, and that's what I'm trying to tell you," I said. I reached over and took her hand, expecting her to yank it away. She let it rest there. It felt sweaty and warm.

"Demonee, I'm sorry, I know that you care a lot for Petal, because she likes you for you. I know she tries to treat you special, and everybody wants to feel needed, but, Demonee, people who care for you don't get you in trouble. They don't turn you into a thief or a liar, or a thug. If Petal really cared about you, she wouldn't have ever got you involved with all this Ms. Hopkins drama. If she wanted to do something mean to her, she would have done it herself, and left you out. It wasn't cool for her to drag you into this mess. It's not the way you treat folks who mean something to you."

"How you know that?" she asked.

"I know, because I been in love with your cousin Brian for as long as I can remember, and he cheated on me with another girl. He pulled me into a real drama with Shell and a kid that he now says ain't even his. I can't tell you how much that hurts, but what hurts most is not knowing that he could hurt me like that. I didn't know who Brian really was. I didn't see it, but you looking right at it in Petal. You just gonna pretend that you ain't seeing what you seeing?"

"I just don't want Petal to be taken away from me."

"Demonee, she's gonna go, and you can trust me on that. The question is what is gonna happen to you? Where are you gonna go? All I can say is sometimes all you get is wrongs in life, and you done had a bunch of them. This will be one more, and all I'm asking you to do is try to save yourself. You can't do nothing about your mama and grandma throwing you out, and you can't do nothing about your uncle not wanting anything to do with you. But you can do something about how you live the rest of your life. You can stick with Petal and let her take you down, or you can tell the truth and hope somebody takes pity on you."

"I don't know if I can do that, Maxine. I don't wanna lose my friend," she cried.

"Then you gonna lose yourself, and me. You know your uncle ain't gonna do nothing to stop them from locking you up." I squeezed her hand. "I don't want that to happen, Demonee. I just lost one person I care for. I don't want to lose another one. I can't make you do it," I said, "but I think your life is gonna be pretty awful if you don't. I'm gonna go make some dinner, you think about what you want to do," I said.

I walked in the house and sat down on the sofa. I didn't want to go into the kitchen to make dinner. I didn't even want to move, and I really didn't want to lose Demonee. I didn't really get along with Mama, and then there was Brian. What was I going to do about him? If I asked him to stay, he would be stuck in limbo trying to see if he could get back together with me, and I would be stuck trying to see if I would ever trust him again. I didn't want that for either one of us. I didn't know why he wanted to go to the military, but I was deciding to let him. That left just Demonee for me to worry about. She wasn't even gone yet, and I could already feel the loss. It had just been me and her for so long, getting on each others nerves and fighting about everything. Why should I even care about losing her? As odd as it sounds, I felt at home with Demonee. When I unlocked the door to our little house, I always felt like I was coming to the place I was supposed to be. It wasn't that way with Brian. Deep down I always felt like we were just playing house, and with Mama a part of me has always felt like I was standing in the way of what she really wanted for her life. I think she was much happier when I was in foster care. No, my home was with Demonee. We had settled into a new life, started healing, and learned to count on each other. Things weren't perfect, but it was home. It was the only place that I had ever really been comfortable. I loved Brian, but from the beginning nothing was right living with him, and with Mama nothing could ever be right, as long as her men came first. I got up from the sofa and went to the front window. I looked out toward the steps. Demonee was sitting there with her chin in her hands deciding her future, our future. "Please make the right decision, Demonee, please," I whispered.

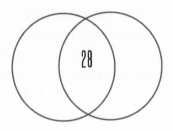

28

When I first ended up in foster care, I was so depressed and scared that I would only eat one thing: mac and cheese. I ate it because I remembered when Mama used to make it sometimes for me and Tia after I had a hard day in school. It was what grownups call comfort food, and helped me recall nicer times, when I was hanging out with Tia or watching TV or something with Mama. That's why I ate it, but after a while I realized that Mama wasn't coming to get me, and that knowledge turned everything sour in my life, including the mac and cheese that I loved so much. I hated my favorite food, as much as I hated Mama for letting me go into a stranger's home. I wanted to be home with her, not living in a weird place. I thought that Demonee would feel that way too. I just knew she would tell the truth about her girlfriend and help herself. I was sure of it, but then when I walked her over to Ms. Hopkins's room that afternoon, she refused to do the smart thing.

Instead of asking for forgiveness and saying she would do anything to help herself, Demonee told Ms. Hopkins that she wasn't gonna do one single thing Ms. Hopkins asked her to do. "I ain't telling nothing on Petal. She my best girl, so whatever you gonna do, you have to do to both of us," is all she had to say, with all kinds of defiance on her face. I hung my head when Ms. Hopkins said, "Demonee, you just made the wrong decision. Honey, you're going to be in a lot of trouble for this. I'm not all that worried about my car. I have insurance, but you don't. Your only insurance is to tell the truth."

"I just told you," Demonee said.

"Yes, I guess you did," she said.

I sighed and didn't say anything. I had already told Demonee what I thought she should do.

We all went down to the office where things really blew up. Petal had already been pulled out of her after-school program, and all the guardians had been called. Demonee's uncle was there, burning. He was so hot I wondered when the wooden chair he was sitting in would turn to ash. He kept giving me pissed-off glances. I stayed in the room anyway, thanking God that I was pretty much ignored by everyone else. Everybody was focused on Ms. Hopkins and the two girls.

"Can you explain why you would do such a thing?" the principal asked.

"Whatever," Petal said.

The principal was stunned. "Is that all you have to say, little girl?" he asked.

"That's all I said, wasn't it?" Petal shot back.

"Petal, please, explain yourself. Do you know what kind of

mess you done got yourself in? Why do you have to cause so much grief? You know I'm not well," Petal's mother said. I felt sorry for her. She really did look sick. She was a tall light sister, with sallow skin and huge dark circles under her hazy brown eyes.

"What else is new?" Petal said.

The principal turned to Demonee. Demonee just folded her arms across her chest.

"You don't have anything to say either?" the principal asked.

"Nope, I ain't got nothing to say," Demonee said.

I expected her uncle to get up and start screaming at her to tell the truth but he just sat there looking angry.

The principal tried a couple more times to get something out of Petal, then he called the police.

"Please don't take my child!" Petal's mother cried when the officers showed up.

Demonee's uncle had a different response. "There's no good in that girl. Lock her up, do whatever you have to do. I'm not going to do any more for her! What's the point?"

"I don't want you to do nothing for me! I don't need nothing from you!" Demonee yelled.

"Good, because you're not getting anything," her uncle angrily said. Her uncle looked at the principal. "You see what I have to go through. I've tried and tried, but nothing helps," he said.

"Demonee, do you understand what kind of trouble you're in?" Principal Chang asked.

Demonee rolled her eyes and said nothing.

I thought about what Demonee's uncle said, that he had tried with Demonee. It wasn't true. He hadn't tried with

Demonee at all. He gave her to me to fix, and because I couldn't do it, he was passing her on to someone else, the juvie system. It made me sick. I left the office and went home.

I was there about thirty minutes when Demonee's uncle came storming in. He slammed the door hard and stood there steaming at me in his best business suit.

I knew he was getting ready to throw me out. I thought about being humble and begging him to let me stay in the house, but all I could think about was Demonee being locked up. He had let them take her away. I didn't want to hear a word he had to say about the situation. "Look man, don't even try starting up with me," I said, looking up from the couch from where I was sitting. Now he was stunned.

"Do you know who you're talking to? Don't start with you? You got some hell of a nerve, Maxine. We had a deal. You watch out for Demonee, and I pay all of the bills. It was a simple bargain to keep, Maxine. Why the hell couldn't you keep it? How hard was it to make sure the girl stayed out of trouble!" he hollered.

"I don't know, why don't you tell me? Oh no, you can't because you weren't the one running after her trying to clean up her mess. You weren't the one trying to make her feel like she wasn't twisted, even though her whole family threw her out like trash." He was really pissed with that comment. His face looked like he could punch a hole in the wall.

"I didn't throw that girl out. I put her with somebody I thought was responsible. I put her with you, Maxine. I thought you were an adult," he said through gritted teeth.

I remembered how good-looking I thought Brian's dad

was when we first met, with his handsome face and nice body, but soon everything about him was distasteful to me.

"You thought wrong. I'm not an adult. I'm a student, just like Demonee, that's all. When she'd be doing her homework in her room, I'd be doing mine in my room. This never made sense," I said, shaking my head. "I couldn't be no mama to nobody. I didn't even know what I'm supposed to be doing."

"You were supposed to be looking after Demonee, that's what."

"Desmona, that's her name, but I guess you knew that— and didn't care?" I spat.

"I care that she's a liar and a thief and her mother say she's trying to become some sort of freak," he said.

"How can you say that about your own niece? She's not a freak!" I shouted. "She only wants to find a place where she feels loved and comfortable, just like Brian."

"Just like Brian, are you kidding? My son knows I love him," he snapped.

I looked at him and smirked. "Really, is that why he's joining the military?" I asked.

He looked like that wall he wanted to punch had just fell on him. "What? What are you talking about? Brian isn't joining the military. He's never even acted interested in doing something like that. And besides, there's no way he would do that without letting me know," he said.

"He most certainly would. I know that for a fact, but I guess he wasn't *comfortable* enough to tell *you* what he was up to," I said, rubbing it in. I wanted the wound to cut deeply, maybe he could feel some of the pain Demonee was gonna feel when they stuck her in a strange place.

"That can't be right. Brian knows that I want him to go to a good college. After that, I plan on him coming and working with me for a while, before going on to earn a higher level degree. That's what I want for him. I wasn't even going to let a young marriage or a baby set him back, he knows that. I haven't always been there for Brian physically, but he's my son, and I love him. There's nothing that I wouldn't do for him, even help take care of his abandoned wife. It's got to be a mistake."

"No, it's not," I said.

"I don't believe you. I can't," he said. He took out his fancy phone and dialed Brian's number. I just held my breath and waited for him to answer. It took a few seconds, but sure enough Brian picked up.

"I need to talk to you now," Brian's dad said.

"Dad, what is it? I have some place I need to be. I'm rushing out of the door right this minute," I heard Brian say on the other end of the phone.

"Well, you can just rush your behind over to Maxine's house. I'm here, and I need for you to be here too, right now!" he said.

"All right, I'm on my way," Brian said.

I shook my head. I wasn't in the mood for any more drama. I really, really wasn't.

Brian took his time coming to my house. In the meantime, his father decided that his conversation with his son was best held outside in the yard, where he felt he would have a little more privacy. I didn't care. I didn't want to be in the middle of whatever they had to say to each other. As soon as I heard the faint sound of Brian's voice through the door, I ran to the window. At first I couldn't hear much of anything. Brian's dad was obviously trying to keep his voice low, then things erupted.

"How do you know what I really want? It's always been what you want for me, what about what I want for myself?" Brian said.

"What about it? What about being dumb enough to go off to the military during a time of war? What about throwing away your future?" his father roared.

"Your future," Brian roared back, "not mine. I've been trying to tell you that for years, but it's been a little hard. You're never at home, and when are, you just won't listen."

"So, this is your way of making me listen? I can't believe it. Son, all you do is stupid things."

"What's that mean?"

"What do you think it means? Getting married young, getting put out by your wife, lying about your child, or being lied to about another child? Brian, you have a whole laundry list of stupid!"

"Maybe, but I know what I'm doing now isn't dumb or stupid. I know that this is the right thing to do, even if you don't. I'm not a little boy anymore. You can't control everything that I do."

"I wish I could. I would stop you from screwing up everything you touch!" his dad yelled. The words hit Brian hard. I could tell because his face looked like he had just ran into a door.

"I gotta go, Dad. I need to handle my business," Brian abruptly said.

"You're not going anywhere."

"Yes, I am, and no matter how much you yell at me you can't change it," Brian said, and started to walk off.

"This isn't over. We're not through discussing this," his father said.

"Ain't nothing to discuss," Brian said, and left.

I held my breath as I saw him going down the street. I couldn't believe what I had heard, and seen. Brian—my Brian—had seriously told his dad off, and walked away, just left. I had never seen that happen. Sure, every once in a while Brian stood up to his dad, but things always ended with his dad somehow gaining the upper hand. It never ended with Brian just walking off, refusing to let his father manipulate his actions. Brian really had changed, or was trying to. I loved him for that. I wasn't with him anymore, but I still felt so much love when I saw him standing up for himself. I moved away from the window and waited for Brian's dad to come back inside. I figured that he would come in angry and start throwing stuff around the place. I braced myself for what was coming next, but when he walked back in the door he looked like *he* had gone to war and came back shell shocked.

"He's really going. I didn't believe it, but my boy is leaving. I don't understand how this happened. Where did he even get an idea like this?"

"I'm not sure, but Great-aunt Freda says that he's been talking to a recruiter down at the Redesign Center for a while."

"That place where he tutors? Maxine, those recruiters are there to help students who don't have any options in life. Brian does. I'm not saying that joining the military isn't an honorable thing to do, but why would he choose a career where he may get bombed or shot at? What if he doesn't come back? What the hell is he thinking?" he asked.

"I haven't talked to him about it. But my Aunt Freda said that he told her he would stay if I asked him."

"She's right, he'll stay if you ask him."

"Probably, yeah, I'm pretty certain of it."

He studied on it a few more seconds. "Then that's what you do. I don't want to lose my son. We don't always agree, but I don't want to see him dead somewhere from a war, or in some country far away from me. He's all I got."

"I know that," I said.

"Yeah, and you know I'm willing to do whatever I have to keep him. I'll let you stay—and Demonee," he said. "I won't tell them to put Demonee in foster care. When she gets out of trouble, she can come back here and stay with you, like before. I just need you to talk to Brian and tell him you don't want him to go. If you do that, I'll keep up my end of the bargain. You just need to give him some hope. I know he'll stay if he thinks that eventually you two would get back together. It's the only thing that I think will make him stay. Believe it or not, I never knew his true feelings about going to college or coming to work with me. I always just thought that he would eventually want to do it, especially since he already has some business sense, on his way to becoming assistant manager of a store. Anyway, help me out with this, just ask him to stay, and I'll do what I can to get Demonee through this. I'll make you a deal."

I slid to the edge of the couch and stared at him. The reality of it hit me. I didn't like the deal. It was the same one we had before, the one that didn't work because I didn't know how to keep *my part* of the bargain, and I still didn't. De-monee living with me was no good. She needed more supervision than I could give her. If she didn't get it, she was probably going to end up in jail for a very long time.

"Demonee doesn't belong with me. She needs somebody who can really look after her. I can't do it, and I shouldn't have to. I care about her, but she needs her mama."

"Her mother doesn't want her back, you know that," he said.

"Then you take her. You're her kin, and you can at least make certain she don't keep doing what she's doing and end up in prison."

"Maxine, I can't take care of that unruly little girl," he angrily said.

"Why not? She's your flesh and blood just like Brian. You standing up here talking about not losing him, but the truth is you done already lost him. He don't live with you no more. He moved in with me, then when he got tired of me he moved in with another chick. Now that situation ain't working out, so he ready to go again. He's all grown up. He don't need you like he used to, but Demonee does. She's going in all kinds of directions and maybe you can teach her the right way to go. All she needs is some understanding and love."

Some regret came to his face. "I can't love that girl, not the way she is. I'm sorry, but I've always been taught that some thing's just aren't right. Besides, she reminds me too much of my sorry sister, Jessie. I don't know how much you know about her, but my sister Jessie, Demonee's mother, is a real magnet for trouble—drugs, alcohol, stealing, at one point or another she's been involved with it all. I can't tell you how many years I've spent trying to get her to do better, but she's never really wanted anyone's help. I know you think that I just stuck you with Demonee, and I'm not saying that it isn't true. However, I did want to give her a better life. She's the second oldest girl in her family. The first daughter got involved with cocaine and ended up in prison for distribution. I didn't want that to happen to Demonee. She's a difficult child, but when I look at her I see some potential in her, that's why I was trying my best to get her a decent life. I didn't want her to be like her sister, or my sister. Jessie's never done anything in this world but get in trouble and produce children for the state to take care of."

"I've heard that," I said.

"The problem is each time I see Demonee all I can think of is her mother."

"I get that, and Demonee has been in trouble, but she ain't produced no children, so she's not your sister. She's a kid herself, just a child who wants somebody to be there for her. I don't know why her mama can't do that. If she living her life like you say she is, who is she to judge? Anyway, it don't matter. All Demonee needs is somebody to care for her like she a human being, and I can do that. If you take her back, I'll still care about her, and I'll love her just the way she is."

"I get that, but you understand that I'm not home as much as I like. I may not be there as often as she needs me to."

"Then I'll be there. When you're not home, I'll keep an eye on her just like I used to, but she needs to be someplace where she can't just do what she wants all the time. She needs to know that she's in a house where she has to act right. No matter what I did she never seemed to get that living here with me. Anyway, that's our deal. I'll ask Brian to stay and you let Demonee come home with you," I said, like a true businesswoman. It looks like I was actually learning something in my Marketing class.

Demonee's uncle didn't look too happy about my new talent, but he caved. "If that's what you want, I'll do it," he said. "I know a good lawyer. It won't be easy, but he can keep her out of the system. I'm sure he can get her community service, or something like that."

"Are you sure?"

"Maxine, nothing is certain, but I will tell him to do everything he can to help."

"Thanks," I said.

He left the house, and I went to my room. I sat down on the bed I used to share with my husband, and I was maybe about to share it with him again. I didn't know how I felt about that. But I had made a deal, and a deal was a deal. I was going to ask Brian to stay for me. What that meant I didn't know. I loved him, there was no doubt about that, but could I ever really be a wife to him again? I think I could try, my heart still loved Brian. If I just let my heart lead me there was no way that I couldn't take him back. It was my mind that was giving me the trouble, a mind that couldn't let go of all the ugliness that he had brought into my life. If I could just stop thinking about him with Shell perhaps everything would all work out. It sounded so easy when I said it to myself, but it wasn't. Nothing about what I was going to do was easy.

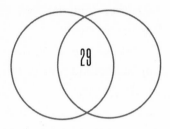

I wore a blue-and-white-polka-dot dress to the hearing the day that they took me away from my mother. I had forgotten that, but this morning it came back to me when I was getting ready to go to Demonee's hearing at the courthouse. I remembered the dress because it wasn't mine. A social worker had pulled it out of a Goodwill bag just minutes before my hearing and forced me to put it on. It was a pretty dress, but I felt out of place in it, as out of place as I felt sitting on a cold hard wooden chair waiting for my mother to say that more than anything she wanted to take me home. The words never came, and I told myself that it was because of the dress. My mother hadn't purchased it for me, so perhaps she simply didn't recognize me in it. I made myself believe this lie because it was much easier than believing that Mama had so cruelly rejected me. It was just too mean, but I think not nearly as mean as what happened to Demonee. Her mother didn't even bother to show up. It was just her uncle there and an older white-haired lawyer who looked like he had been around when they wrote the first law book. I felt awful for De-monee. I couldn't imagine not having your mama show up at all. Even Petal's mother was there, all sickly looking. Her light brown skin was yellowed, and her body looked wobbly and weak. She looked like she might fall out of her seat at any time, yet she had managed to make it there for her daughter, because that's what a real mother does. I sat on the opposite side of the courtroom and waited.

First up was Petal. She looked syrupy sweet in a soft pink skirt set with two inches of white lace around the hem. Some-body had taken a long time to twist her shoulder length hair into baby doll curls. She looked more like a foster kid going before the court for an adoption, than a girl who was in front of a judge for threats of violence against her teacher, felony theft, and willful destruction of property. For a moment I thought the judge might be taken in by her innocent appear-ance, but as soon as she stood up I saw the frown on his wrin-kled face. It stayed there while her public defender, an attractive brunette in a designer suit, painted a picture of Petal that would have made you think that she had a pair of wings growing out of her back. She went on and on for several minutes, talking about how popular Petal was with the other students, extra curricular activities she had been in since elementary school, her good school grades, positive tests scores, and of course her devotion to her sick mother.

"She's had some behavioral problems for the past couple of years, but overall she's a fine student, who helps take care of her family, and does her best to try and have a life of her own."

"Apparently that life includes lying to her peers, taking money that doesn't belong to her, and causing several thousand dollars of damage to her teacher's property."

I smiled inside when the judge said that. "You go judge," I said to myself.

"Petal, you are a very pretty young lady, and I believe for the most part a good daughter, but you're not a good person, because good people don't do the things that you've done, no matter how many personal issues they might be experiencing," he continued.

"It wasn't my fault. She wanted to do that stuff," Petal said, pointing to Demonee. Demonee looked like she wanted to say something, but her lawyer gave her a 'Don't say anything look.' "

"I sincerely doubt that this wasn't your idea, Petal. I've read your school records and Ms. Blis's school records. I know both of your histories, but I've also been doing this for many, many years. I have a strong sense about the young people who come to my court. This was your idea. I'm certain of that," the judge said, pushing his wire framed glasses up over his nose.

"No it wasn't. I didn't do nothing. I'm not even like that," Petal said, this time her lawyer gave her the look. She got quiet, and that sweet face of hers turned bitter.

I smiled at that too.

"Take a seat,"the judge said to her. She sat down and Demonee stood up with her lawyer.

I waited to hear what he would say about her. Unlike Petal's lawyer, he didn't even attempt to bring up anything positive from Demonee's past. He talked about Demonee's poor school record, and the negative things that were in her school file, including her suspension for class skipping, and the book she threw at Ms. Hopkins's head, and several other incidents that I hadn't even heard about. He concluded his speech by saying that Demonee was a troubled child. "This young lady was abandoned by her mother early this year. She is the second oldest child in a large family, and I believe that her mother simply decided that she didn't want the responsibility and expense of taking care of her. Her mother has a history of drug abuse, and lives a less than favorable lifestyle. I think it was just easier for her to get rid of what she calls a problem child."

"That is an understatement," the judge said. He pointed at Demonee. "Tell me what you have to say for yourself, little girl. Explain to me why you took part in this sad affair."

"I don't know. I don't have much to say. I wasn't trying to take nothing or hurt nobody. I just like Petal, that's all. I don't have a lot of friends. Petal, she was real nice to me," Demonee said.

"I'm sure she was, but tell me about the other students at your school. They aren't friendly with you?"

"Maybe one or two, but mostly nobody hangs out with me, just Petal. That's why I was doing what she wanted me to do. But it was my fault too. I know I shouldn't have let her talk me into taking that money, and I didn't have no business threatening Ms. Hopkins, and tearing up her car."

"That goes without saying, but let me ask you this young lady. Would you have actually hurt Ms. Hopkins, if you and Petal hadn't settled for destroying her car?"

"I don't think so," Demonee said.

"But you did throw a book at her head."

"That wasn't my idea. I just did it because."

"Because why? I saw in your school records something about possible drug use. Were you using drugs when you did any of these things?" the judge asked.

"No sir, I just wanted her to like me," Demonee said.

"Do you like yourself?" the judge asked.

"Sometimes, not really," Demonee said.

"I see. I see. You may have a seat," the judge said.

Demonee and her lawyer sat down.

"Is their teacher here? Ms. Hopkins?" the judge asked.

I turned and noticed that Ms. Hopkins had been sitting a couple of rows behind me the whole time. She looked like she really wanted to be somewhere else, but she stood up and came to the front. She took the stand, sitting right next to the judge, the way I did a long time ago when the judge asked me about the beating that Mama's boyfriend gave me.

"I want to know a few things from you," the judge said, and started to question her about factual parts of the incidents.

Ms. Hopkins started telling it all.

Again, I waited, and so did Demonee's uncle. He looked as nervous as I felt. He kept adjusting his tie and turning his big diamond and gold pinky ring. He was scared. He had kept his word and got Demonee the best lawyer, but maybe it wasn't going to be enough. The judge seemed pretty hard-core. It was hard to tell if things were going to go her way.

"Your honor, may I finish by saying that I really like both of these girls. I never wanted to see either one of them here, but they needed to be aware that there are consequences to bad behavior."

"Yes they do, and for the record I don't like seeing them here either. Each day I pray that I'll walk into this courtroom and it will be completely empty, but that hasn't happened yet. So, let me ask you a few more questions."

"Dang, what more is there to ask?" I said to myself. I wanted it over. I wanted Demonee's fate decided, but I also wanted to get out of the room because it was bringing back way too many memories.

"Ms. Hopkins, neither one of these young ladies have outright denied that they did what they did. I just want to know from you what you think of this whole sorry mess that we're here about."

"What I think is that deep down both of the girls are good girls, or can be. Life is hard at their age, and it's even worse if you are dealing with personal and family issues beyond your control."

"Like the people who they stole from?" the judge asked.

"I suppose," Ms. Hopkins said.

"Let me ask you this, as a teacher of these two young ladies, what would you have me do with them?"

"I'm honestly not sure what to do. They are two very distinct girls, with different personalities. I think that Petal is outgoing and smart, but also manipulative, and sometimes quite mean. In contrast, until she started hanging out with Petal, Demonee mostly stayed to herself and never caused any problems. I do worry about her nature. She's a follower, and I believe that her constant troubles at school are the result of that. I think she could do much better with a more positive influence in her life."

"She needs to choose her friends more wisely," the judge said.

"Yes sir."

"Thank you, ma'am, you can go back to your seat," the judge said.

Ms. Hopkins walked back to place and breathed a sigh of relief. She clearly didn't want to appear to play favorites. She hadn't openly said that Demonee deserved a second chance, but she had made it clear that Demonee was the kind of kid that could be easily led down the wrong path. It wasn't much, but maybe it was enough.

"I'm ready to rule. Stand up girls," the judge said.

"I think Ms. Hopkins is right. I could see from reading your school records and the way you presented yourself here that you are very different girls, and so I'm going to punish you accordingly."

"Ms. Sprint, will you please take your client Petal and her mother outside," the judge said. I sat up straight in my chair. I was expecting that. I watched them leave nervous and confused.

"Stand up Ms. Blis," the judge said to Demonee, after they had left the room. Demonee and her lawyer both stood up, and Brian's father adjusted his silk tie again.

"There's a place called New Start that I think you can really benefit from. It's a program where girls like you can get some one on one counseling and learn how to take control of their own destiny. I'm going to send you there for a month and let you get your feelings about everything sorted out. You have some major self-esteem issues, and I don't think that you will ever succeed in life if you don't rid yourself of them."

"Yes sir," Demonee said.

"I'm not finished. I'm also sentencing you to a year of

community service, because you need to know that your actions can have real consequences. You don't get to be a thief and hoodlum, just because your life isn't exactly what you want it to be. Do you understand me?"

"Yes sir," Demonee said.

"Of course you do. That's all," he said to Demonee. He turned to her lawyer. "Mr. Coleman, see my clerk about her paperwork. She will be checking into New Start today. You will also need to pick up a list of places that she will be doing her community service. Please make it clear to her that if she doesn't complete her entire year, I will have to think of a more severe punishment."

"She'll do every bit of it," her uncle spoke up.

"I believe you, sir. By the way, I want to commend you for taking on the responsibility of this young lady when no one else would step up to the plate. It's very admirable of you to try and make up for her mother's lack of parenting," the judge said to Brian's dad.

"She's my niece. I knew she would be better off with me. I couldn't let her end up in foster care," he said.

"No, I couldn't," I said under my breath.

"Thank you for everything," her lawyer said.

And just like that it was over. I grinned from ear to ear. Demonee wasn't going to skate, but she wasn't going to be locked away with a bunch of hard-core girls either. I got up and gave her a big hug before they took her out of the courthouse. She hugged me back hard, and I realized how much I was going to miss her for that month she was away. However, as soon as she exited the courthouse doors I realized that I couldn't stand being in the courtroom one more minute. I said goodbye to Ms. Hopkins and whispered a word of thanks in her ear. She simply nodded.

I walked outside the courtroom and saw Petal sitting between her mother and her lawyer. That sweet smile on her face was gone. She was realizing that being judged the ring leader meant that things weren't going to go very well for her. I felt kind of sorry for her. I knew what it was like sitting outside a courtroom, waiting to find out the fate of your life. After Mama said that she wasn't going to kick her boyfriend out, the judge ordered my social worker to take me outside. I sat there sad while the judge spoke to Mama. When I was finally let back in the court, I got the horrible news that I couldn't go home. Petal was going to get some bad news too, but I suspected that the news was going to be more awful for her sick mother, who probably wouldn't have her around to help for a while. I avoided looking at them as I made my way to the elevator. I had had enough of worrying about other people's problems; I still had some of my own to straighten out.

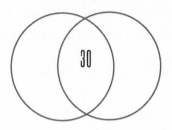

30

S ometimes you get something totally unexpected, but it's
exactly what you want. Demonee left three days ago.
She packed her stuff and went to live with her uncle. It
was because of the agreement that me and her uncle
came to before her trial, but I didn't expect her to go along
with it. I was really surprised when we sat down on her bed to
discuss it and she handled it with maturity.

"I don't wanna go, but I know I have to, because I didn't
do so good living with you," she said, stuffing her cotton shorts
into her suitcase. I took them out and folded them.

"You did all right, but I think you'll do better with your
uncle. I know he can be a real pain sometimes, but I really
think that he'll look after you," I said, placing the neat stack
beside a small heap of mismatched socks. I took them out and
folded them as well.

"He didn't before," she said.

"Yeah, he did, at least I think he was trying to. He really

did think that you would be better off here with me, but my mind ain't together right now, Demonee. I'm just a kid like you, and I got to figure out what I need to do for myself. Your uncle, he's different. He's already all grown up."

"I know, but will he care about me, just for me? Do you know what I mean?" she asked.

"I know what you mean, and I think he'll try, and that's all we can ask."

"My mama didn't, and neither did my grandma."

"I know, but he's neither one of those people. I've seen him with Brian. He can be harsh, but when he cares, I mean really cares, he can give you the world."

"You mean like he did with this house?"

"Yeah, and with you. See I didn't know it, but I needed somebody here with me after Brian left. I needed somebody to keep my mind off of him, and somebody who I could talk to."

"We fought a lot."

"Yeah, but that's still talking, and sometimes any kind of talking helps."

"I don't wanna leave, Maxine, but I will," she cried.

"I'll be over and see you all the time. You're just leaving my house, that's all, and nothing else."

"For real?"

"For real," I said.

We let the conversation go on that note. There really was no more to say. We both knew how we felt, and we both knew that it was time for Demonee to be somewhere else. I was very happy to know that as soon as she settled into her uncle's place she was going to be going off to New Start. I had looked it up online, and it seemed like great place for Demonee to learn to love and support herself, even if her family was having a hard time doing it. As for her friend, Petal, the judge saw right through her lie and her pretty face. He gave her three months in juvie. Demonee told me that when she gets out she's going to be moving to another school district. That's the best news I've heard in a long time. Demonee doesn't need Petal in her life, and Petal doesn't need Demonee. They are both screwed up, and being together makes things worse, especially for Demonee. She doesn't need a girlfriend like Petal. She needs someone that she can turn to like Tia. I called my best girl and let her know everything as soon as I heard about Petal leaving.

"Girl, that is good. Let that little heifer be someone else's headache," Tia said.

"Girl, I feel the same way about it, but I know it made Demonee sad to see Petal go. To help her feel better, I sent Madona over to talk to her about how she was dealing with missing her sister. They talk all the time now, and I feel good that they can share their troubles and not be so sad."

"So what about you? How you getting along, girl?"

"I'm fine. I'm okay with it being just me."

I have to be. Brian is going into the Marines after all, even though I told him that he could come back. His explanation for going was logical and rational, and it reminded me so much of why I fell in love with him.

"Maxine, I told my daddy, now I'm telling you. I'm gonna go ahead and join the Marines. I thought about it a lot, and I decided it's a good thing to do. I've been running around lost for a while. I was with you, then I was with Shell. She lied to me about the baby, and already left me for another dude."

"The baby's daddy?"

"So she say. I don't really know or care. That's not why I'm going. I just need to learn some stuff, you know, grow up. I should have been honest with you about Shell. I should have told you what was up with us, and that I wasn't ready to get married."

"Yeah, you should have. You really hurt me, Brian, but it was my idea to get married. I wanted to leave home and I wanted you. I thought getting married was my way to get both. It never even occurred to me that things could turn out to be such a big disaster."

"It don't matter. I was hot for the marriage too. But when it happened, I didn't want to accept who I was. I didn't want to be a husband. I was a selfish little boy."

"You was still in high school. You *was* just a boy, and I was a girl, who wanted to spend all her time with you. I wanted to be wherever you were. I wanted that ever since we was little. I was clinging too hard. I shouldn't have been holding on so tight."

"Naw, I should have understood that I was already caught. I love you, Maxine, only you, but it was hard for me to realize that," he said, caressing my hand.

"Well, how is the military going to help you get it, Brian?" I asked.

"It's not, and right now that's cool, 'cause I ain't about that. I've decided that I don't want to get with nobody. I want to get with myself."

"And you think the Marines really will help you do that?"

"I think they'll give me focus and some job training. I took some tests. They'll probably hook me up with some computer programmer skills. They say I have an aptitude for that, and when I get out, maybe we can try again. I already told my daddy this, and you know he still mad as hell about my decision, but he ain't gonna take it out on you. He said he would take care of you and Demonee and he gonna keep up his end of the bargain."

"Good, I guess that's the only nice thing that came out of our marriage. I won't have to go home to Mama, and Demonee will have a better home, and someone to pay attention to her needs."

"Yeah, I'm glad you stuck with Demonee. You're the first one who ever did. Here," he said, pulling something out of his pocket.

I opened my hand, and he placed it into my palm. When I looked down, I noticed that it was my little silver promise ring, the one that he had given me years ago.

"Where did you get this? I thought it was in a shoebox in my closet."

"It was. I took it out the day that you threw me out. I've had it ever since."

"Why?"

"I don't know. I was all confused over Shell, but I knew that I just couldn't let you go. I wanted something of yours to hold."

"You could have held me, if you hadn't screwed up."

"Yeah, I know. Anyway, now I want to give the ring to you, you know, like when I gave it to you for the first time."

"I shook my head. No, you keep it. I don't want it back, Brian. I love you, but I don't trust you, so I can't promise you anything."

"Not even a small promise?"

"Ain't no small promises, Brian. A promise is just a promise, and when it comes to you, mine are all used up," I said.

"Do you remember what you said when I gave it to you? Do you remember how you went all silly in the face?"

"Yeah, I remember. You gave me that ring right after I got a D on my English exam. I was bummed, and I knew Mama was gonna be pissed. Then there you come with that ring, and I just suddenly started feeling better."

"You can feel that way again," he said.

"Naw, I can't, not just with no little ring. It won't make everything go back to the way it was. Brian, I can't wear that ring again, and I can't promise you anything."

"Okay, I can't argue with your feelings, but I'll change your mind in the next few months. I'll go away and soldier up. *I promise* that I'll be somebody that you can be proud of when I come back."

"Don't come back for me, Brian, just come back," I said. I kissed him on the cheek and he left.

As I saw him step off the porch, I knew that I would miss him, and I also knew that when he came back we would just be good friends. It was hard, but I had learned that I could be okay without Brian, and I intended to keep things that way. He was going away to grow up, and I was going to do the same. Still, I would always remember the good times we had when we were children, the simpler times, the ones before two foolish teenagers in love decided to get married.

That's the story.